Dear Reader,

Welcome to this Centennial Edition of *Great Lakes Romances®*, historical fiction full of love and adventure, set in bygone days on North America's vast inland waters.

Like other titles in this series (see descriptions at the back), *Sweet Clover: A Romance of the White City* relays the excitement and thrills of a tale skillfully told, but does not contain explicit sex, offensive language, or gratuitous violence.

Because *Sweet Clover: A Romance of the White City* was written by an author with strong Christian values, it contains a subtle message of Christian faith that evolves naturally from the tale of a heroine who adheres to her Christian upbringing.

We invite you to tell us what you would like most to read about in *Great Lakes Romances®*. For your convenience, we have included a survey form at the back of the book. Please fill it out and send it to us, and be sure to watch for the next books in the series, coming in Spring 1993.

Thank you for being a part of *Great Lakes Romances®!*

Sincerely,
The Publishers

P.S. Editor Donna Winters, who is also the author of several books in the series, would love to know your reaction to this reprint of an 1894 romance novel. You can write her at P.O. Box 177, Caledonia, MI 49316.

ABOUT THE AUTHOR

Clara Louise (Root) Burnham, a tall, slender woman with blue eyes, blond hair, and an outgoing personality marked by her enjoyment in meeting people, embodied all the characteristics of a perfect heroine for the sweet romances she wrote from the 1880's through the mid-1920's.

Born May 26, 1854, in Newton, Massachusetts, she was raised the daughter of musicians, and planned to become one herself. At age nine, she moved to Chicago. Her writing career began when as a prank, her brother locked her in her room, telling her she could not come out until she had produced a poem.

Before the age of twenty, she was wed to lawyer Walter Burnham. The couple took up residence in an hotel apartment overlooking Lake Michigan, where she spent from nine until noon at her writing desk producing first short stories, and eventually the novels for which she is most famous.

Mrs. Burnham spent three months every summer at her Maine cottage, "The Mooring," on Bailey's Island, well off the coast, and brought both East Coast and Great Lakes settings into stories that garnered a loyal following until her death on June 20, 1927, at age 73.

SWEET CLOVER

A Romance of the White City

Clara Louise Burnham

Great Lakes Romances®

Bigwater Publishing
Caledonia, Michigan

SWEET CLOVER: A ROMANCE OF THE WHITE CITY

Abridged Reprint. First Published 1894: Houghton, Mifflin and Company, Cambridge.

Great Lakes Romances® is a registered trademark of Bigwater Publishing, P.O. Box 177, Caledonia, MI 49316.

Library of Congress Catalog Card Number 92-70330
ISBN 0-923048-80-4

Edited by Donna Winters
Cover photo restored and hand-tinted by Rose Summers, LaClaire Laboratories, Inc.
Fabric frame by Judy Groendyke, Rainbow's End, Inc.

Printed in the United States of America

92 93 94 95 96 97 98 / CH / 10 9 8 7 6 5 4 3 2 1

INTRODUCTION

Welcome to the Centennial Edition of *Sweet Clover: A Romance of the White City*. With the 500-year celebration of Columbus's discovery of America, and the one-hundredth anniversary of the World's Columbian Exposition held in Chicago in 1893, this seems an appropriate time to reminisce about the Fair. Regardless of the original intent of its planners, the event became known as much for the carnival-like atmosphere of its Midway Plaisance (giving rise to a new noun in our vocabulary—Midway) and the appearance of the first Ferris Wheel (named for its inventor, George Washington Gale Ferris), as for its superb neoclassical architecture and hitherto unmatched exhibitions of industry and the arts.

When the fairgrounds were opened on May 1, 1893, the shores of Lake Michigan had given rise to a "White City," so designated because all the major buildings and very nearly every smaller one had been spray-painted white. With angelic sculpture adorning many of the edifices, the euphemism, "Dream City," was also applied to what soon became known to American Victorians simply as "the Fair."

Not far from the excitement of the exposition grounds, a thirty-nine-year-old writer set pen to paper creating a romantic story woven around the events of that memorable summer. With innocence, humor, and a dash of her Christian moral convictions, Clara Louise Burnham spun a tale of a sweet heroine down on her luck, her impertinent but lovable younger sister, and the two heroes who would capture their hearts with their persistent, but always respectful wooing.

In editing the story for today's *Great Lakes Romances* reader, I have tried to remain as faithful to the original work as possible, while centering on the action that involved the lake setting. In so doing, I have summarized in the prologue the first ten chapters, much of which took place in the East and was slower-paced.

Our written language has changed from one-hundred years ago. Capitalization, punctuation, and spelling differ from standard practice today, as do the meanings of certain words. I trust the reader to interpret "gay" as it was originally intended during the 1890's, meaning lighthearted fun, and to indulge references to period literature and music which are not well-known today.

One of the great entertaining aspects of this novel, however, is its representation of the Victorians as they moved, spoke and thought in their fictional world, an insight I believe today's readers will find charming, captivating, and quite possibly educational as well!

Donna Winters
January 1992

Characters

Clover Bryant Van Tassel—The twenty-three-year-old widow of Richard Van Tassel, out of mourning when the story opens.

Mildred Bryant—Clover's twenty-year-old sister.

Jack Van Tassel—A friend of Clover and Mildred from childhood. His father, who had grown up with Clover's parents, had taken Clover as his second wife and provided for her and her fatherless family when they were destitute. Shortly thereafter, he died of a stroke.

Gorham Page—Jack Van Tassel's cousin, a laconic Boston lawyer not known for his effusiveness. Jack, a Harvard graduate, reads law at his firm.

Lovina Berry, aka Aunt Love—Elderly aunt of both Jack and Gorham, with whom she has established a reputation for her cookies. Her permanent residence is in Pearfield, Massachusetts.

Blitzen—The mischievous terrier who adopted Aunt Love and won't be without her!

Robert Page—Gorham's older brother, a wholesale drygoods merchant with whom Gorham resides.

Hilda Page—Robert's wife, an inveterate matchmaker and spoon-collector. She's a congenial soul with a sisterly fondness for Gorham.

Prologue

An outline of the opening chapters of the original novel.

The story opens in 1889 at Harvard, where Jack Van Tassel, athletic, tall, slender, with wavy black hair scrupulously parted in the middle, and brilliant brown eyes, has just graduated. His father, Richard, asks probing questions about his son's intentions regarding the young ladies in his acquaintance and discovers his son holds no particular attachments, not even for Clover Bryant, the young woman who has been his friend from childhood back home in Chicago.

Several weeks later in Chicago, twenty-year-old Clover Bryant, with soft brown hair and sparkling blue eyes, and her seventeen-year-old sister, Mildred, a tall, broad-shouldered young creature, learn the sole means of support for their household which includes a sick mother and a younger brother and sister, has been cut off. Payments on a debt owed their deceased father by his brother can no longer be met.

Richard Van Tassel, a longtime close friend of the Bryants, having concluded an extended business trip East, calls upon Clover. Jack has not yet returned from the East when the elder Van Tassel takes the young woman, who is deeply burdened with the care of her family, for a drive through Jackson Park. Reluctantly, she reveals the news of her uncle being unable to continue his loan payments.

The following day, Clover accepts an invitation to go sailing with Jack Van Tassel, who has returned home for the first time since graduating from Harvard. Through the course of conversation, Clover reveals that she has accepted a marriage proposal from Jack's father, thinking Jack already has knowledge of the circumstances. She is surprised to learn that, not only did Jack not know of the engagement, he has designs on Clover himself!

Out of sorts over circumstances between Clover and his father, Jack Van Tassel returns East, and he and his bachelor cousin, Gorham Page, a Boston lawyer, embark on a trip to Europe, where Jack remains for an extended stay while his cousin returns to his Boston law practice.

Within a year of Clover's marriage, her mother, youngest sister, and little brother pass away, and her husband suffers a stroke. At the elder Van Tassel's request, his son is not informed of his illness. Clover, accompanied by her younger sister Mildred, takes her invalid husband to his aunt's home in the East to nurse him back to health, at which time Page's path crosses with that of the younger Bryant sister.

In October, Van Tassel passes away, and Page, his lawyer, is summoned to Chicago, where he meets the widowed Clover for the first time, finding her a much more sympathetic creature than his imagination had led him to believe. He takes upon himself the responsibility of notifying Jack, still in Europe, of his father's death, and of the fact that Clover and her sister will be leaving Chicago for an extended trip to California, should Jack wish to again take up residence in the old family home in the Hyde Park section of the city.

Jack returns immediately to Boston. There, he begins reading law at his cousin's office. Through the course of time, with the intercession of Aunt Love, Miss Lovina Berry, with whom Clover and Jack's father had stayed the previous summer, Jack comes to understand that Clover had brought great happiness to his father during their brief marriage.

As time passes, Jack learns that Clover and Mildred have followed their California sojourn with one to Alaska, and another to Europe. Through Aunt Love, he sends word to Clover and Mildred that they should return to the Van Tassel home if they desire.

At about the same time, an agreement is reached to hold the World's Columbian Exposition in Chicago very near Van Tassel's Hyde Park home, a decision in which Jack's father had played a part, and Jack insists his cousin accompany him there for the dedication of the buildings at the fair grounds in October, 1892.

CHAPTER 1

THE DEDICATION

The twentieth of October, Chicago was to be clothed in bunting, and the great men of the country were to be drawn by prancing steeds through her streets. On the twenty-first, the Exposition buildings were to be dedicated to their splendid use, and Jack Van Tassel told his cousin that they must both be present at the ceremonies. Page demurred, but Van Tassel had his way, and ten o'clock of that sunshiny, clear, Friday morning found the two men entering the grounds, where a sense of roominess was the first sensation, after struggling in the city's crowd.

Jack felt his breast swell with pride in the fair scene, incomplete, yet already inspiring; but he forbore from being the first to comment. Let the Boston man speak; and he finally did. Page's eyes slowly took in an overwhelming impression of the general scheme—of what had already been, and what would be accomplished. Then he spoke:—

"This is great—so far."

The words were a balm to his companion.

Page went on.

"But Eastern men designed these palaces. Eastern

art"—

"Now look here," burst forth Jack. "Don't try to apologize for Chicago's achievement. She hasn't got there yet, but she is arriving. She had sense enough to make this Fair a national and not a local business. You're surely not surprised at that? She understood it that way from the first. They are not all Chicago men who have laid the brains of this country under contribution, and whose indomitable energy has been the steam which has actuated the vast machinery of construction from the beginning, and will do so to the end. Don't explain it, my friend; just say it is stupendous, and pass on."

Page, as he silently obeyed, remembered Mildred Bryant's prophetic words when he had met her by chance on the train the summer Jack's father had gone East to recover from his stroke. *It is very fortunate for the country that we have taken the Fair.*

It began to look that way; still herculean tasks remained.

Jack had received an invitation to witness the parade from the loggia of the Mining Building, and the cousins bent their steps thither, between the lines of waiting spectators. At present, the building was used as barracks for troops. The two glanced down the neat perspective of soldier beds, as they ran up the broad flight of steps leading to the gallery, then they came out upon the balcony that faces north, and looked with interest upon the scene. Flags in great numbers were flying from every roof. The waterways and Wooded Island lay before them in the October sunlight.

They were talking of the names of buildings, and discussing the fabulous measurements of the mountain called

Manufactures and Liberal Arts, when a new party appeared from the gallery doorway. The new-comers advanced to an arch a couple of rods from where the young men were standing, and Jack, who was profoundly interested in his subject, merely received an impression of beauty and fashion as he glanced at them, and then, looking back, returned to his statistics.

"If they can only have good weather the coming winter," he went on, "The thing will be ready May first, in spite of the croakers."

Soft laughter and happy voices came from beyond the massive masonry, which half concealed their neighbors.

"Jack," said Page, in a low tone, "Mrs. Van Tassel and Miss Bryant are with that party."

"No! Why, I didn't see them."

"Yes. Mrs. Van Tassel has some kind of a gray and white dress on, and Miss Bryant"—

"I want to get out of here, then."

Page answered him sharply.

"Is it your intention to play the role of Indian toward those ladies the rest of your life?"

"No, nothing of the kind," returned Van Tassel uncomfortably. "I am more willing to see them than they probably are to see me. I don't blame Clover, if she chooses never to meet me again. I suppose she remembers as clearly as I do some of the last things I said to her. Whew!" for in changing their positions one member of the party had stepped back into plain sight, "what a stunning girl they have with them!"

"That was Miss Bryant," said Page.

"No, no. You didn't see the one I meant. Splendid creature; carried her head as though the Fair was built expressly for her."

"Yes, that was Miss Bryant. I have met her a number of times. Perhaps I had better go over and speak to her."

"Don't think of it till I am out of the way," and Jack grasped his cousin's arm. "That, Mildred? Milly *Bryant?*" he added incredulously, looking reminiscently into that young woman's past, and seeing a combination of tanned countenance, rough hair, and old clothes revealing surplus wrist and ankle; a picture which refused to have relation to the trim and elegant young creature who had caught his eye.

This revelation increased to a panic Jack's desire not to intrude upon these friends. As though to enlighten him still further, Mildred insisted that her sister should step back also, and see some vista, which her own movement had brought into range.

Jack instinctively shrank more closely into the shadow of his pillar, while Page sympathetically followed his example, and both stole glances at Clover's pleased, unconscious face; a changed face from that which either of the men knew as hers. Jack saw in it the sign of a greater maturity and life-experience, as well as the subtle charm which exists in a lovely woman whose advantages are set off by tasteful and fashionable attire. Page saw what still seemed to him an angelic countenance, only made earthly by the tints of healthy youth, alert with interest; these smiling lips were but distantly related to the rigid, delicate mouth he remembered.

Clover vanished again, recalled by her companions' interest in a company of cavalry who galloped in golden glory across a distant bridge.

"I wish I was out of this," exclaimed Jack. "They may

all take it into their heads to come over here any minute. If the girls were alone, I shouldn't mind it. They could behave as they pleased then; but with mutual friends it would be very awkward for them. Dick Ogden is in the party. I can hear his laugh this minute. I'm going, Gorham."

"Very well, I too, then. Here comes some governor and his staff."

"Yes, it is Russell. The crowd is safe to cheer now and wave handkerchiefs for five minutes. It is our chance. We shan't be noticed. Come."

Jack started across the loggia with Page beside him. As ill luck would have it, the only one of the party by the balcony who turned idly curious eyes to look after the pair was his friend Ogden.

"Why there's—it *is* Van Tassel!" exclaimed the latter. "*Oh,* Van."

How Jack anathematized the cheerful, loud voice. He turned a deaf ear and hastened on.

"Van Tassel!" bawled the other. "Here, what's the matter with you? They're here, old fellow."

There is no creature so difficult to escape as the man who is convinced he is doing you a favor.

Jack could hear the legs of his persecutor's chair grate on the flooring as he sprang to his feet. He paused and turned around, knowing that if he persisted, his misguided friend would not hesitate to pursue and capture him in his zeal.

"They're right here," repeated Ogden explanatorily, his ingenuous florid face beaming. "Wasn't it curious you should have passed by, so near and yet so far?"

Van Tassel and Page advanced, the former with a rigidly impassive countenance. It seemed long to him that he was crossing the ten feet of balcony which lay between him and the young women whose reception he feared sensitively.

Ogden, and doubtless their other friends, supposed them united by ties of intimacy. Much as he disliked to obtrude himself upon them, to permit strangers to suppose that he was not pleased to meet these ladies would set many tongues wagging and was not to be considered. Better to risk a snub than to appear disloyal to those his father had honored.

But he need not have feared. Clover and Mildred were not the inexperienced girls of his acquaintance. They had taken in the situation as keenly as he had done, and when he reached them were ready to greet him and Mr. Page in a matter-of-course manner, calculated to divert suspicion had any existed. The circumstances, moreover, were favorable. The common interest of the parade at once claimed the attention of all, and after Page had been introduced to the strangers of the party, Jack drew a breath of relief that at any rate the ice was broken.

He stood near Mildred, looking down upon the gay plumes, uniforms, and prancing steeds of the procession, and wished she would address him. Was this the girl who had always been eagerly ready to act as crew of his boat, whose strong arms had not been of contemptible assistance in bailing her out? Who had received his invitations to sail in a thankful spirit, being thereby richly repaid for her physical exertions? She had sometimes needed to be snubbed out of too energetic participation in his own and Clover's plans. She had been a good fellow always, Jack remembered, even if occasionally inconveniently effervescent in the matter of spirit; had been an honest, fair antagonist, with a brave love of sport.

It struck Van Tassel as very curious that he should be so meekly desirous now of a crumb of friendly notice from one who had looked up to him so long and loyally.

He wished he could forget some of those heated things he had said to Clover on that miserable afternoon. Of course she had repeated them to her sister; and he felt uncomfortably sure that the memory of them was even now seething beneath the jetted crown of Miss Bryant's hat.

He envied Page the unconsciousness with which he could lean toward either sister, making and receiving comments. Clover's sweet face moved him with a tide of thought that gave his eyes a sad expression, which she caught on the only occasion when she looked up into his face.

On the whole, it was an uncomfortable half-hour which Jack spent in that loggia. The talk and laughter of the others gave him a feeling of remoteness and isolation. He wanted Clover or Mildred to speak to him, and they did not. He could not address them without a bit of encouragement. It was a relief to him when it was proposed to forsake the interminable lines of militia which were filing by the Transportation Building, and adjourn in search of luncheon.

Page seemed determined to accept Dick Ogden's urgent invitation that the cousins should continue of the party, and indeed Gorham started off gayly with Mildred, as though it were a matter of course that Jack should follow. The consequence was that, feeling a good deal as though the whole experience were a bad dream, Van Tassel found himself after a while placed next to Clover at the table. On her other side sat Dick's mother, a lady remarkable for an imposing figure and a fluffy pompadour of curling white hair. As this personage declared that the morning in the open air had given her an alarming appetite and proceeded to apply her full attention to its demands, conversation with her languished. Jack observed this, and renouncing the nightmare idea with an effort, endeavored to make necessity serve him.

"You have been abroad all summer, I believe," he remarked to Clover.

"Yes, longer than that," she returned. Her self-possession seemed untroubled; but in reality she suffered, too, from mingled emotions. She pitied Jack, but resented the fact that circumstances had forced them together, and his presence evoked memories overwhelmingly bitter and tender.

"Gorham Page and I did the lake regions of England and Scotland this year," he went on. "Did you happen to be in that vicinity?"

"No, we stayed in Switzerland during the summer months."

"You have seen much of the world in the last two years."

"Yes. Mildred and I feel ourselves quite experienced travelers."

"Shall you be satisfied to settle down now for a time?"

"I can hardly tell. We have formed a dangerous habit."

"Are you"—Jack looked busily into his plate—"Are you stopping at home—at the old house?"

"We have no home yet. We mean to settle down some day and make one."

"Why have you parted with that dear old place, Mrs.

Van Tassel?" asked Mrs. Ogden sonorously, helping herself again to chicken salad.

"Mrs. Van Tassel finds it rather large for her purposes, I fancy," answered Jack quickly, "and our housekeeper mourns her defection; but we haven't parted with the place. I was there in January, Clover, and Jeanie shed a few tears in her homesickness for you. I haven't seen her yet this time. Page and I only got in yesterday, and we went to the Great Northern."

Jack did not add that this unusual step was taken because he hoped that Clover and her sister might have returned and taken advantage of the invitation he sent them long ago through Miss Berry to take up residence in the family home, if they desired.

"Do you know how steadily I have clung to Boston of late?" he continued.

"Aunt Love wrote me you were there with your cousin," Clover replied. "Are you going to adopt it as your home?"

"No indeed. You will think, Mrs. Ogden," leaning forward to speak across Clover to her neighbor, "that Mrs. Van Tassel and I are very poor correspondents. Here we have both been roving about for the past year and waiting to meet in order to learn details about one another's movements."

"You can't tell me anything about young men as correspondents," replied Mrs. Ogden feelingly. "When Dick is away, the most I ever expect from him is a telegram every day or two."

"We're a bad lot," admitted Jack. "No," speaking again to Clover, "I am a Chicagoan, and just now prouder than ever of the fact. I fancy that we shall all come home like straying chickens on May first, '93. Of course you intend to be here during the Fair?"

"Yes. Mildred and I both anticipate it highly."

"I tell you, Mrs. Van Tassel," put in Mrs. Ogden, "if you don't want to use your house next summer, you can make a fortune renting it. In that situation, within walking distance of the grounds, you can get anything you like to ask for it."

Clover for a second time was about to disclaim any right or title to the homestead, but Jack besought her with a glance.

"I think we shall find it too convenient to be dispensed with," he said hastily.

After luncheon the party separated; their invitations to the dedicatory exercises in the Liberal Arts Building admitting them to different situations.

The scene was such as one is glad to have assisted in for its uniqueness if nothing more. Even seeing it, one could scarcely grasp the vastness of an auditorium covering forty acres; through whose outer corridors companies of cavalry passed now and then without making a noticeable sound within. Theodore Thomas's orchestra with its attendant singers, a company of six thousand in all, made but a little bright bouquet in one spot, and the leader was obliged to telephone to the platform half way down the hall in order to be informed when a speech had ceased and a musical number might take its turn.

At the end of the building opposite from Thomas, the Mexican band enlivened the meditations of the few thousands, fifteen or so, who were near enough to enjoy their martial strains. Mammoth banners and flags made gay the grand arches that supported the roof, and each tassel on those which were so decorated weighed as much as a woman.

Only a Bobdignagian could have felt at ease in such surroundings, yet wonderful order was maintained amid this largest audience ever gathered together under one roof.

Clover and Mildred were near enough to the singers to hear the *pièc de résistance*, Chadwick's inspiring, moving ode, and as Clover listened her eyes grew moist under the stress of the day's emotions.

"Jack is evidently very friendly," Clover said that night to her sister, when they were alone in their room at the Auditorium.

"He ought to be," returned Mildred shortly.

"He behaved very well and kindly," continued Clover. "The situation was odious."

"Odious. I should think so," remarked Mildred. "I never disliked that bawling Dick Ogden as I did when he kept on calling Jack like that. Don't begin to praise him to me," added the girl, turning toward her elder a glowing face. "After Jack Van Tassel has dragged around on his knees a good long time I am going to forgive him. Not before."

Clover looked troubled. "But it might all have been so awkward for us had he chosen to behave differently," she protested. "It is much easier for us to lock injuries in our breasts that the world knows nothing of, than it would be to have a gossiping set of people wondering and staring. Jack has grasped the bunch of nettles and saved us from those stings. You can feel as you please about it, but I am grateful."

"I wish he would go away. I wish he'd go to Kamschatka," exclaimed Mildred hotly. "I can't rid myself, when he is present, of the idea that he is considering how very differently we should be situated now if it weren't for dear Mr. Van Tassel."

"Well, it is true."

"Don't be tiresome, Clover. Of course it is true; but Jack has grown so grave and quietly observing, I feel that I shall not be able to endure having him about. I like fine clothes and fashionable life generally, and when I am soaring in my natural element, if Jack is going to give me those meditative, suggestive stares, it will ruin my pleasure. It is just as if one had a string about a bird's ankle and could twitch it down whenever he liked."

"I think you feel so because you haven't talked with him yet, Mildred. You know Jack was always generous."

"Was he?" the young girl faced her sister. "Was he when he accused you and insulted you?"

"Oh, I've forgiven him, Milly," returned the other gently, making a repressive gesture. "I have considered his standpoint a great deal since then; and we enjoyed his father and benefited by him when the only son was far away. We even had the priceless privilege of serving him in his last days, while Jack was unwittingly defrauded. Oh, I should not have been at all surprised if he had been unable to take me by the hand today. Don't be hard on Jack."

CHAPTER 2

GORHAM PAGE'S COMMISSION

A few days afterward a bell-boy brought Gorham Page's card to Mrs. Van Tassel's parlor. It was followed shortly by the young man himself, who felicitated himself upon his good fortune in finding her at home.

"My stay in Chicago will be so short, that had you been out I fear I should not have met you again," he said. "I am happy to see, Mrs. Van Tassel," Gorham inspected her with kindly, shortsighted eyes, "that travel has done all for you Miss Bryant hoped. Your face has quite a new color and contour."

"No, just my old one," she answered lightly, indicating a seat near her own. "I am sorry my sister is out; but she is a popular girl," with a little smiling sigh. "Where ever she is, somehow a number of engagements seem to crop up."

"Yes. One can see that she is charming company. I should like to have seen Miss Bryant. However, my errand is with you especially today."

"Oh, it is an errand that has brought you? How unflattering!"

"Not necessarily. It argued nothing unflattering when

John Alden performed his famous errand to Priscilla."

Page looked argumentatively into his hostess's amused eyes.

"Haven't you gone a long way afield for a simile?" she asked.

"No, I think not. I was quite as reluctant as poor John to accept the mission."

"Then decline it even at this late hour. I am the least curious of women."

"Impossible." Page shook his head. "Miles Standish is waiting for me over there at the Northern, and he is in a great state of mind."

"You tempt me to wish I had been out when your card came up. Perfunctory visits are very uncomfortable. I think you had better return to your friend, and tell him that Priscilla would not allow you to speak."

"I'm not making you uncomfortable, am I?" asked Gorham looking up and half laughing. "You see it is this way. I wanted to come to see you, and as soon as Jack learned my intention, he burdened me with this business. He told me to be eloquent, and not being in the least so, I am overwhelmed by my responsibilities. I had a presentiment, and told him so, that I should make a mess of the whole affair; but he insisted upon trusting his messenger as blindly as the Puritan captain of old."

Page had a way of lapsing, as he talked, into a meditative manner.

"And do you insist upon refusing to be warned by John Alden's failure?" asked Mrs. Van Tassel.

"Oh, I mustn't fail," he returned with prompt simplicity. "That is, if I do I shall take a room here in the Auditorium for the remainder of my stay." Page knotted his brow reminiscently. "Jack outlined a plan for me. He suggested a number of arguments with which I was to lead up to the main idea, but they are pretty well muddled in my brain now." Gorham gave a short, desperate laugh. "After this confession of weakness, Mrs. Van Tassel, you will be obliged, if only out of generosity, to send me back with a 'yes.' Now, let me see; I'm confident this ought not to come first, but Jack wanted me to say that he was certain that Uncle Richard left the homestead to him instead of to you, at your own instigation."

Clover, who had not been able to imagine what was coming, acquiesced gravely. "Mr. Van Tassel would probably have acted as he did in any case, but I wanted to make certain that Jack's dear old home should be secured to him."

"It humiliates Jack to feel that you avoid the place for fear he might go there."

"This *is* an unpleasant errand for you, Mr. Page."

"Please don't use that tone. Jack means so well, I couldn't refuse to be the go-between. He asks, he even begs, that if you intend to remain in Chicago now, you will go back to your home. It is comfortable. All your belongings remain there. His father made every arrangement for you. Jack feels sure he would be grieved to have you leave it. He himself is going back to Boston. The housekeeper is alone at his father's home and is pining for you. I forget whether that was to be an argument, but the fact remains. Jack thinks it would save a lot of talking among your friends if you were to go on in the old way. Naturally, he has no use for such a big place. It would be too lonely to endure under the circumstances, and it is hardly the thing to leave the house tenantless year after year. Of course all this is under Jack's supposition that you have no prejudice against the home as a home. If that is false"—

"No. I have a strong attachment for the locality and the house itself. Mildred has also."

"Then you will say yes: and I will promise to take my success as meekly as you could desire."

"Shall I do it Mr. Page?" asked Clover, looking perplexed.

"By all means, if you ask me. Here is the Fair coming on, and the difficulties of suiting one's self in a home in Chicago are going to be many, I fancy."

"I don't want to think of that. We should be able to find a comfortable place."

"Then consider that suggestion unmade, and let me take your consent to Jack. Do you still hesitate?"

"Yes. I had quite made up my mind to do without Jack, and this would change all that."

"Jack does not at all wish to be dispensed with."

"I consider," said Clover with grave gentleness, "that I owe him any favor he chooses to claim; but it seems quixotic on his part to call this one."

"And yet he does. We cannot always understand the vagaries of youth, Mrs. Van Tassel."

"Jack was always willful," she returned, smiling sadly. "Tell him I thank him, Mr. Page, and that Mildred and I will talk it over."

An hour after Gorham's departure, a note was brought to Clover. It was from Jack. He said:—

I thank you for considering my proposition. I have a feeling that in the end you will not refuse me. I have suffered for every unjust word I ever said to you, Clover, and now the only peace possible for me is to be in friendly relations with those my father loved. Only when you are living again under his roof shall I feel that I have won his forgiveness as well as yours. The selfish jealousy of you which has made my heart sore had gone, and gratitude has taken its place. We have both lived long in two years, and suffered much. We can feel for each other.

Forgive your old comrade, Jack.

Clover's tears fell upon this abrupt note, and her heart went out to her friend. She did not need now to talk the matter over with Mildred. She had decided to return to the home by the lake.

Jack went back to Boston without seeing her again; for although he called, the sisters were both away.

CHAPTER 3

MAY DAY

What Chicagoan will ever forget the winter of '92 and '93! It was as though the elements had joined with the majority who frowned down their city's audacious effort. The newspapers recorded the storms and their damage. What an unthinkable thing it was to undertake a World's Fair in such a climate! Certainly if one wanted an allegory of discomfort one had but to visit the Garden City at that season, and witness the teaming through torn-up streets, the building, and the elevating of railroad tracks, while the sense of shortness of time sent men to labor and often to die in exposed places when the mercury was lost below the zero mark. Roads were either ironbound, or deep in the mud of a thaw, and blizzards descended furiously upon the glass portions of Exposition structures, destroying in an hour the work of weeks.

As the first of May approached, more stinging grew the criticisms upon the authorities who had failed to have the Columbian Exposition entirely ready to keep its engagement; but though on the great day Chicago was still in an undeniably uncomfortable condition of unfinished hotels and bad weather, the White City rose like a perfect superb lily from its defiling mud, and the great crowd that swarmed into Jackson Park on the morning of May first found so much to marvel at that they were good-natured and eager under a chill gray sky, and unmindful of clinging soil into which they sank at every step.

Jack Van Tassel had arrived in town a couple of days before, and after registering at his hotel had called immediately at his old home.

The girls received him cordially, although he was unexpected. One or two letters had passed between Clover and himself during the winter, and she now asked him to leave his hotel and take possession of his old room. He declined with thanks, stating that his plans did not yet permit of a prolonged stay in the West, and that it would not be worth while to make the change.

"I am afraid he saw that I hesitated when I asked him," said Clover to her sister after the guest had departed. "I wish we had known that he was coming, then we could have thought the matter over and arrived at a decision. I really didn't know whether I was doing a proper thing or not."

Mildred, who had seen and been amused by her sister's perplexity all through the call, laughed mischievously.

"It is an odd thing if you can't invite your son to visit you," she said.

Clover regarded her helplessly, but she could not help smiling too. "I don't know whether we should be outraging conventionality or not," she repeated. "He will be coming back again in a little while. If only Jeanie hadn't deserted us. It was such an inconvenient season for her to be overwhelmed with homesickness, but she said it was the first time that she had not been really needed here."

"You remind me of Iolanthe," said Mildred wickedly. "I couldn't help thinking of it all the time Strephon was here." And then she sang:—

"'I wouldn't say a word that could be construed as injurious,
But to find a mother younger than her son is very curious,
And that's the sort of mother who is usually spurious;
Tara diddle, tara diddle, tol lol lay.'"

The color rose under Clover's clear skin as she joined reluctantly in her sister's laugh. "Perhaps we had better procure a dragon," she suggested.

"Oh, wait a little," returned Mildred, loath to alter their present mode of life.

But Jack, before he left, had agreed to call for his friends on the morning of May first to take them to see the opening exercises in the new city whose completed splendor they had not before beheld.

The three walked down through the grounds in the dull gray weather, and joined the half million of souls who waited in the Court of Honor to see President Cleveland touch the electric button.

Clover gazed at the white magnificence of architecture, and felt a thrill at the solemn stillness pervading all, which the fine orchestral music only accented.

"It seems to me like the story of Galatea," she said to Jack. "We are waiting to see the breath of life breathed into the statue."

Van Tassel looked down the Grand Basin to where the heroic Republic stood veiled in white from the eyes of men. The low-hanging sky hung its pall above all.

"I think the button may start the clouds as well as the machinery," he remarked. "They look as though they were only waiting some signal to pour down."

"We shall need a shower-bath to put out the fires of our enthusiasm," exclaimed Mildred, who looked as excited as she felt. "Oh, Jack, aren't you glad you are a Chicagoan? Aren't you glad that we've gathered goldenrod right in this very spot in front of the Administration Building?"

Jack protested that he shared this subtle joy fully; and at the moment a new shiver of expectation passed through the throng. The music had ceased. The President had begun to speak. It was a solemn moment, a triumphant moment, when at last the electric button was pressed, hitherto motionless machinery suddenly throbbed, and the vast pulses of the stately, statuesque White City began to beat.

Clover and Mildred unconsciously clasped hands, and their breath came fast as they stood facing the majestic Peristyle, its marble columns surmounted by the solemn, glad, immortal declaration: "Ye shall know the truth, and the truth shall make you free."

Jack stood beside them, his head bared before this beginning of a new era; for at the touching of the signal, down fell the veil from the golden Republic, up streamed the enormous jets of water from the fountains; color and movement thrilled along the roofs of the snowy palaces; flags of all nations unfurled gayly from myriad staffs; the boom of artillery thundered from the lakeside; and as the multitude, swayed by mighty feeling, rent the air with cheers, the sun burst from a cloud and blessed the scene with new splendor. The World's Columbian Exposition had opened.

Van Tassel accepted Clover's invitation to dinner that

afternoon when they reached home, chilled with much standing about in the spring wind.

The impersonal common interest of the day had done much toward re-establishing the old easy relation among the trio.

"So Jeanie felt a call to visit her own kin, did she?" said Jack as they sat at table. "She is so much a part of the house I miss her."

"Yes; she could not be tempted from her project even by the prospect of the Fair. 'What do I want with the Fair?' she asked contemptuously. 'Chicago's just got unbearable since they started it.' But she wanted me to promise to take her back when all the excitement is over and she returns to America," said Clover. "Of course we miss her very much; but at present we get on finely."

"Yes," remarked Mildred, "I don't know that Jeanie would be pleased to know how well. I believe she was right. No doubt a person of her sort would be more fatigued than interested by the Fair."

"I was wondering this morning," said Jack, "while we were waiting down there, what Aunt Love would say to it all."

Clover smiled. "I think Chicago and everything connected with it seems as far off to her as the Sandwich Islands;" but as she spoke a novel thought came into her mind, and after Jack had gone she imparted it to Mildred.

"I have had a brilliant idea," she announced.

"That is nothing new," returned her sister. "A quarter, please," holding out her hand.

Clover loftily ignored both the compliment and the request for prompt recompense.

"We can't selfishly keep this comfortable house just for

our own two selves the next six months."

"I could, just as easy," returned Mildred nonchalantly, dropping into an armchair. "Aren't you glad now that we have lived a life of resorts for two years, and are not under obligations to anybody? Moreover, that we haven't had time to make any intimate friends anywhere? Why, everybody we know here has either rented his house and fled, or is wondering how servants and expenses are to be managed through the summer."

Clover looked serious. "I feel that we ought to do exactly what Mr. Van Tassel would do if he were alive."

"Yes, that is so," agreed Mildred promptly; "but I don't see how you are going to find that out."

"Why, it is perfectly plain that he would entertain his near relatives."

Mildred raised her eyebrows thoughtfully. She began to sing softly again from Sullivan's opera:

"'To say she is his mother is an utter bit of folly,
Heigh-ho, our Strephon is a rogue!
Perhaps his brain is addled and it's very melancholy,
Tara diddle'"

"Stop that nonsensical song."

"My dear, Gilbert never writes any nonsense. It gives me the utmost pleasure to warble his lines. He is the only librettist in the world who says just what he wants to say, and it happens to rhyme. Pardon me if I appeared to be personal. That was another happening. So you think you ought to have sonny at home. Anybody else?"

"Certainly. Mr. Page."

Mildred pursed her lips into a noiseless whistle.

"Mr. Van Tassel's sister's child," went on Clover firmly. "He has a right to expect an invitation. What is the matter? Don't you like him?"

Mildred made her favorite grimace of faint repugnance, and her head dropped to one side. "I've had a good deal of him by proxy," she answered. "I'm very much afraid he's a worthy young man."

"Well, what of it?"

"Oh, you know I can't endure worthy young men," smiled the younger sister provokingly.

"Jack says he is a noble fellow," declared Clover with dignity.

"Of course; but alas, if that was only one of those things that go without saying! His sister-in-law adores him madly. Well, then we are to have sterling cousin Page. Anybody else? It seems to me you are drawing about us a possibly charming, but certainly unconventional family circle."

"No, no. There are the other Pages. Of course we must ask the married brother, just as much as Gorham, and we are under obligation to Mrs. Page for kindness to you."

"So she is to be the chaperone. Is it your expectation that she will wish to stay here all summer? What a perfect goose you were, Clover, not to have your bright idea before you let Jeanie go. After you have thought up three meals a day for guests, for about three months, your opinion of the brilliance of that idea will probably decline and fall."

"Just wait," said Clover triumphantly. "You haven't even heard my bright thought yet. It is Aunt Love."

Mildred looked into her beaming eyes uncomprehendingly. "It is nothing to me," continued Clover, "whether Mrs. Page stays one week or six. I am going to ask Aunt

Love to come and take Jeanie's place all summer."

"Do you suppose she will do it?"

"Yes, I do. I shall ask her, anyway, before one day more passes over my head,—that is, if you agree, Mildred."

"Oh, if I agree!" repeated the latter with light scorn. "I notice you didn't trouble yourself to consult me about Strephon and cousin Page."

"You would like to have Aunt Love, of course," persisted Clover.

"Yes; but she must be sure to bring Blitzen," she insisted, remembering how well the elderly aunt's mischievous terrier had entertained her during her summer out East.

There was only one subject discussed throughout the length and breadth of Pearfield, twenty-four hours after Mrs. Van Tassel's letter reached Miss Berry.

Lovina Berry was going to the World's Fair. Pearfield would be represented, after all. It was a dangerous undertaking. Everybody felt that. The postmaster made himself quite unpopular by doubting whether Loviny ran more risk from desperate characters in Chicago than she would in any other large city; but his heretical opinion was accounted for by a well known contrariness of nature.

Many and solemn were the leave-takings and warnings bestowed upon Miss Berry at the outset of her pilgrimage. She was somewhat astonished herself at her own calmness at the prospect.

"It must be I don't sense it," she declared as she gave her lisle-thread glove a parting wave from the car window. She had planned by letter to have Gorham Page meet her in Boston, and take her to an inexpensive boarding-house where she might remain until she was fitted out for her wonderful trip.

It was a tired and harassed woman that Page met that afternoon, hugging to her, as she stepped from the car, a straining, excited, furry bundle that jumped eagerly to the end of his chain as she permitted him to leap down.

"Such a time as I've had this day," she exclaimed. "I guess I've broke most o' the laws ever made by God and man. By good luck I knew the conductor,—he came from near our place, and he, seein' that Blitzen rampaged dreadful in the baggage-car, let me hold him in my lap. I lost my temper before I'd been out o' Pearfield half an hour and I haven't found it since. I'm just tuckered out. Miss Bryant made a great point o' my bringin' Blitzen, but mercy, before I'd have the care o' him from here to Chicago I'd give up the whole undertakin'." Miss Berry looked anxiously at the dog as he bobbed about at the end of his tether as though to expend the energy stored in his lively legs during hours of inaction. "I don't know how I could leave him in Boston," she added, "and yet"—

Page smiled. "You know very well if you left him he would walk on the ties to Chicago. Don't worry, Aunt Love, I'll send him safely for you. You shall not have any trouble."

Miss Berry looked half hopeful, half incredulous.

"Yes, by express. It will be all right," and Page held open the door of a cab, into which Miss Berry stepped with the nervous and astonished Blitzen again caught in her strong clasp.

"I haven't thanked you a word," she said when the horse had started, "but you can't think what a help it's been to me to have you manage about the boardin' place and all."

"You know my sister-in-law. Hilda wouldn't hear of your going anywhere but straight to her," returned Gorham.

"Oh, that is too much," exclaimed Miss Lovina, flushing with pleasure; and the warm welcome she received when she arrived at Mrs. Page's dainty apartment completed her relief from care and embarrassment.

"I'm sure you never counted on Blitzen," Miss Berry said anxiously, in return to her hostess's greeting.

"But I am glad to see him," responded Hilda. "It is well known that a dog who can wag his tail can knock over lots of valuables in a flat, but Blitzen is a safe and welcome guest, seeing as how his tail has been cropped."

"We'll let him run in the street all he wants to. Perhaps he'll get lost," said Miss Lovina of the stray who had adopted her a few years back. She regarded the small animal darkly in spite of the confiding and questioning gaze he was bending upon her, as though begging to understand today's erratic movements.

"Much more likely to be stolen," remarked Gorham. "I had better send him on to Chicago very soon."

Mrs. Page proved of great assistance to Miss Berry in adding the right articles of dress to her wardrobe, and completing her preparations. It was with a light heart that Aunt Love finally shook hands with Page after he had settled her comfortably in her section of the Chicago train, and when the latter glided slowly and smoothly from the station, Miss Berry leaned back in the cushioned seat and felt happy though excited. She had never been in a sleeping-car before, and every convenience about her excited her wonder and admiration.

She was traveling at Mrs. Van Tassel's expense, and simply followed the explicit directions Page had given her;

so she went into the dining car for her meals, a proceeding which filled her with wonder. Her practical soul yearned to examine the compact kitchen arrangements.

Gorham had charged the porter to attend to her wants, accompanying the exhortation with the only sort of persuasion which appeals to the species, and innocent Aunt Love was in consequence gratefully impressed by her new friend's assiduous attentions.

There is no denying that the gentleman of color had something to endure from the time the train crossed the last state line and entered Illinois. It had been impressed upon Miss Berry that she was to alight at Hyde Park, and her porter earned the money Mr. Page had given him before that station was reached.

"You don't want to get out till you've passed the World's Fair," he said at last in desperation; and Miss Lovina clung to this definite clue with such concentration that when the usual stentorian announcement was made—"World's Fair Buildings on the right," she scarcely cast a glance toward the labyrinth of roofs and domes, but clasped the handles of her bag and shawl-strap, and sat on the extreme edge of the seat.

Soon the porter arrived, took possession of Miss Berry's belongings, and in another minute she stood on the platform, where Mrs. Van Tassel and Miss Bryant met her with open arms.

At least one of Mildred's hands was extended in welcome. The other kept firm hold of a chain to which Blitzen was attached. Instantly the little dog's leaps and grins monopolized the attention of all three. He whined, he actually howled in the fullness of his joy at finding the mistress he had despaired of seeing again.

"For gracious sake!" exclaimed Miss Berry, much embarrassed. "There, there;" she stooped and patted the terrier sparingly. "Yes, here's my trunk-check, Mrs. Van Tassel. My, but you do look well, child. For pity's sake, Miss Mildred, take the chain off'n that dog, and maybe he won't trip me up. Be still, can't you?"

Mildred laughed as she stooped and unfastened the hook from the smart new collar which had gilded Blitzen's misery since his arrival. "Yes, he will not need chains now," she answered, "but we have had to keep him a prisoner for fear he might go back to Boston. It would have been such a pity for you to cross each other on the way."

CHAPTER 4

CLOVER'S INVITATION

Those who wished to continue to point out the defects in Chicago and her Fair had ample opportunity through a large part of the month of May. It was indeed Chicago's Fair then; no one else claimed it. The exhibits were not all in place, the electric effects were not complete, the weather was cold, Orientals had to wear American overcoats above their white gowns, and they sneezed lugubriously under their turbans. The pleasantest spots in the White City at that season were the open fires in the dignified or dainty club-houses known as State buildings. Only the Eskimos were really comfortable, and some of those poor women wished the incoming and outgoing visitor would not allow the northeast wind continuous entrance to their homes.

But the month was nearly out by the time Miss Berry arrived in Chicago. It was the beginning of that marvelous summer whose weather every Chicagoan will always proudly consider an exhibit worthy to be ranked with any wonder it shone upon. The natural elements, like the human ones, gradually admitted that the Columbian Exposition was not only a worthy but an overwhelming success, and in place of buffeting wind and destructive storm, sent week after week a warm blue sky and a cool east breeze to add the crowning charm to the White City's bewildering loveliness.

Had the human element been as prompt in succumbing, thousands of those who strove in the madding crowd of October might have reveled instead in the fresh beauty of June; but the general confidence had not yet been gained. The same journal which had pictured the vulgar young city vociferating for the World's Fair bouquet had not yet declared that it took off its hat to Chicago, adding that all other shows bore the relation to the Columbian Exposition which Jersey City did to Imperial Rome. A comparatively small army of explorers came from the East as yet, to spy out the land and carry back reassuring reports to their skeptical or timid friends.

Miss Berry, in her comfortable, novel quarters, was from the first charmed with her surroundings. The bright bracing air, the frequent tally-ho coaches that passed the door, their scarlet-coated buglers piping with cheerful unsteadiness, the expanse of tumbling blue-green water that constantly gladdened her eyes, all seemed as festive as the fine house which was her temporary home. She enjoyed the playing of the orchestra every morning on the piazza of an adjacent hotel, and was soon able to hum "After the Ball," that unavoidable, omnipresent accompaniment of the World's Fair summer.

Only one thing puzzled her for the first few days after her arrival, and this perplexity she set at rest one cool evening, by watching her opportunity and walking clandestinely to the sands at the back of the Chicago Beach Hotel. There she stooped to the water's edge, dipped her finger in an incoming wave and transferred it to her mouth. Tasting it critically, she looked thoughtful, and after a moment repeated the operation.

"I suppose I've got to believe it," she murmured, rising. "'Tain't salt."

The more cultivated and traveled one was, the more wonderful and beautiful the White City seemed to him. Upon a woman of Miss Berry's narrow worldly experience, its unique characteristics dawned but slowly. For some weeks it is quite certain that the housekeeping duties which Clover at once placed in her hands were more attractive to the good woman than the marvels which lay so near her. She was not insensible to the privilege of being within walking distance of Jackson Park, and now and then she made pilgrimages thither.

"It's somethin' like knowin' there's a big plum puddin' standin' near by, and that whenever I want to, I can go and pull out a plum;" she said; "but mercy! it would take a whole lifetime to see what they've got down there, and every time I go I realize it more."

Clover carried out her hospitable intention as soon as Aunt Love was fairly domesticated; and one morning a letter from her was handed to Mrs. Page at her breakfast-table.

Her family had just been talking about the World's Fair, and Jack had been answering questions concerning the best locality in which to secure accommodations.

"There is nothing like having an ardent Chicagoan in the house to make one attend to these matters in time," remarked Mrs. Page.

"I am very much afraid you will find you are not in time," returned Jack discouragingly. His advice, given a couple of months before, had not been heeded, and he now proceeded to state a series of facts and figures which were rather appalling.

"You will have to do something about it, Jack," remarked Mrs. Page's husband, who is not so designated on account of any inferiority. He was a stout, sandy-haired individual with a good digestion and disposition, who was accustomed to allow Hilda and Gorham to think for him in all matters not related to the wholesale dry-goods business in which he was engaged. "You say we ought to see the Exposition," he went on placidly, "and it is your affair, in the interests of hospitality, to tell us where in—Chicago we can find the proper quarters."

"I impressed upon you some time ago that you ought to attend to it," returned Jack rather stiffly. The air of lightness and condescension with which his cousin always treated the subject of the Fair grated upon him.

"Yes, he did, you know, Robert," declared Mrs. Page, always inclining, like most of Jack's feminine friends, to side with him.

It was at this juncture that the arrival of the mail created a diversion, and Hilda opened Clover's letter.

She glanced down its pages. "Why, how lovely! How kind!" she exclaimed from time to time. "Listen to this. You are all interested. It is from Mrs. Van Tassel."

My Dear Mrs. Page,—I have been wishing for some days to find the right moment in which to thank you for your kindness both to Aunt Love and me in rendering her so much assistance in coming to us. She seems happy and at home already. I am the more pleased to have secured her that it makes it easy for me, in the absence of my old housekeeper, to entertain guests during the coming eventful summer. I hope you and your husband have not already committed yourselves to another plan for seeing the Fair, for our house is most conveniently situated, and my sister and I would be pleased to have you come to us. Will you extend my invitation to your brother as well? As for Jack, it is not necessary, I am sure, for me to write a separate invitation to him. His room is ready for him, and I count upon his taking possession of it for as long a time as he can make it convenient. Indeed, I wish you all four to choose your own times and seasons for coming, for I have no plan to entertain any one else, and I beg you to consider the house always open to you, and a sincere welcome always ready.

Mildred wishes me to send you her love, and we both hope soon to receive favorable word of your plans.

Cordially yours, Clover B. Van Tassel.

Mrs. Page, upon finishing, let her pleased gaze rove from one to another of her three companions. Jack's face was eager and happy, Gorham's interested, but her husband was the first to speak.

"I foresee that I am going to fall in love with that woman," he remarked, breaking open his third muffin and handing his cup to the maid for a second cup of coffee. "That is a charming letter."

"Just an ordinary Chicago production," said Jack exultantly. "What do you say, old Reliable?" he added, turning toward Gorham.

"We are in great luck," returned the latter.

"Now, I will admit," said Jack, "that I have been trying to provide for us all at the Chicago Beach; but I will cease my struggles gratefully."

"When do you want to go, Hilda?" asked Robert Page.

"When can you go, is a more pertinent question," she answered.

"July will, I suppose, be the best time. Would it be heresy, Jack, to inquire if the thermometer in Chicago rises above sixty-five degrees in July? I have understood that it does."

"I know of no city in the country where there is no hot weather in summer," returned Jack shortly. "Chicago is, however, a summer resort."

"I suppose you mean a place where summer resorts. That is what I have heard."

"Perhaps you would better not risk your life there."

"Tut,tut, my boy. I am going to see the writer of that whole-souled letter."

Jack, who had already excused himself from the table, here left the room without deigning a reply, and Mrs. Page immediately looked toward her brother.

"What do you think, Gorham? Of course this is a delightful invitation, but ought we to accept it?"

"I don't quite see your objection," he answered. "It is charming of Mrs. Van Tassel, but it is so evidently a sense of duty which impels her to give such an invitation to a mere acquaintance like me, and a stranger like Robert."

"Look here," remarked the latter, looking up vaguely. "I don't think I want any flaws picked in that invitation."

"Now you keep still, Robert, like a dear. You don't know her at all, and Gorham does. She is just doing this in Uncle Richard's name; I know it, and I am not willing to impose upon her."

"May I see the letter once again?" asked Gorham.

"Certainly?" Mrs. Page handed it to him with alacrity. He read it through from beginning to end. It sounded like Clover. He could hear her pleasant voice in every phrase.

"She is a thoughtful, deliberate sort of person," he said as he handed the letter back. "Whatever her motive is, it is a sufficient one, and one thing that would influence me to advise you to accept is the effect on Jack. Their relations have been a little strained, and I think it would make things still pleasanter than they are now, if Mrs. Van Tassel and Miss Bryant were to become better acquainted with his people."

"Yes, that is what I think," remarked Mr. Page; but his wife frowned upon him.

"You, and Robert, and Jack, go," continued Gorham. "I won't. That would be rather too much of a good thing; but I can get a room at the Beach Hotel, and that is near by. I propose to spend a good deal of time at the Fair. I want to go through it with some degree of thoroughness. Of course no one will really see half of it. I understand that, giving one minute to each exhibit, it is estimated that it would take thirty-two years for a man to get around."

His brother groaned. He was stout and not energetic save in the matter of wholesale dry-goods.

"Thank Heaven it won't take thirty-two years to see Mrs. Van Tassel," he remarked devoutly.

There were no doubts or scruples in Jack's mind as to accepting his invitation, at least for the present. Indeed, this reconciliation between himself and the Bryants, as he still often found himself calling his old friends, altered the whole trend of his life. He felt a new satisfaction in living; a new desire for home; a willingness which amounted to necessity to shake the dust of Boston from his feet, and once more to make of Chicago a permanent abiding-place. His sense of loneliness, an aching one still at times, abated. His own place waited for him. The friendship of these cousins, kind and helpful in their way, could never be to him like that of those girls, the only sisters he had ever known, who had so long divided with him his father's affection and care. He was going home. It was the first sensation of the sort that he had had for years.

He did not try to conceal his satisfaction from Mrs. Page when he said to her his *au revoir*. He expressed sincere gratitude for her kindness and hospitality, but she saw that he was not sorry to have no plan for returning to Boston, and felt a little piqued despite Jack's enthusiasm over the plan which would soon make them a reunited family party.

"I have not seen Jack so gay since Uncle Richard died," she said that night to Gorham.

"No. His alienation from Mrs. Van Tassel and her sister has worried him a good deal, I know," responded Page. "This final burial of the hatchet must be a great relief to a fellow so sensitive as Jack is."

But this explanation was not sufficient to account to Mrs. Page for Van Tassel's jubilant spirits. He had not sprung up three stairs at a time, and whistled and sung over his packing, just because of obtaining the forgiveness of two young women whose feelings he had outraged.

"Men are stupid," she soliloquized. "I *know* that Jack is in love."

With this truly feminine solution of her cousin's conduct she was the better satisfied because she would so soon have opportunity of verifying her own perspicacity by ocular proof. But her diagnosis would have been a surprise to Jack. No over-like haste mingled with the impatience he felt at the lateness of his train on the June afternoon when he reached Chicago; and when finally he found himself on the familiar home street, even its unfamiliarity seemed representative of the pleasant new state of things which had come into his life. His flying visit during the bad weather of six weeks before had not shown the old neighborhood in its present finished condition.

Van Tassel smiled as a coach and six rattled by him, the notes of its "mellow horn" breaking in impertinently upon the strains of an orchestra at the adjacent fashionable hotel. "Can this be quiet little Hyde Park?" he asked himself.

How the long June evenings of his boyhood came back to him as he sauntered down the changed street! How the thrushes used to sing here at this hour! How the boys and girls who could muster anything to navigate, from a scow to a trim canoe or sailboat, used to launch their craft, early in these long evenings, and sometimes lashing the boats together, a dozen in a row, would drift over the rocking waves and sing by the hour beneath a moon which electricity had not yet forced out of a long-established business!

The wild shore was changed, cultivated, and trimmed into order according to fashion now, like the young people who once disported over it in free country fashion.

Jack could not whistle the scrap from "Carmen" against the insistent rhythm of "After the Ball" which was being performed by a uniformed functionary from the hotel who passed him under the old familiar elms.

But Clover was on the piazza to meet him, a gracious genius of home in her blue gown, with the welcoming light in her eyes.

"I told you not to stay for me," said Jack, coming up the

steps, his hat in his hand.

"I know," returned Clover, looking down into his happy, handsome face. "I stayed for my own sake as well as yours. I have been at the Fair all day, and did not feel like going down this evening. Mildred went from town with the Ogdens on their drag to take supper in Old Vienna. She wished me to give you an extra shake of the hand for her."

"Thank you, Clover," he answered, and he held her hand a moment as they interchanged a look that had in it reminiscence, but reminiscence from which all bitterness was gone. The sweet summer air seemed throbbing with their love for him with whom every part of this home was connected.

Miss Berry appeared at the house door. She started at the pretty tableau she saw, and recalled the time when she had pleaded with a heart-sore man to understand that Clover had given his father much happiness in his last days. The memory passed like a vision across the fair June scene.

She would have withdrawn, but Van Tassel saw her. "How do you do, Aunt Love?" he said, and then she came forward to return his cordial greeting.

"Isn't this a queer thing, for me to be in Chicago, Mr. Jack?"

"It is just as it should be," he returned. "Now when we get Gorham and Mr. and Mrs. Page here, we shall be a complete party."

"Mr. and Mrs. Page promise me July," said Clover, "but your cousin Gorham seems to think he would better stay at the hotel. We won't quarrel with him at this distance." She smiled. "Well, Jack, will you go upstairs? Is it to be hammock or Fair this evening?"

"I can scarcely wait till tomorrow for the Fair, yet I don't like to leave you at once."

"Don't mind that. I should enjoy seeing your first view, and should have saved myself for tonight except that I could not escape personally conducting a friend today who was very kind to us last year."

"Come in and eat something first, Mr. Jack," said Miss Berry, so anxiously that Van Tassel laughed.

"I am sure, Aunt Love, if I have the good luck to meet you in heaven, the first thing you will do will be to urge upon me some manna or angel's food, or whatever may be on the bill of fare."

"Hush, child. Come straight in, for daylight is precious."

"Thank you, but I knew that, and so I took lunch in the train. I expected only to carom on the house as it were, and then make a bee-line for the great show. We did have the first view of it together, Clover, you know."

The dimple dipped in Clover's cheek just as of old. "It will seem different to you tonight," she answered. "That was impressive and solemn; but now—No, I won't be so foolish as to try to describe what is incomparable. I will only say, Go. You will be grateful for whatever feeble standards of comparison you have gained by travel."

CHAPTER 5

THE COURT OF HONOR

Jack jumped into a Beach wagon as it rolled along from the hotel, and drove down East End Avenue, approaching the gigantic failure known as the Spectatorium, whose bulky, half-clothed skeleton upreared against the sky like a type of blighted hope.

Following Clover's advice, he entered the park at the Fifty-seventh Street entrance. A band was playing on its aerial perch above the Eskimo village, and Jack smiled to hear the gay, assured strains of "After the Ball" soaring above a vigorous drum accompaniment. He walked across the bridge and looked down where the Eskimos in their white robes with the peaked hoods propelled their slender canoes noiselessly amid the darkening shadows of the willows.

Straight before him to Michigan's brink stretched an electric-lighted avenue, flanked on one side by State buildings, and on the other by that lion-guarded Greek Palace of Art whose columns, even pictured, send a thrill of grateful delight to the hearts of those who have passed within its portals.

The fresh verdure of the lawns showed living green, as Jack passed on to the right until he gained the waterside of the Art Building, and there paused to gaze across at the edifices on the opposite shores. Towers and domes of all shapes and sizes showed amid the June foliage. Every beauty of form and tint surrounded him, divided by broad spaces of rippling water. He was in a city of preternatural loveliness. What wonder that a noiseless boat came gliding to his feet in answer to his wish to explore these distant, fairy vistas. He stepped within, and silently the little craft sped on.

The white loveliness of Brazil, the alabaster lace work of the poetical Fisheries,—Van Tassel glanced over his shoulder as they were left behind, and in a minute more the lofty, winged angels of the Woman's Building blessed his sight.

The dainty conceits of Puck and the White Star melted from his vision to make way for the glories of the Horticultural treasure house, surmounted by its illuminated crystal dome. Lilies, red, yellow, and white, were asleep in the stone-guarded lakelet, upon which smiled the wreathed marble beauty of women and babies on the façade; and in contrast, next sprang to life in electric light the alert equestrian figures of cowboy and Indian controlling restive steed, and peering forth into the night.

But an exclamation escaped Van Tassel's lips as the Transportation Building was passed, and the arched grandeur of the Golden Door shone down upon him. The launch turned, and thus ideally, without sound or effort, he was borne on between Wooded Island and the homes of Mines and Electricity, approaching the vast expanse of the Liberal Arts Building, only to turn smoothly again beneath the bridge, and glide on toward that Mecca of all Exposition pilgrims, the unique Court of Honor.

Jack stood there once in a still, chill time of waiting, and had seen the dead marble city quickened to life. Now the heart which began to beat that day had made all the whiteness to glow. He forgot to breathe as, passing beneath the last bridge, he emerged where the sea horses reared wildly above cascades that went splashing down the stone steps beneath Columbia's triumphal barge.

Through pink and purple, the rippling opaline water in the Grand Basin was losing its sunset hues, and paling, as the fairy boat passed on. The gold of the statue of the Republic was turning to silver. The figures on the snowy palaces that faced the four sides of the lagoon still stood white against the darkening background. Angels poised on soft, strong wings, seemed vivified as the day died. Jack saw their beckoning hands through a mist. He heard the penetrating tones of their silver trumpets through the lingering sweetness of a serenade that proceeded from a distant pavilion. Strange influences were about him, and he was glad that no mortal friend stood by.

His father had worked and planned and striven for this. Did he see the result? Could he know the success that had crowned the efforts of his confrères?

Suddenly, across the spontaneous regret that sprang in Jack's heart at the realization of what Death had snatched from his loved one, came an idea which was like a glimpse of new light. Since such a miracle of beauty as now lay about him was possible in this lower world, might it not be indeed true—

Jack's thoughts became confused. They had followed so long and yearningly out into that unknown country where his father had gone, and about which he had never before troubled himself, that he had grasped for his won consolation a belief that it was a reality; and now something in this stately and beautiful place built with men's hands made him recall vaguely the Bible declaration:—

"Eye hath not seen, nor ear heard, neither have entered into the heart of man, the things which God hath prepared for them that love him."

It was with reverence and a species of awe that Van Tassel gazed about him. The Court of Honor had given him his first approach to a realization of the possibilities of the Celestial City.

Only gradually the details of his surroundings impressed him. His boat glided toward the Peristyle, and he began to notice that the water was picturesque with gondolas, propelled by their bright-sashed oarsmen.

Beneath a massive arch he could look out upon the great lake, his lake, his old playmate, now grown grandly alien as guardian of this mystical city. He knew every tone of its voice. He had braved it in its stormy strength, and gone to sleep at night to its lullaby.

Now its surf, breaking against the outer stones, appealed to his moved heart in the song of a past gone forever, and he did not know whether its proximity, the voice of this single friend in a place of strangers, gave the crown of pain or of joy to his tender ecstasy.

And now the royal palaces so lavishly decorated with painting and sculpture began to assume their further nightly decoration of jewels. Tiny incandescent lights ran swiftly in diamond necklaces and diadems about cornice and pediment of buildings, and glittered in long lines close above the waters of the lagoon. The crown of the Administration dome shone out in immobile fire, while torches of flame, "yellow, golden, glorious," flared across its façades.

Van Tassel had no well-meant descriptions of this view to contend against. No one had endeavored to prepare him for what he was to see. To him these wonders were appearing for the first time; one after another spontaneous, unexpected change of scene forming a *crescendo* of loveliness. More and more unreal grew the fairy spectacle. Less and less did he try to realize the impossible fact that he was in a familiar locality.

He left the boat mechanically because his quiet fellow-passengers—figures also of a dream—did so; and when he paused again, he was standing near a giant horse and plowboy near the water's edge. Behind him stretched the spaces of lawn in front of the Liberal Arts edifice, softly green in the rays of many arc-light moons. He gazed westward toward the Administration Building, before which three great fountains played, and suddenly its regal jeweled dome became more splendid in the surrounding darkness. The cameos upon its surface shone out clear-cut and white in the night. A moment thus, then the carving disappeared, and again the electric jewels stood alone against the sky. That magic, all-revealing light flitted to rest upon the great central fountain where the Muses propelled the barge of Progress through musically plashing waters; and while the erect figure in the chair of state still looked proudly out into the night, all other brightness faded. Even the jewels vanished. The palaces stood dark and mysterious beneath the stars. All at once a light was thrown upon the group which surmounted the Peristyle.

Columbus in his four-horse chariot shone white above the shadowy columns, driving in from the broad waters toward distant, glowing, advancing Columbia.

Van Tassel, spellbound, yielded still more to the mystery of the place and hour, and a subdued murmur caused him to glance again westward. The fountains which flaked the great barge on either side had ceased to play, while a strange beam of light shot heavenward from either one. At last at the foot of the beam a bright liquid bubbling began, which seemed to gather strength, and at last leaped from both fountains high in the air. This vivid red changed to violet, to gold, to emerald, to molten silver, breaking in brilliant showers and mists. Apart from the lofty middle jet in each one, circled low whirls of bright water with such swiftness as to stand like sheaves of wheat placed in a ring about the central cascade.

Van Tassel wished to have a fairer view of both fountains, and changed his position to another side of the great horse. Around him were other shadowy beings whom he did not regard. Near his new standpoint and rather in his way was a woman seated. He did not look to see upon what she sat. In his present state of mind he would have supposed it a throne had he thought about it at all; but he did not think about it, and the throne was in his way, so he unconsciously leaned slightly upon it in his effort to see.

The figure in the chair turned her head. "Did you find them?" she asked, then added coldly, "Excuse me," and turned back again.

Van Tassel started like a somnambulist wakened from sleep. Another familiar voice had spoken to him out of the past. At the same moment the search light which had been upon the Quadriga sped to the angel above the pediment of the Agricultural Building. So light her poise, so strong her wings, so beneficent her outstretched arms, it seemed impossible in that mystical irradiation that she should not quit her lightly touched support and float downward to waiting mortals.

A need for sympathy upsprang in Van Tassel's heart. Involuntarily he spoke;

"Is that not beautiful Mildred?"

"Jack!" The exclamation in amazed tones as the girl sat up alertly in her wheeled chair. "I was just wondering if you had come. When did you arrive?"

He took the hand she offered. "I don't know," he answered slowly. "Do you see that angel?"

"Indeed I do. That is my angel."

"Our angel then. Let me share it."

"You shall," replied the girl generously. She waited a moment in smiling silence; "but that isn't our hand," she added at last. "That is mine. Haven't you had it a good while, considering it is a loan?"

"Have I? Well," and Jack slowly released it. "I am in dreamland, Mildred. I am glad to meet you here, whether you are a reality or not."

"Oh! You remind me of those creepy shades in Vedder's picture where one asks the other who he is and the second answers shiverily that he doesn't know. 'I only died last night,' is what he was inconsiderate enough to reply. I have never forgiven him."

Jack stood at her side and leaned an arm on the back of her chair.

"This is a sort of No Man's Land too," he answered, "and when it grows dark here one feels that these marble creatures gain life. See that population on the Peristyle! They belong here. We are only strangers."

"I see the spell of the White City is upon you, else you

would certainly express some surprise at finding me alone."

"It is only one of the good and wonderful things that have befallen me tonight. It seems perfectly natural. I needed you, Mildred. I needed some tie to the time in which life was worth living to assure me that it is so still, and that there is perhaps more use in it than there would be in sinking into the opal water and dying rapturously in this enchanted place."

"Why Jack, kindred spirit; you have it as severely as we have!"

The girl extended her gloved hand impetuously, and Van Tassel accepted it with alacrity.

"Are you going to take it away again immediately?" he inquired, slowly waking to the situation. "I was enjoying holding it before more than I realized until I was bereft. One must have sympathy in a place like this."

"Oh I know it," she said, speaking hastily as she withdrew her hand and looked over her shoulder apprehensively, "and I am afraid every second that Mr. Ogden will come back. When our party left Old Vienna, we separated and promised to rendezvous by the plow-horses, *I* thought, but Mr. Ogden understood that it was to be at the Liberal Arts entrance, and he has gone now to see if they are there. My chair-boy is over yonder resting his weary bones on the steps. I never can endure to have the poor things stand around any more than they have to."

"I trust the Liberal Arts entrance is a sufficiently ambiguous term to detain our friend some time," returned Jack. "Isn't there some white magic that could be practiced on him? Of course no black art would be possible here, but I must say I should have come down by easy stages before I could converse with Ogden tonight, and I don't want to leave you."

"I don't want you to, either. I— especially don't. And I told Mr. Ogden that if we met you here I should have to go with you---Yes, I put it that way, for I told him we expected you, and it wasn't quite the thing for me to come away; but of course I hadn't the least idea we *should* meet you."

"And you told him that too, I suppose," remarked Jack dryly, all his dreaminess departed. "You declared it would be your duty to go with me if we did meet, but of course such a calamity for Ogden was improbable. I know just how you put it. Girls know how to smooth a man the right way. Now that we have met, and Ogden is out of the way, you tell me you especially want me to remain with you, and don't want him."

Mildred looked up at the speaker, and after a moment burst into a mirthful laugh.

"Where is our angel?" she asked

Jack glanced across the lagoon, but all was shadow save for the rosy glow in the colonnade of the Agricultural Building.

"Vanished!" exclaimed Mildred. "Frightened back by your naughty temper just as she was about to fly down to us."

"I don't like to think of you as the least bit of a coquette," said Van Tassel.

"Then don't. It is extremely disrespectful. Oh, Mr. Ogden, you are back again. The unexpected always happens, you see, and truth is stranger than fiction. Here is Mr. Van Tassel, after all."

"Well, Jack." The two men greeted each other, each endeavoring to conceal his dissatisfaction. "It *is* possible to find a needle in the haymow, then," said Ogden. "Miss Bryant told me you were expected about now. Your first visit? What do you think of our little show?"

"Can't say yet," returned Jack shortly. "I am just going to see another part of it."

"The fireworks, I suppose. They will start, now the fountains have stopped."

"Fireworks? No!" exclaimed Van Tassel in genuine repugnance. What sacrilege for pyrotechnics to paint the lily! His eyes fell upon a revolving glove of light inside a window of the Electricity Building. Its color changed with each revolution. "I think I will wander over in that direction," he said.

"The fireworks are always fine," remarked Mildred. "Are you sure you would not prefer to come to the lake shore and see them? The reflections in the water give beautiful effects." As she spoke, the girl left her wheeled-chair.

"Oh, don't rise, Miss Bryant," begged Ogden hastily. "I will find our pusher. The rest of the party did understand that we were to come to the Liberal Arts entrance. They will meet us at Baker's Chocolate House."

"Don't let me detain you," said Van Tassel courteously. The electric jewels were again running in lines of light around the buildings. Jack could see the expression in Mildred's face as she stood before him.

She waited a moment and Ogden stepped aside to find the guide.

"I don't want to see a rocket go sputtering over this place," explained Jack, for the girl's eyes demanded something.

She gave a short laugh. "You poor, provincial Bostonian," she remarked. "Go your way; and when you discover what the fireworks of the White City really are, perhaps your fastidiousness will not be shocked. Certainly, Mr. Ogden, I am ready. *Au revoir,* Jack."

"Good-by, old fellow," said Ogden, as Mildred resumed her position in the chair. He was beaming again with relief from the apprehended loss of Miss Bryant's society.

Van Tassel moved away in the opposite direction from that they took; but no amount of attempted concentration on his surroundings would restore to him the dreamy delight of half an hour ago. He saw continually the reproach and surprise in Mildred's eyes.

"What right had I to take her away from Ogden?" his thoughts protested. "It was all nonsense for her to think that hospitality demanded it."

Then his reflections passed over from the indignant hazel eyes to Miss Bryant's cavalier. The latter's uneasy devotion had been apparent even in the few phrases Jack had heard him say. The eagerly bent head, the short nervous laughs with which he interspersed his sentences told the story; and instantly curiosity leaped up in Van Tassel's heart as to Mildred's real sentiments toward her admirer.

She had said she especially wanted Jack not to leave her tonight. What did that mean? Jack walked a little faster because he suddenly knew that it was the fact that she had said that, coupled with Ogden's lover-like manner which had made him hold aloof.

He had made a point of giving Ogden his chance, and now he felt ashamed of it. Why should he have felt injured because Mildred had an admirer? Probably she had a dozen, and what wonder if she had?

He felt humiliated, and convicted of disloyalty. Milly

Bryant had wanted defense from something, and appealed to him in vain.

Jack had passed along the side of the Electrical Building and crossed the bridge to Wooded Island by this time, and, deciding to postpone further exploration, determined to walk straight up through the Cornell Avenue entrance and so home. But as thousands of people know to the cost of their groaning muscles, getting on Wooded Island and getting off it are two very different things. Jack wandered about for some time before he found another bridge, and when he did so, it led off to the east, and his aimless walk brought him to the lake shore. Cannon-like reports were sounding upon the air, and superb bombs bursting high above the water broke into lavish showers of emeralds, rubies, and diamonds. The shore was black with a watching multitude, and Van Tassel found himself drawn to its outskirts to watch and wonder with the rest. Volcanoes and serpents of flame, bouquets of a hundred rockets at once, filled the night with brightness, paling the stars, and illuminating the surging water; and when a succession of fiery white cascades slowly unrolled their graceful curves and stood poised in air, showering a light as of day upon the scene, Jack joined in the cheers that with whistles from a congregation of boats saluted the gorgeous spectacle.

"I'm a fool," he said, as he resumed his walk northward. "I am sure Mildred would have given me her hand again on that."

CHAPTER 6

A MASSACHUSETTS CELEBRATION

"I see by the paper there's some sort o' doin's at the Massachusetts house today," observed Miss Berry to Clover, as the two stood in the dining room one morning after breakfast was over.

"A day when you ought to visit the Fair then, surely," replied her companion.

"Why, yes. I don't know but I will," returned Miss Lovina ruminatively.

"And you ought to make an early start, Aunt Love. You are not the only loyal Yankee in town."

"Just so," said the housekeeper placidly. "Mrs. Van Tassel, we must have a chocolate puddin' pretty soon. Mr. Jack was fond o' chocolate from a child. I well remember"—

"Yes, I want to hear all about it some time; but you know how hard it is for you to get an early start for the Fair. Let me attend to your department today, and you go down to the Massachusetts house and have a good time."

"My dear, I shall get there in good season. Don't you worry a mite. Independence is won. The country's safe and my bein' on hand at just such a minute don't signify. I'd rather go through my reg'lar routine. I'm happier that way."

Thus it was that when Aunt Love stepped leisurely through the Cornell Avenue turnstile, taking her way down between Kentucky and West Virginia and around Pennsylvania's edifice, she saw that the Massachusetts Building was surrounded by a crowd.

"That's clever," she murmured, in no way disturbed by the evident fact that she could not approach near enough to hear the speeches. "There's plenty o' folks to show an interest."

The wreathed façade of New York's palatial home rose beside her, and she ascended the broad marble steps, passed through the hall, and out upon the eastern porch. A fountain plashed coolly in its centre, wicker rocking-chairs stood about, dull blue portières were looped between its pillars. Miss Berry was warm and tired from her walk. The chairs looked inviting. She sank into one of them, and listened to the lulling tone of the fountain while she looked across the street at the more energetic patriots or more curious idlers, who lined the way to the Hancock house in the hope of seeing the dignitaries of the occasion pass in and out.

A fine band stationed in the yard of the mansion began to play inspiringly. As Miss Berry grew refreshed under the influence of the silvery falling water and her comfortable chair, her anxiety to see and hear increased. Her point of view was unsatisfactory, and yet the idea of joining the crowd of spectators was not attractive.

"I wonder if they'll let you go upstairs in this grand, big place," she pondered. "One o' those blue fellers 'll stop me quick enough if I can't. They know a good deal better what a body can't do than what she can."

Miss Berry might be excused for grumbling. She had made her acquaintance with the Fair City at a date before the Columbian Guards had learned their points of compass; and she would have to become lighter on her feet before she could forgive them the unnecessary walking which their blundering directions had caused her to perform.

She left the shady stone porch, and, passing through the spacious apartment which led to the hall, began to ascend the stairs. No one protested, and she took courage to remark her surroundings.

"The New Yorkers seem to like any color so it's red," she mused, noting the Pompeian glow of the wall. Of course a Massachusetts woman on this day must not be uncritical of her neighbor's efforts.

But when Miss Lovina entered the banquet hall she stood amazed. Only for a moment, however. It was an unrighteous place. She felt it. She refused to be dazzled by its prismatic glass and its painted cherubs. There was an unholy luxury, a theatrical suggestion about its velvet boxes. Miss Berry, looking straight before her, hastened swiftly as she dared across its polished floor and through the light room beyond, out upon an upper balcony which overlooked the festivities of her own substantial and respectable State.

Yes, Miss Berry could breathe out here. Coming from the seductive shadow of the dim hall, the sunlight seemed doubly clear. The heavenly blue of the firmament bent above snowy and golden domes, flying flags, and winding waterways, while the bewitching sparkle of lake Michigan's electric blues and peacock greens seemed more vital as one listened to the rhythmic harmonies poured forth on the summer air by the musicians below. It was a season of delight. The whole atmosphere seemed charged with gayety.

A man leaning his elbows on the rail of the balcony was thinking this when Miss Lovina emerged from the doorway. She glanced at him, then glanced again, then gazed.

"Of course 't ain't him; but if it don't look like him!" she mused.

The more she looked, the stronger grew the resemblance of that back to one she knew. The man was interested in the celebration over the way. Why should she not stand beside him a minute?

Acting on the impulse, Aunt Love also leaned her arm on the rail, and waited a second before stealing a furtive curious look at her neighbor's face. Their eyes met. In a moment both her hands were being shaken.

"For the land's sake, Mr. Gorham!"

"Hurrah for us," he answered, laughing. "To think that I should have come unexpectedly upon this celebration and you. What more could a Bostonian ask?"

"You might ask to be in the Massachusetts house instead of over here in Gotham."

"I fancy only invited guests go in there today; but at any rate I have only just arrived, and this is a fine place for the general effect. So that is the old Hancock house."

"Yes. I remember the real one very well."

"How well the grounds look. I am anxious to get in. You have visited it, of course."

"Yes, I have. I must say to you, Mr. Gorham, I had to laugh to see some o' the stuff they've put in a glass case over there. I've got some things in my attic in Pearfield they could have had and welcome."

"Perhaps they would have been glad of them," remarked Page.

Miss Berry laughed. "I never thought before o' puttin' Aunt Jerushy's old calash under glass for a show," she said. "It would 'a' looked simple to me; but there's papers in one o' the downstairs rooms that are interestin'. There's no doubt about it. It does make a body's blood boil to see the old superstitions down in black and white, and think o' the past sufferin's of innocent folks. There's one paper there makin' out a case against some poor critter for havin' dealin's with the devil, 'way back in Salem times."

"I want to see everything in that house," returned Gorham, with anticipatory relish.

"Well, give an account of yourself," said Miss Berry, after a moment's silence. "Have you been to Mrs. Van Tassel's?"

"No, not yet."

"But you are comin', ain't you?"

"To call, certainly."

"But you've been invited to stay?"

"Yes, I know; but I have taken a room at the Beach."

"Why, what's that for? Mrs. Van Tassel will think that's queer."

"She will have guests enough without me."

"It is your Uncle Richard's house," persisted Miss Berry.

"Yes, that is just the trouble," returned Page quietly.

Aunt Love sighed. "Well, I was 'lottin' on helpin' to make you all comfortable."

"I haven't a doubt of it, you dear soul. Be sure that only stern principle drives me from under your wing, and please get me an invitation to dinner soon, won't you? How is Jack?"

"He's lively. I heard 'em at breakfast talkin' about all comin' down to the illumination tonight."

"I wonder if I might join the party."

"Of course. Nobody knew you were comin' out so soon."

"I didn't expect it myself. It was a sudden determination."

"They are goin' to have their supper down here at six o'clock, I heard 'em say at breakfast, at the Marine—Caffy, I think they call it. At any rate I know the house first-rate; and if 't wan't for the Art Buildin' I could show it to you from here. It's brown, and that's queer enough in this place, and then it's all covered with candle snuffers. Just as soon as I once sensed it that the Columbian Guards were put here to look pretty and didn't know where anything was, I made up my mind if I didn't learn the g'ography o' the place I'd be a cripple; so I buckled down to it and I'm most ready to stand an examination. Miss Bryant told me when I first came down that if I'd just take the opposite direction to what a Guard told me, I'd find myself all right; and that did work pretty well, but it's better yet to know your own way around and not have to make calculations."

Page nodded smilingly.

"It does beat all," Aunt Love went on, "how when you're at this north end o' the Fair, the Art Buildin' is just across the street from everything. It does seem sometimes as if it hadn't any end; and when you once get into it. My!"

"Yes, I suppose so," said Page, "but," he added with the courage of a new-comer, "I propose to see all that's in it; and speaking of thoroughness, have you looked over this building?"

"I just glanced as I came along," replied Miss Berry cautiously. "It's pretty worldly and glitterin', just like the folks that built it. That hall in there with the slippery floor"—

"A ball-room, yes. Let us go back and examine."

"Oh, it's a ball-room, is it!" said Miss Berry, following the young man back into the lofty apartment where sunlight sifting through caught in the prismatic chandeliers and lay in rainbows on the floor.

They stood at the rope-guarded door of the dainty tea-room. Page pointed out to his companion the beauties of wreathed pillars and mural decorations in the lofty hall, but he observed that the light of suspicion still shone in her eyes.

"Let us try the roof, Aunt Love," he remarked "You can see the Hancock house again from there, and I'm sure you will be more comfortable."

"Oh, I know this is all elegant, Mr. Gorham, and it's a great thing to have such riches opened up for everybody to see. Why, downstairs there's a gold piano, and velvet and silk curtains' but folks don't want to set their hearts on gold pianos and diamond chandeliers. You ain't goin' to take that elevator, are you?" she added, dropping her virtuously impersonal tone for one of anxiety.

"Certainly. You must have learned the importance of economizing steps here."

"Better get lame from walkin' than break your leg in a fallin' elevator," remarked Miss Berry. "Accidents in the papers do scare a body." But she consented to run the risk, and soon was standing beside Page in one of the square towers on the roof, with the Fair City spread out around them.

"I suppose you have visited the Midway," remarked Page, looking over to where the Ferris wheel revolved, slowly and steadily.

Miss Berry threw up both her hands. "Yes, all I want to," she returned sonorously.

"Don't say that. I expect you to pilot me to all the shows."

"You'll be disappointed, then. Civilization's good enough for me. If I'd had a call to minister to naked savages, I s'pose I'd 'a' been given grace to conquer; but to listen to 'em yell, and see 'em dance, is a mighty queer thing for Christians to seek for entertainment, it seems to *me*. If I could go into that Midway with plenty o' hot water and Castile soap, and some sensible clothes, and could help those poor critters to a more godly way o' livin' that would be a different thing; but when I want a good time I ain't goin' to try to get it bein' trod on by camels and yelled at by Turks, all the time smellin' smells I don't know the name of and would be afraid to. No, sir."

Page laughed. Miss Berry looked as though Michigan's breezes were powerless to cool her.

"Perhaps the Midway Plaisance is an acquired taste," he said. "You may like it better, later."

"No, I've seen enough of it if I can't be a missionary, but I'm glad all the natives have got it warm at last, anyway."

"Which natives?"

"Oh, all those foreign folks. They're all natives of some place, I s'pose, and they do say when 't was rainy and cold and muddy they had a forlorn time of it in the Plaisance."

"Yes; we used to read about it, and my brother Robert nicknamed the street then the Mudway Nuisance. We all laughed at the joke but Jack. It is against Jack's principles to jest at sacred things like Chicago and her Fair. I shall have to get him to show me the fine points of the Midway. He won't refuse me."

"No, indeed. There's plenty that like it. The place gets more crowded every day. Why, Mr. Gorham," Miss Berry dropped her rather sad, musing tone, and spoke feelingly. "That Midway is just a representation of matter, and this great White City is an emblem of mind. In the Midway it's some dirty and all barbaric. It deafens you with noise; the worst folks in there are avaricious and bad, and the best are just children in their ignorance, and when you're feelin' bewildered with the smells and sounds and sights, always changin' like one o' these kaleidoscopes, and when you come out o' that mile-long babel where you've been elbowed and cheated, you pass under a bridge—and all of a sudden you are in a great, beautiful silence. The angels on the Woman's Buildin' smile down and bless you, and you know that in what seemed like one step, you've passed out o' darkness into light." Aunt Love paused thoughtfully. "It's come to me, Mr. Gorham, that perhaps dyin' is goin' to be somethin' like crossin' the dividin' line that separates the Midway from the White City. I've asked myself when I've passed under that bridge and felt the difference down so deep, what did make it so strong? 'T ain't only the quiet and the grandeur o' those buildin's compared with the fantastic things you've left behind; I believe it's just the fact that the makers o' the Fair believed in God and put Him and their enlightenment from Him into what they did; and we feel it some like we'd feel an electric shock."

Page nodded. "You make me more interested than ever in my prospect of sightseeing," he said. "Now I propose that you show me the way to that café where you say the others will come this evening, and we will take lunch together there. Not a word of objection, Aunt Love. This is a great day. United we stand, divided we fall. Let us charge on the café under the candle-snuffers."

The two friends descended to the street, and Page, submitting to Miss Berry's guidance, was led through the archway running beneath the eastern corridor of the Art Building. "I won't attempt to take you through the buildin' itself," said Miss Berry, "'cause I know well enough I shouldn't get through before the middle o' the afternoon; partly 'cause you'd stop to look at the statuary, and partly 'cause the first thing I always do when I get in there is to lose myself. I've thought, up to this summer, that I had a pretty good bump o' locality; but land! let me turn around in that place a few times and all those signs, 'East Wall,' 'North Wall,' and the rest, don't mean any more to me than Greek would. You'll see how 't is when you try it."

Page was only half listening. He paused by the brink of the water, fascinated by the sparkling, shining, noonday beauty before him. Gondolas were stealing from beneath the bridges, and electric launches passing and repassing silently and smoothly over the changing waves.

"We must get into one of those boats, Aunt Love," he said with enthusiasm.

"You can't sail to the restaurant. That's right over yonder." observed Miss Berry practically, indicating with her parasol the many-towered roof of the Marine Café.

Page sighed. "Do what you like with me," he answered resignedly. "I can see already that the summer will be too short."

"If your breath ain't, that's all you need fret about," returned Miss Lovina, as they started eastward, along the bank of the pond. "Many's the time in the last weeks I've wished I only weighed one hundred. Don't those ducks and swans have it comfortable?"

Page watched the undulating motions of the pretty birds that eyed them as they passed.

"No, I didn't bring my lunch; hadn't the least notion o' stayin'," replied Miss Berry over her shoulder, to the graceful followers who soon veered away, secure of dining sumptuously every day.

"These here steps," remarked Aunt Love, as she climbed up to Costa Rica's entrance and down on the other side, "do seem an awful aggravation when you're tired, which I ain't now, of course. There's no gettin' out of 'em except by walkin' all around Robin Hood's barn."

Page found his companion surprisingly intelligent as to the names of the buildings they passed lingeringly on the way to the café, and once arrived at that haven, they proceeded to take a leisurely lunch, after which Miss Berry allowed herself to be easily persuaded to ride around the lagoon in an electric launch.

Page found so much to interest him in this initial trip, the quiet gliding motion, cool air, and constantly stimulating panorama were so charming, that he scarcely knew when to abandon this certain good for one more doubtful. At last, however, he and Miss Berry found themselves roaming beneath the gilded towers of the Electricity Building. Miss Lovina gazed benevolently and uncomprehendingly upon one and another evidence of marvelous achievement, waiting patiently whenever Page paused to examine and question.

"There's one place here," she volunteered at last, "where I will say for 'em they've done a cute thing. They've harnessed chain lightnin' so it pulls up and down a zigzag path just as tame as my cow'll go to pasture. Come and see it, Mr. Gorham."

So Page was piloted through the spectacular southeast portion of the building, where color and movement thrilled through every phase of intensity, from the steady glow of the living green pillars of the Egyptian temple, to the various whirling globes and wheels, and the racing bubbles of changing light which sped along their irregular tracks.

"Ah, here are the telephones," remarked Page.

"Yes; do you know, Mr. Gorham, till I came to Chicago I'd never seen a telephone? I find folks don't make anything of 'em here. Mrs. Van Tassel ain't any more afraid of her telephone than she is of her sewin' machine. When I first came I used to jump a foot every time that sharp little bell rung; but I made up my mind that I was havin' advantages, and that I wasn't goin' to slight 'em. I made up my mind I was goin' to speak into that box, no matter how fast the chills traveled up my back, and I did it; it makes me as weak as a kitten yet, but I just will be up with the times I live in if I get a chance; and ain't a telephone a perfect wonder now?"

"It is, indeed, and they are improving them all the time. I see there is a long-distance telephone. How should you like to talk to New York?"

"I shouldn't like to make a fool o' myself that way or any other, Gorham Page."

"But really, Aunt Love"—

"Save your breath, Mr. Gorham. I know this building's

full o' queer doin's and it's a good place to play jokes on a body, but there's limits to even a greenhorn's credulity."

I was never more in earnest, I assure you. It is possible to talk to New York."

Miss Berry regarded her companion severely. "Then it's blasphemous. That's all I've got to say."

"Why, I don't see that."

"Do you s'pose the Lord would have put New York a thousand miles away from Chicago if he'd expected 'em to talk to each other?"

Page laughed. "I never thought of that before as a reason for the antagonism between the two cities. Nonsense, Aunt Love; the world moves, and you must move with it. You shall speak to New York and be proud of yourself ever afterward. you know it is to be expected that science will do everything possible toward annihilating space."

Page ascended the steps toward a silk-curtained cabinet; a uniformed boy opened its glass door.

After remaining in the closet a minute and speaking a few sentences into the telephone, he beckoned to Miss Berry who had remained standing at the foot of the steps looking very apprehensive.

"Now, Aunt Love," he said encouragingly, as she slowly approached, a do-or-die expression on her face. Had Miss Berry been of the Romish church instead of being a "Con'regationalist in good and regular standing," she would assuredly have crossed herself before entering that tasteful little apartment.

Page smiled into his mustache as he placed the receiver in her hand, fervently wishing that he might hear both sides of the impending dialogue.

"Mr. Gorham," said Miss Berry, addressing him over her shoulder impressively, "think of the miles, the hours, I traveled; the rivers and lakes I crossed; the mountains I tunneled"—

"Yes, yes, Aunt Love; but don't keep our New York friend waiting."

"I feel prickly, Gorham. I think I'm goin' to faint."

"Oh no, you're not. Just say Hello," returned Page cheerily, his eyes twinkling.

"Hello," quavered Miss Lovina, and promptly the answer came:—

New York. Is this Miss Berry?

Miss Berry. How did you know my name?

New York. A gentleman just told me to expect you. I am happy to meet you, or to hear you, all the way from New York.

Miss Berry. Go away!

New York. Aren't you a little unreasonable, madam? I'm a good way off already.

Miss Berry. How am I to be sure you ain't in the next room, sir?

New York. Do you hear me so distinctly?

Miss Berry. It is the most wonderful thing in the world if you are real.

New York. Oh, I am real, I assure you, madam. I see you have been making trips to the Midway, and your confidence in human nature is shaken.

Miss Berry. You're just right there. I should like to talk to you about the Midway. Have you been to the Fair yet?

New York. No; and alas, I'm afraid I'm not coming; but if I do, I'm going to the Midway the first thing.

Miss Berry. Now, young man, you just stand there a minute, and I'll convince you—"Hey?" for Gorham was pulling her sleeve.

"There are some more people waiting to speak, Aunt Love."

"What? Oh," Miss Berry looked dazed, relinquished the receiver, and moved like a somnambulist out of the cabinet.

"You might have said good-by to your new friend," suggested Page.

"Mr. Gorham, tell me," spoke Aunt Love beseechingly. "If I was ever good to you, if you ever liked my cookies, tell me the truth. Was that all hocus-pocus, or was it genuine?"

"Why, it was genuine, Aunt Love. It is done every day in business."

"Well," Miss Berry stepped off energetically. "All I can say is, I've capped the climax o' my life. I don't calc'-late to ever call anything wonderful again."

But she did. Page took her upstairs to the gallery where a door opened by magic when her foot touched the threshold; where the tel-auto-graph reproduced a writer's chirography while transmitting his thoughts; where a metal rod, passing along a person's spine, caused blue flames to leap forth, crackling and spitting in Mephistophelean fashion, a cure which Miss Berry thought worse than any known disease. She saw there, too, the smallest steam-engine in the world, reposing its miniature perfection in a walnut shell, and displaying its exquisite mechanism only beneath a magnifying glass.

But the cooking of food and the hatching of chickens by electricity appealed to Aunt Love so engrossingly that, after repeated vain efforts to woo her away from both these attractions, Page finally took his leave of her there, and his parting view showed Miss Berry gazing through the side of an incubator where chicks were in every stage of existence, from the first thrust of a yellow beak through the eggshell, to the freed and bedraggled little wretch whose sole aim in life seemed to be to half hop and half tumble across the incubator until its wet body rested directly upon an incandescent light. These eventful journeys, with their apparently suicidal goal, so absorbed Miss Berry that she could do little more than wave her hand after Page as he set briskly off for pastures new.

CHAPTER 7

THE BRONZE BABY

Somebody says that we only really live when we do not know that time is passing. If that be true, Miss Berry lived intensely during the period she passed in the gallery of the Electricity Building that afternoon.

"I wonder how late it is!" she asked herself at last with a start. "The folks 'll think I'm lost. I must hurry home directly."

But she sighed as she said it. To "hurry home" from this city of magnificent distances was but a form of words.

"If I could only borrow the wings off'n some o' those angels!" she murmured as she hastened down the nearest flight of stairs; but doubtful as she was of the lateness of the hour, she could not keep her mind from straying back to the strange scenes in the miniature world she had been watching. Next the incubator had been a little sandy enclosure in the midst of which stood a small curtained house where the young chickens could be brooded at will, and across whose front ran the defiant legend, "Who cares for mother now!"

"I wonder how soon electricity 'll take the place o'

folks," she mused. "Seems if 't won't take long. Yes, yes," she went on in answer to a faint peeping that came from beneath her wrap, "we'll get home some time tonight," and she hurried faster still, a pleased smile breaking over her face, for Aunt Love was not alone. She had at the present moment one of those emancipated chicks in a pasteboard box pressed to her side.

"I believe I'll take the Internal Road, and then the cars," she said to herself. "There'll be an awful crowd at Sixtieth Street, but I can stand consid'able squeezin', I know I'm late."

She was late. Not that it mattered. She was to dine in solitary state that evening in any case; but she had meant to reach the house in time to carry the information of Mr. Page's arrival and his plan to meet his friends; and in this she was disappointed. Only Blitzen was left at home to give her his customary boisterous greeting, and she had before her the difficult task of explaining and introducing to him her ball of yellow fluff and impressing its sacredness upon his volatile mind.

Jack was the first to arrive at the rendezvous that evening, and to his satisfaction Mildred was second. She sauntered up to the steps accompanied by a young army officer at whom Jack stared down from his post on the balcony. He had, however, sufficient self-control to swallow his discontent. Mildred had somehow taught him this self-control in the short space of a week, and he managed to walk to meet her with an air of nonchalance suited to that with which she slowly mounted the steps after dismissing her escort.

"Who is the military?" he asked lightly.

"A cousin of Helen Eames. He has been showing us

over the Battle Ship."

"Indeed? I was there this afternoon too."

"Were you? It is awfully stuffy down below in that museum, isn't it? Our party was glad to retreat to a private room and have a blueberry cobbler. Everything is beginning to be crowded now."

"What interests me," said Jack, placing a chair by one of the tables for Mildred as he spoke, "is to know how soon you are going to give me a day."

"Oh, any time," returned the girl as she seated herself.

"Any time! That is what you always say, but when I try to pin you down you slip away."

"Wouldn't anybody?" smiled the other. There was something about the curves at the corners of Mildred's upper lip and its downward dip in the middle that made her smile more provoking than other girls'.

"There! You are slipping away again."

"No, indeed. I am far too tired and this is too comfortable."

"You have had an engagement every day since I have been here. You can't deny it. What sort of a way is that to treat a guest?"

"You aren't my guest, you are Clover's."

"Clover is a daisy and always was," exclaimed Jack, regardless of paradox. "She is the sweetest girl in the world."

"Of course," returned Mildred, raising a glass of water to her lips as coolly as though she liked this.

"I ought to have gone with you that first evening," said Van Tassel gloomily.

Mildred set down her glass and looked at the speaker with an unfathomable expression as she spoke slowly:—

"'There is a tide in the affairs of men
Which, taken at the flood, leads on to'"—

"Would it, Mildred?" Jack broke in with a sort of earnest excitement. "Would it have led on to fortune?"

The girl colored under the glowing gaze.

"If I had gone with you, would you have had fewer engagements and more time for me since then?"

"How can I tell?" she returned, with a low laugh of enjoyment. Jack was fairly dramatic. He was really entertaining.

"I didn't know exactly what my feeling was then; but I knew afterward," he went on. "Ogden wasn't any part of our past. I didn't want to share you with him that night."

"He didn't want to share me with you either, so you were both satisfied," returned Mildred demurely.

"Was he satisfied?" asked Van Tassel savagely. "Methinks not. I notice that whatever your engagements have been this week, he has not been in them."

"How observing you are!"

"Yes. He is done for. It would be interesting to know how many scalps that makes, Mildred."

"Look here, Jack," the girl was not smiling, and her eyes darkened as she met his. "If you will practice conservation of energy now, I will give you a capital opportunity to air your talents in amateur theatricals next winter. You are the very man we have been looking for."

"Can I court you?"

"That depends on your versatility."

"Or my patience in standing in line. I've been standing in line all the week. Don't you think it is about time I got to the front?"

"What do you call this?" Mildred gave him a tantalizing glance from under her half-dropped lids. "I arrive early at the rendezvous. We sit *tête-à-tête*, and how do you make use of the time?"

Color flashed all over Jack's face.

"I am a fool," he agreed.

"That must be why you always speak the truth so indiscreetly. I never thought of that as the reason, really. Now let us decide what to order before Clover comes. What can make her so late?"

The fact was that Clover, wanting to stop a minute to look at some pieces of old china and silver in the Louisiana house, had had the usual curious experience in World's Fair minutes. In a city of enchantment, how could it be expected that sixty seconds should be of the conventional length? She had set aside plenty of time also just to walk through the middle of the Art Building; and as every woman knows, it was always impossible to pass so near "The Young Athlete" without pausing, if but for a brief acknowledgment.

Gorham Page had just been admiring the bronze, and had stepped aside to look at the photographs on a neighboring table when Clover advanced. He was short-sighted, and she wore an Eton suit and a sailor hat, the garb of ninety-nine out of every hundred women in the summer of '93; but he knew her at once, and paused. After a moment's watching he approached her.

She colored faintly with surprise as she returned his greeting.

"The subtle differences in the nature of man and woman are more interesting than the obvious ones," he said.

"What are you leading up to now?" she asked. "I

expected your first words to be an explanation or an apology, or both. How does it happen that this is the place where we first meet?"

"You were very, very kind, Mrs. Van Tassel, and I hope I assured you of my appreciation in my letter; but I found I could get a room at the hotel near you, and then affairs taking a favorable turn I left Boston suddenly, and none too soon; I have been here all day. How stupendous it is! You are on your way to the Marine Café. May I go with you?"

"Oh, you have seen Jack, or my sister."

"No."

"Then how comes it that you are so well informed?"

"Happily for me, I ran across Aunt Love."

"Oh, that explains her prolonged absence perhaps. Usually, it is hard for us to persuade her to spend a whole day down here. We must hurry a little, I think." Clover laughed. "Hurrying is the normal condition of people who try to keep appointments at the Fair."

They threaded their way amid groups and figures in plaster and marble, and emerged from the southern entrance.

"What I started to speak of when I first met you was the contrast of a man's and a woman's way of approaching that bronze," said Page. "I went up to it and especially noticed the muscles and veins of the man's hand and the truthful way the fingers sink into the flesh of the baby it supports. You approached it and took hold of the baby's hand and patted his leg. Now why didn't I want to pat that little fellow's fat leg?"

"I give up," laughed Clover. "I can only say you had very poor taste."

"No, there is a deep reason for the difference. Of

course it is a woman's nature to pat a baby."

"What a deep discovery! I congratulate you on the result of your explorations. Do you think you shall write a book about it?"

"I amuse you, Mrs. Van Tassel."

"Yes, you do, I won't deny it." Clover was a trifle ashamed of having been caught in her loving ebulliation toward the soft bronze, and was willing to laugh it away.

"Still it is interesting," Page went on musingly, "to observe how affection is outward with women and inward with men."

"That doesn't sound complimentary to us, Mr. Page. I hope you mean well."

Gorham's pensive eyes met her merry ones.

"Yes. I revere the wise arrangement by which it takes a man and a woman to make one complete being; and the more I observe and understand refined human nature, the more I think I see the possibilities, and what it was intended that marriage should be. You are a good walker, Mrs. Van Tassel."

"Yes; I am thinking how impatient Mildred and Jack will be with me. I will give you a subject for your analytical mind. Make a record of the broken appointments at the World's Fair and discover the reasons for them. You would have a psychological study of absorbing interest."

"All phases of human nature are interesting."

"Even that where vials of righteous wrath are poured out upon you for delinquency when you know you haven't any defense to offer? You are my defense this time."

"What do you want me to say?"

"Oh, I wouldn't trust you to say anything. I am morally certain that you would tell the truth."

"That isn't so very damaging, is it?"

"Why, certainly. You would tell them that I stopped to caress the bronze baby; and if Mildred heard that, hungry as she is by this time, you would soon have to formulate exceptions to your rule that women are all affection outwardly. By the way, what a fortunate experience yours has been."

Page smiled philosophically, and looked approvingly at his light-footed companion.

They arrived at the café shortly after Mildred had directed her companion's attention to the menu, and the apparition of the unexpected guest entirely diverted from Clover any comment upon her tardiness.

The cordiality of his welcome pleased Page. He could not know the reason for the nervous energy of his cousin's greeting. The four sat for an hour at table and then took their way by boat to the Court of Honor, where they remained in the launch during the playing of the fountains. Clover, sitting next to Page, watched his attitude toward this first view of the evening's spectacle with some curiosity.

He caught her amused gaze once as it rested upon him.

"Sumptuous! Delicate! Wonderful!" he said, breaking a long, absorbed silence.

"What?" returned Clover. "But you haven't suggested yet going down beneath the electric fountains to find out the why and the how of it all; and I am sure you will not rest until you have been on the roof of the Manufactures Building and made friends with the man who manipulates the search light."

"No." Page smiled vaguely and shook his head. "I do not want to go behind the scenes."

"Then the Court of Honor is a wonderful place," said Clover.

"Poetical! Marvelous!" gasped Page.

A gondola decked with soft lanterns stole by. One gondolier swept his oar lazily through the water, the other stood with his hand caught in his bright sash, and poured forth the "*Dammi encor*" from "Faust" with true musical intensity.

Again Clover and Page looked into one another's eyes, but there was no badinage this time in her glance. It was a place of dreams. Showers of golden mist fell beneath the stars. The massive buildings softened away into distant shadowy suggestion. The sculptors' creations shone out thrillingly.

In heavenly beauty stood the Agricultural hall with its foreground of gleaming water, the pure white of its columns defined against the tempered rose-color of its inner wall,—a vision glowing and pure; as far above its sister palaces in beauty as its use was set apart from theirs; for here were displayed the works of God rather than the imperfect marvels of man's handiwork.

Amid the majestic splendor of the night rolled the passionate appeal of the gondoliers' love-song, become an impersonal voice now as the boats drifted apart. Little wonder that Page forgot to be abstractly analytical, and that the soft spontaneous sympathy of his companion's eyes exercised enchantment borrowed from the environment. He smiled upon her with a bright tenderness which transfigured his thoughtful face.

For a long time they were silent, but when he gave her his hand as she stepped from the launch, he spoke out of the depths of his enjoyment:—

"That was a never-to-be-forgotten experience for me."

"I think no one ever forgets his first evening in the Court of Honor," returned Clover.

"Well, what are we going to do now?" asked Mildred, as they ascended the steps. "My! How the wind has sprung up from the lake. They will hardly dare to have the fireworks."

"Then let us take a brisk constitutional home," proposed Jack.

"Come, children. Follow your leader," commanded Mildred, turning and addressing Clover and her companion.

"Hurry her by the chocolate houses, Jack," said Clover," that is, if you can."

"He can't," returned Mildred. "I have my eye on Baker's now."

She insisted that they all stop and partake of the cup, more potent than tea to cheer when the east wind blows, served by the pretty, uniformed girls, who by this time in the evening were inclined to be pessimistic and severe, small blame to them. They must easily believe that the human body is largely liquid.

Leaving the little circular temple, the quartette started up the lake shore on the stone walk. The dark waves were tumbling and dashing, tipped with foam in the sudden gale. The battle ship and large excursion boats were gay with electric lights.

"Oh, Mrs. Van Tassel!" exclaimed Page. "See the search light on the Quadriga." They turned to view the group with its mounted heralds and champing, prancing horses, distinct and unearthly fair in the surrounding blackness.

"Could we walk home backward, do you think?" he

asked.

"No," replied Clover. "I can answer with certainly, for I've tried it more than once."

"I suppose we do in course of time get past the Manufactures Building? What an incomprehensible, colossal thing it is."

"Yes, a good deal more so to me now than it was a month ago."

"Have mercy!" exclaimed Page with a groan.

Mildred and Jack were walking in front of them.

"Isn't this like old times, Mildred?" asked the latter with a relish, clapping his hat on tighter as the sweep of the wind threatened it.

"Just about as unlike as we could imagine. Sorry to disagree with you, Jack."

"Don't mention it. You don't disagree with me, my child. I have enjoyed this first evening with you immensely."

"First evening is pretty good, isn't it?" suggested the girl, and they both laughed. "You didn't use to quarrel for my society," she added.

"I want you to understand that I wasn't quarreling with you there, a few hours back, at the Marine Café."

"Oh!"

"No, I was merely making the excusable protest of an old friend,—speaking in a brotherly way, you know."

"Oh, it won't do, Jack." He knew exactly how she was smiling in the darkness. "It is my unalterable rule never to be a sister to any of them. I can't break over it for you."

"Them!" exclaimed her companion. "I don't thank you to class me with Tom, Dick, and Harry, and the rest of these late arrivals. Remember, I was the first-comer into your friendship."

"You *were* a pretty good sort of fellow."

"Yes; you probably can't conceive of what a healing thought it is to me now that I have snubbed you many a time, young lady. I had to. Your attentions were so persistent in those days. Yes, mademoiselle, I had to hold you off, or I should never have had any peace of my life. I remember it well. Perhaps you don't."

"Oh yes, I do, perfectly," sighed Mildred. "Wasn't the that little boat of yours, the *Flirt*, the staunchest little dear that ever spread a sail? And to think that is all over! I don't feel nearly so much elation over going with Mr. Eames on that yacht party tomorrow as I used to in nagging you into consent that I should sail the *Flirt*."

"Is that the infantry officer?"

"Yes; and he is very nice. I should like you to meet him. If I knew him a little better I would have procured you an invitation. You should remember that virtue is its own reward. If you had not preferred smoking in the hammock to coming into the parlor and making yourself agreeable the other evening when Helen Eames and her mother were calling, they would surely have asked you to join the party. 'If you would be loved, be lovely.' That is what my mother used to tell me." Mildred laughed to herself.

"Then why don't you obey her?" returned Jack curtly.

"I don't want to be loved," returned the spoiled girl. "I'm loved too much already."

After this they marched in silence for a time, their springy steps carrying them by the foreign buildings, Ceylon, France with its green, fountain-sprayed court, Spain, and Germany. It was not until they turned beside

Iowa's pavilion and left behind them the waves dashing on the sea-wall that Mildred spoke again.

"It gives me the blues, Jack, every time I see our boat-house stranded high and dry behind that nightmare of a Spectatorium."

"I don't see how you can call anything dry that is as full of beer as that is."

"Oh," exclaimed the girl indignantly, "what a fall from its old estate! To think of our playhouse being turned into a saloon! Do you remember the dance it was christened with? I was allowed to go, and you made me perfectly happy by waltzing with me once."

"Humph!" returned the other. "And now it is a great question whether you would make me perfectly happy by waltzing with me once."

"Oh, Jack," Mildred laughed out now, "don't be cross. Don't grudge a girl her 'little brief authority.' My observation of life has taught me that her queenship is brief enough. She blossoms out of awkward childhood into an attractive womanhood, and then after a little space yields up her sweet liberty to some lord of creation whom she has to pacify and wait on ever afterward. Moral: Let her keep her authority as long as possible."

"You seem to have been rather unfortunate in your married masculine acquaintance," returned Van Tassel dryly.

A sudden thought sent the color flying to Mildred's face, and her customary complacent poise was shaken.

"There was one exception," she said, so timidly and meekly that her companion was struck by the change; but she had not the courage to be more specific, and there was no need. Jack understood her.

When the four reached home they found Miss Berry in the sitting-room reading by the light of a lamp.

Blitzen was sitting on a rug, and did not, as usual, run to meet them. On a chair reposed a bird-cage with some white stuff in it.

"What is this, Aunt Love?" asked Clover. "Have you some new pets?"

"I've got one," returned Miss Berry, smiling placidly. "I'll give you all three guesses. It's a World's Fair souvenir."

"Tell us, Blitzen," said Mildred, kneeling on the rug beside the small dog and shaking his tousled head; but Blitzen, as soon as he could free himself, withdrew in unwonted dignity. Evidently there was that within him tonight which could not brook flippancy.

"A live souvenir?" asked Clover, perplexed.

"Mr. Gorham can guess," remarked Miss Lovina, glancing again down the columns of her newspaper, and shaking in a comfortable silent laugh.

"I?" said Page; then, after a moment's cogitation, "You surely didn't bring home one of those chickens?"

"I did. In that cage, my dears, there is an electric chicken." Miss Berry looked over her spectacles impressively. "The same power that runs the internal railroad and shines in the rainbow fountains, don't disdain to hatch a chicken. If you doubt it, there's the chicken."

She gestured toward the bird-cage.

"I brought it home in a box; and I said to myself that most everybody had an old cage, so I went up garret, and there I found that one. On Blitzen's account I thought best to use a cage tonight." Her gaze descended on the terrier, whose head descended beneath it.

"Blitzen," asked Jack with deliberate, stern solemnity, "what do you think of the chicken?"

Blitzen rose with a crushed air, and slowly, as one who would not attract attention, crept across the room and retired under a remote sofa.

A shout of laughter followed his unostentatious disappearance.

"We've had some words," explained Aunt Love. "He barked cruel at the poor little thing when he first saw me with it."

"Have it out, have the chicken out," said Mildred; and Miss Berry, yielding to the general urgency, produced her prize from the depths of the cotton wool. It began to struggle and peep vigorously as soon as its beady eyes saw the light, and there came a muffled howl from under the sofa.

"What are you going to name it?" asked Clover.

"I don't know what name would be good enough for such a smart critter."

"Why, Electra, of course," remarked Jack. "Nothing less for such a star among chickens."

"Sounds well and suitable," observed Miss Berry placidly, "whether it means anything or not."

"I wonder if it has any unusual springs," said Mildred. "If I should touch the button do you suppose it would give us a rest?" She advanced a finger toward one of the bright eyes, but Miss Berry removed her squeaking prize from harm, and tucked it away again in the cotton from which it struggled several times before finally settling down with a diminuendo of peeps.

CHAPTER 8

CLOVER'S DIPLOMACY

Mr. and Mrs. Page arrived duly, even a little earlier than they had at first anticipated. Jack met them at the station and drove with them to their destination.

"You see it was simply impossible, Mrs. Van Tassel, for my wife to curb her impatience after Gorham began to write home," said Mr. Page to his hostess in explanation of their change of plan. "Gorham doesn't very often gush, as perhaps you know."

"And I assure you that Mr. Page was not difficult to persuade," added Hilda. "Your last kind letter determined us. And I am really in Chicago!" she went on, looking about her. "Jack, congratulate me!"

"I do, sincerely. I think you, Hilda, will appreciate your advantages."

Mr. Page gave his contagious, quiet chuckle. "That is the way he goes on," he said, turning to Mildred. "Jack is very severe on me always. I am going to show you, Miss Bryant, several lists of adjectives, carefully prepared, very carefully and thoughtfully, one for every day in the week, that I am intending to use on the World's Fair to mollify my cousin."

"You might have trusted safely to the inspiration of the moment," returned Mildred gayly.

"Oh, you don't know Jack. One single false move, one expletive out of place, and it would be all over with me."

"Poor Robert, I feel for you," remarked Van Tassel.

"Why, that is mysterious," replied his cousin. "Anybody who compassionates me just now doesn't understand economizing his emotions." The speaker sank back in his roomy wicker chair and took a glass of lemonade from a salver which Miss Berry was passing to the company. The crushed ice jingled pleasantly against the crystal, and the couple of straws that emerged from each glass were alluring to a stout and thirsty man. "Aunt Love, it is very pleasant to see you here," he added. "We shall have to renew our old acquaintance. We had no time in Boston."

"That's so, Mr. Page. I guess I can jog your memory about a good many things."

When later the husband and wife were shown to their own room and the door was closed, Robert looked at Hilda with large eyes. "Whew!" he said softly. "Uncle Richard was all right. What pretty women!"

"I told you so. I told you that Mildred was a perfect Juno, and that you were very unfortunate to be out of town when she spent that week with me at the beach. As for Mrs. Van Tassel"—

"Why, she's an angel,—she's an angel! I knew it from her letter. I felt it in my bones."

"As if you knew anything about your bones, you dear old cushion. Stop praising those girls—calling one a goddess and one an angel. Come and apostrophize the lake. Isn't it beautiful?"

"It was you who called Miss Bryant a goddess, remember. Yes, this is every bit as good as the ocean, for all I see," walking to the window and putting an arm around his wife's waist. "We are in great luck, Hilda," continued Page, glancing about their spacious room. "This isn't much like the discomforts we read about in connection with World's Fair visiting. I don't wonder," he added after a pause, "that Jack was cut up by being at cross purposes with those girls."

"H'm. There is one exhibit I have come out here to see that isn't inside the White City," returned Hilda. "I've come to discover which one of them Jack is in love with."

"Both, of course. How can he help it?" replied her husband promptly.

Gorham took it upon himself to launch his brother and sister on their Fair pilgrimage that very evening.

When they came home again, hours later, Clover and Jack were sitting alone in the parlor and rose to meet them as they entered the room. Their tired, excited faces were a study.

Hilda dropped into a chair. "Well," she exclaimed, "I never expected to go to heaven till I died; but I've been there."

"Jack," added Robert meekly, "get in your fine work now. I've nothing to say, absolutely nothing. I've dropped my jaw so often since six o'clock that it isn't in working order, any way."

"Say no more," returned Van Tassel, waving his hand grandiloquently. "We Chicagoans are nothing if not magnanimous."

"I thought I knew what I was going to see, that is the queer part of it," said Robert, looking perplexed; "but it seems I didn't know anything at all about it. I feel there is an unlimited feast in store for me, Mrs. Van Tassel."

Clover smiled at his enthusiastic tone. "You are in the first-day frame of mind, I see."

"What is that?"

"Oh, eagerness and hopefulness."

"And what is the second?"

"Despair; yes, overwhelming, stony despair."

"What is the third? Suicidal tendency?"

"No indeed. Resignation. At first one expects and determines to see everything; soon finds that to be so impossible that he yields to his bewilderment, and at last accepts the inevitable and sets himself to see what he can, and be rapturously content therewith."

"Thank you, thank you! Forewarned, forearmed. Perhaps we may even skip the second stage."

A few days later, Clover, her guests having scattered on various quests, went to the noon orchestral concert in Festival Hall. This wonderfully generous free exhibit attracted a large audience, many of whom embraced it as an opportunity to rest from the fatigues of sight-seeing, while many others, coming perhaps from the country where "hearing a band" was a rare privilege, were drawn thither by the hope of attractive music.

Possibly one half the number came intelligently to the feast, and greeted the conductor when he entered upon the stage. Clover joined in the applause as Theodore Thomas passed before his players with that quiet, characteristic grace, which had power to thrill with anticipation a greater number of America's music-lovers than the movement of any other man.

It interested her as it had many a time before, this

summer, to note the effect upon certain of the audience of the number with which the programme opened. She saw pleased hopefulness give way to apathy in many faces, as strange harmonies and dissonances fell upon uncultivated ears. She noticed one patient-faced countryman who waited through two numbers, evidently discovering nothing but a wilderness of sound. He then examined his programme, and not finding "After the Ball" on it, arose and departed from the hall more in sorrow than anger.

Blessings on the man, by the way, who introduced the noiseless paper on which those programmes were printed. There were two girls sitting next to Clover, chewing gum while they listened for some melody they could recognize, and Clover congratulated herself that all the foldings and drummings of their programmes were unaudible; but alas, as soon as the maidens discovered that the music they were hearing was unworthy the name, they cheerfully set about doing the next best thing, which was to prepare for the afternoon's campaign. This was a free concert anyway, so no matter if it wasn't worth much. They would not leave at once, because this was a better place to rest than they would be likely to find soon again; so they unfolded their maps of the grounds, not printed on absorbent paper, far from it, and proceeded to discuss their plans.

Clover caught sight of Jack standing across the hall. He discovered her at the same moment. His concentrated look flashed into a smile as they exchanged nods.

At the close of the number he came around to where Clover sat in the front row of the circle, and leaned his arm on the railing in front of her.

How handsome Jack can look, when he is happy and interested, she thought, and instantly became aware that her neighbors had ceased their planning, and were nudging each other in silent absorption.

"Wasn't that great!" he exclaimed. "Are you going over to the Music Hall this afternoon?"

"Indeed I am. They are going to play the Tschaikowsky Symphony."

"That settles it. Suppose we go up in the wheel after lunch, and then go over to the concert together."

"All right. I'd like to. Why, there is Mildred on the left, down there near the front. I didn't know she was coming."

"Nor I. Shall I go and speak to her?"

In a minute Jack was back, just as the music began again. The girls who had constituted the thorn in Clover's side during the first half of the programme had left their seats as soon as he moved away, so he came in and took the place beside Clover.

"Mildred says she will go with us," he whispered.

When the Intermezzo was finished, Clover spoke.

"Did you ask Mildred to join us?" she asked.

"No, she proposed it," returned Jack, and there was a pleasure in his eyes which did not escape his companion.

"You mentioned last night in our talk that you hadn't seen much of Mildred since you came; that she was too much of a belle for your comfort."

"Yes. It is simply surprising to find her here alone."

Clover's eyes twinkled. She had mentioned to her sister, this morning, that she meant to meet Jack at the noon concert.

"Well, you leave her to me. No matter what I say, don't contradict me. Promise?"

"What's up?" asked Van Tassel doubtfully.

"Oh, Mildred's conceit and a few other things that ought to come down. I want you to myself a part of the time, Jack."

Her companion met her laughing glance.

"I am yours to command, Clover, always."

"Don't forget, then," she answered.

When the concert was over, Mildred came slowly up the aisle, superb as usual in her consciously unconscious carriage.

"Well," she said to her sister as they met, "where are we to lunch?"

"Are you going to lunch with us?" asked Clover in well-affected surprise.

"Of course I am," returned the younger with a half-pouting smile flung at Jack; "and I am going in the Ferris Wheel with you too. I haven't been up in it yet."

"Why, I don't see how you possibly can, Mildred," said Clover coolly. "I heard you promise Mr. and Mrs. Page to meet them in the Art Gallery at two o'clock, and show Mrs. Page some of our favorite pictures."

Mildred expected some protest from Jack, and was disconcerted that none came. "I only told them that if I was at the south entrance at two o'clock I would act as their cicerone," she answered.

"Well, my dear, having said so much," suggested Clover gravely, "I think the least you can do is to be there, considering that they are our guests."

Still Jack did not interfere. Mildred could not forbear hurling one glance at him from beneath her eyelashes, but it might have been a gaze. Van Tassel was absently viewing the dispersing audience.

Her eyes and cheeks burned as they had on the night he

refused to accompany her to witness the fireworks, but as on that occasion she carried the matter with a high hand.

"Very well, then you have lost my company at lunch, too. You and Jack would be sure to make me late, dawdling at table. *Au revoir*," and as they nodded to her, she swept away.

Clover looked at her companion and tried to repress the mirthful laugh that bubbled over her lips.

"Jack, you wouldn't be human if you hadn't enjoyed that."

"Then I must be inhuman," he responded rather ruefully, "for I give you my word I'm scared almost to death."

"Don't you worry, *mon ami*; I know Mildred to the depths of her noble, generous, overbearing, over-indulged soul."

"I don't suppose you realize, Clover," Van Tassel spoke low and jerkily, "but I care very much; absurdly much, you might think, considering the shortness of the time."

Clover looked into his flushed face, and the merriment in her sweet eyes was quenched.

"Dear Jack," she said, laying her hand lightly on his arm, "whatever you wish, I wish. Trust me. No harm has been done. Do you want my advice,—the advice of one who knows?"

"Yes, I do."

"Then don't let Mildred suspect what you have told me. The round world is just a rattle to her now. You are one of the bells on it that jingle for her amusement when she moves you. There are Katherines in existence still, and Petruchios are wholesome teachers for them."

"Imagine me cracking a horsewhip at Mildred!"

"Out, please!" roared a Columbian Guard, exasperated

by the sight of these two loiterers, after the remainder of the audience had drifted away. "As if there wasn't any other place on the grounds to spoon but just this," he muttered.

Mildred, to her credit be it said, devoted her afternoon to Mrs. Page with as cheerful courtesy as though she bore no grudge in her mind against the world. Mr. Page left them together and went off somewhere under his brother's guidance. It was nearly dinner-time when he drove up to the house in a Beach wagon, and found Mildred swinging idly in a hammock on the piazza.

"Your wife is taking a nap," she announced, as he came up the steps.

"Fortunate woman!" he responded, sinking wearily upon a wicker divan. "The only interest I've had for hours in any exhibit was as to whether there was a chair in it; but Gorham is a terrible fellow. Merciless. Each building being one thousand miles from every other building makes it hard lines. I threatened more than once to trip over one of those chains that say, 'Keep off the grass,' and refuse to get up again."

"You and your brother should have taken one of those double chairs."

"Oh, there wouldn't have been any room for Gorham," and the jolly man laughed. "I suppose you have done the Plaisance."

"Partly, yes."

"Gorham and I went into the Dahomey village, this afternoon. Some of those savages were unpleasantly personal. Good afternoon, Aunt Love," as the housekeeper appeared on the veranda. "I was just telling Miss Mildred how those children of nature in the Dahomey village injured my finer feelings today. One of them came for me with a big carving knife, yelling 'Big man, fat man,' and going through the pantomime of taking a slice off my sacred person."

"Dirty critters!" remarked Miss Berry sententiously.

"Isn't it a funny paradox to see an incandescent light over the door of each hut?" went on Page. "There was one big fellow squatted down in the sun, off by himself, playing on a rough sort of harp, and singing monotonously something that sounded like 'Come away, come away, Chicago.' I tried to write down the pitches he sang, and that amused him immensely. His ivories would have made a perfect dentist's sign. I gave him a dime or so to repeat the performance a sufficient number of times, and he was delighted, and kept saying, 'Chicago beer.'"

"Yes," returned Miss Berry bitterly. "They have to come to a Christian land for that."

"Wait till you see the South Sea Islanders," said Mildred.

"We did. Fine, aren't they? There is an exhibition of drill and muscle worth seeing."

"And that *café-au-lait* skin!" exclaimed Mildred. "I am entirely spoiled for white beauties."

"Let 'em wear somethin' more 'n a straw wreath and a piece o' calico then," remarked Miss Berry.

"But Aunt Love," suggested Page, "you must remember how clothing that brown skin is. I am sure you must admit it is an improving sight to see one of those heavy-eyed beauties sit cross-legged and absently scratch one great toe while she sings."

"What are you all laughing about?" asked Hilda, coming out upon the piazza in the freshness of a light organdie gown.

"Your husband has been to the Midway," returned Miss Berry. "Don't be surprised at anything he may say or do; and I don't believe we'd better wait for Mr. and Mrs. Van Tassel any longer, for dinner was ready when I came out here."

"I don't understand Clover's staying so," remarked Mildred, leaving the hammock and trying not to speak severely.

"I go, I fly, to make myself presentable," said Page, slowly dragging himself up from his comfortable resting-place.

After dinner Mildred made an opportunity to address the housekeeper privately. "For pity's sake, Aunt Love, when you are going to speak of Jack and Clover as you did this evening, don't say Mr. and Mrs. Van Tassel."

"Why not?" asked Miss Lovina with exasperating unconsciousness.

"Why, it sound so—so—absurdly married."

Miss Berry smiled. "What shall I say then?"

"Mrs. and Mr. Van Tassel, of course," replied Mildred, making an effort to speak with a suavity she did not feel.

"Well, if that ain't a new idea. Mrs. and Mr.! Do tell!" said Miss Berry good-naturedly. "Oh, I'll learn a deal of etiquette to take back to Pearfield. It's enough to do a body good to see Mr. Jack and your sister so much to each other, ain't it? Seems if they have lots o' pleasure together now; just as it should be."

"I don't know that they are together so very much," returned Mildred coolly.

"That's 'cause you're off so much o' the time. Why, they're just the best friends that ever was; and Mrs. Van Tassel, she's gone back before my eyes from a grave woman full o' care to a merry girl just as free as a bird. It does me good, Miss Mildred. It does me so much good, I'm 'most afraid I shall grow fat on it."

Mildred's bright eyes looked thoughtful for a second, as though she were digesting the housekeeper's words. "There is Blitzen, barking," she exclaimed, and both hastened to see whether Electra's nervous system was receiving some fresh shock.

Gorham Page strayed over from the hotel, as was his habit after dinner, and found the family disposed in various comfortable chairs and hammocks about the piazza.

The autocratic Miss Bryant was feeling a trifle sore, although she did not dream of acknowledging to herself that it was because Clover and Jack still remained away, and in the present sensitive state of her self-love it was a new affront that Gorham did not at once seek her side, but after bowing to her, settled down beside Mrs. Page, who closed the book she was reading upon her finger as a marker.

"Yes indeed, the afternoon was delightful," she said, in answer to his question. "Mildred and I had a charming time among the pictures. You nearly committed fratricide. Do you see poor Robert fast asleep over there?"

"This will do him a world of good. Train down his flesh, and strengthen his muscle; though the poor old chap did say, before we decided to come home, that he had walked so long his feet splayed out like the camels' every time he set them down." Page laughed reminiscently.

"Camels? Did you go into Cairo Street?"

"No, to the Bedouin village; the Wild East show."

"Very well. You have just saved your lives. I understand that Cairo Street is one of the plums of the Plaisance, and if Robert had gone without me, I should have been highly offended."

"Yes, he is well trained. I wonder if my wife will find me as thoughtful. I am afraid not."

Hilda laughed at the sincere meekness of his tone. "No, I'm sure she won't for the simple reason that you will never have one."

"I should be sorry to think that."

"Then why don't you do as nine out of every ten men in your place would do?"

"You mean fall in love? You know, Hilda, how often I've done that."

Mrs. Page laughed again at the gently remonstrant tone. "Your sort of falling in love isn't worth two straws," she declared scoffingly. "Don't take that into consideration at all. The next woman you meet who satisfies you intellectually, propose to her. If she accepts you, marry her. I don't believe you would make her very unhappy. You wouldn't if you were as kind a husband as you are a brother."

"Thank you. You might give me a written recommendation. See how handsome Miss Bryant's face looks against that golden pillow."

"Yes; it is a proof of your hard heart that you withstand her."

"I don't withstand her. You have no idea how much I enjoyed an afternoon I had with her at the Fair last week; but Jack was remarkably short with me that evening, and I fancied I had trespassed on his preserves."

"Not a bit of it. He must be a dog in the manger."

"Why, I'm very sure he is hard hit in that direction."

"Oh, where are a man's eyes, I wonder! I haven't been

here very long, but long enough to discover the truth."

"I suppose you want me to ask you what truth?"

"No, I don't, my dear." Mrs. Page reopened her book.

"You are not hinting at---at---Mrs. Van Tassel?" Gorham spoke in a hushed tone.

"Just observe for yourself," said Hilda sententiously.

"You ought not to have such a thought."

Mrs. Page looked up, wondering at this severity. "Why, if you please? You surely haven't an idea that that young creature is going to sacrifice the rest of her life to a memory of duty done?"

"But Hilda, that is repugnant!" Gorham rose suddenly, and his sister's gaze followed him as he moved away. It was very unusual for him to show so much feeling.

"Wouldn't it be a strange, strange thing if after waiting all these years Gorham should love at last and love hopelessly?" She banished the query with a sigh. Sober second thought assured her that her brother had not meant more than he said. The idea that Jack might wish to marry his father's widow was distasteful to him and that was all.

Page approached Mildred, little realizing how indefensible she considered it that he had not done so some minutes previous. She was too glad of his presence, however, to punish him. It would never do for Jack to come home and suppose that she had not been holding court.

"What beautiful evenings you have in Chicago," he began. "May I take this chair?" drawing one near the hammock in which she was sitting against a nest of pillows, her foot touching the floor gently as she rocked.

"Yes, I never tire of seeing the moonlight on the water as it is shining tonight. When I was a little girl it was a great treat to me to be allowed to spend a summer evening on this piazza, and I enjoy it scarcely less now."

"You enjoy it very seldom, I observe."

"Yes, of course there are lots of engagements this summer, and a quiet evening at home like this seems very welcome occasionally. One likes too, sometimes, to renew acquaintances with the moon. After living among rosy, violet, pale green, and white search lights, and all sorts of spectacular electrical effects so much, one comes back to moonlight on the water as to an old friend."

The girl clasped her hands above her head upon the down pillow, and allowed Page to look at her, which he was not slow to do.

"I miss your sister and Jack, this evening. Where are they?"

"Columbus knows! Since the authorities have been Barnumizing the Fair, as they call it, one is led on to stay, and stay, and stay, to see this race or that dance or the other illumination. I left them after the noon concert."

"You were there, then. Of course you are fond of music."

"I enjoy it very much, although Clover says I don't. She and Jack are cranks about it. I am not."

"They have one strong predilection in common, then."

Mildred did not reply; and Page continued: "The effect of music upon a person who is in sympathy with it is an interesting study. Those involuntary chills that pass over one under the moving influence of good music are rather annoying to me. I do not wish to be moved uncontrollably by anything. I wish to decide just how deeply to feel on any subject. Do you know what I mean?"

"Yes, exactly." The decision of the girl's reply rather

surprised her companion. She let him look deep into her luminous eyes set in the moonlight fairness of her face. "And further than agreeing with you in the desirability of the principle," she added, "I carry the theory into practice."

"Do you mean to say that you are always able to let your head decide what your heart shall feel?"

"Invariably."

"But that is no common characteristic in a woman. With women the heart speaks first usually."

"Not in the case of the well-balanced woman."

"Then perhaps you can tell me," said Page, much surprised and interested, "perhaps you will be good enough to tell me what your ideas are concerning love. There, too, do you think it possible for the head to speak first?"

Mildred let a repressed laugh burst its bounds. "Do you mean, do I think it possible to fall in love head first?"

"Forgive me if I ask too much; but it seems to me very helpful to compare notes with one whose aims and desires are similar to your own."

"Oh, I don't mind telling you, Mr. Page," said the girl, sobering. "My ideas on the subject are clearly formulated, and I know of no reason why I should not impart them to one who will be appreciative. I believe a woman can decide what characteristics would be sympathetic with hers, and when she is sufficiently acquainted with a man to discover if he is possessed of those qualities, she can give rein to her heart, and love him"—the speaker suddenly extended her white hands before her—"love him with all her soul!"

The sudden thrill in her movement and in her low contralto voice electrified her listener by its unexpectedness.

"But can one always love where the head dictates?" he asked; "that is the question."

"Undoubtedly; for when one finds the combination she seeks, she will discover that she has loved it already. I will tell you, Mr. Page, you tempt my confidence because you captivate my judgment. I will describe to you the man I await. He must be good to look upon, for I value beauty of form; but he must be cool and steady of brain, must love to think, to analyze, to look upon life not as a plaything but as something the laws of which must be studied and explored continually. Incidents which appear trifling to others, to him will suggest a thousand questions. He must in short be a student of human nature whose researches I may, by-and-by, as I grow wiser, assist. Oh, proud, happy destiny!" She paused as though overcome, and grasping the sides of the hammock looked with a quick turn of her head toward the moonlight.

Page regarded her in silence, then leaned toward her in his earnestness. "A man like that is not found every day, Miss Bryant; but I congratulate you on your high standard; for the being you describe has surely a great heart to throb for humanity as well as the head to study it, and your affections will not be starved, I am sure of that."

Mildred grasped the hammock closer and caught her lip between her teeth. Page's unconsciousness had turned the tables, and she had sufficient sense of humor, in spite of her vanity, to make it difficult not to smile as he walked unseeing around her net, and it fell, enveloping her own saucy head.

CHAPTER 9

THE FERRIS WHEEL

It was half past nine when the wagonette bringing Clover and Jack stopped before the house. They were received with a chorus of questions, in which Mildred was too clever not to join. She was glad that Van Tassel must see Gorham seated near her, apart from the others, confidentially discoursing in the moonlight, even though Jack did not seem to observe it. He seated himself on the step near Mrs. Page, and leaned against a railing.

"We have had a fine time!" he exclaimed with what Mildred's practiced ear recognized as unmistakable sincerity.

"Oh, The German village by moonlight, Milly!" added Clover, taking a place near her sister. "You really ought to see it."

"We ought to have been there, Mr. Page," said Mildred regretfully.

"I doubt if I could have had a pleasanter evening anywhere," he returned; and if Miss Bryant had had power to decorate him she would have done so on the spot for that timely speech. She trusted Jack heard it.

"We sat there at table, you know," went on the latter, "and the moon came up over those quaint old gables. Oh, it was fine. I declare, we didn't know where we were. Did we, Clover?"

"I thought you were quite certain by the alleged German you entertained me with."

"Alleged German! Well, if this isn't sad! There I wasted Heine's poems by the yard on you. Ungrateful girl! You will never know all the sweet things that were said to you tonight."

"I know you drank a lot of beer and smoked too many cigars."

"Of course, being in Rome I complimented the inhabitants by imitation."

"Mr. Jack," spoke Miss Berry reproachfully, "I remember well that you said once you only smoked on holidays and birthdays."

"Certainly, Aunt Love, that is my rule still. I never break it."

"Whose birthday is this?" demanded Miss Berry, somewhat taken back.

"How should I know? Somebody's, surely." Jack looked up innocently. "I never show favoritism."

"Oh!" groaned Gorham, rising. "I can't stay here. Discipline him, Aunt Love. I am going to my uncontaminated roof-tree."

"Let us all take Gorham home," suggested Jack, also rising. "I'm afraid to be left here with Aunt Love's righteous wrath. Come, all of you. Nobody is too tired to walk to that music."

For the band on the hotel piazza was playing the Washington Post March, which by midsummer was running neck and neck with "After the Ball."

"Come, Robert," said Hilda, shaking the somnolent form in the hammock.

"Hey? What? Don't disturb me. I can die here as well as anywhere. What! Walk home with Gorham? Do you take me for an idiot? Music and moonlight!" with deep scorn. "Oh, go to! Woman, stand aside, or I shall do you an injury. Don't tempt a desperate man."

"Dear Robert doesn't seem to care to come with us," laughed Mildred *sotto voce* to Jack. She was determined that none other than he should walk by her side to the hotel, and of course she had her way.

An hour later she came into Clover's bedroom, brushing her long hair. Her white wrapper fell open at the neck, disclosing her handsome throat, and she looked particularly beautiful to her prejudiced sister.

"Where else did you and Jack go tonight beside the German village?" she asked.

"Nowhere."

"You took supper there and stayed all the evening?"

"Yes. We really couldn't tear ourselves away. It was like being in some romantic old story."

Mildred smiled and hummed her favorite bit from Iolanthe.

"No indeed," answered Clover. "I am not his mother. He doesn't pretend that I am, and he doesn't wish me to be; so your little song doesn't fit the case at all."

She did not look at her sister, but went on with her effort to braid her rebellious hair. Mildred ceased humming.

"I wish my hair was curly," she said at last.

"We all have our gifts," replied Clover. Mildred

thought her tone sounded unusually complacent. It was a novel experience to feel aught but compassion, or tenderness, or reverent admiration for Clover, but now she suddenly found herself regarding her for the first time as another girl like herself, and observing her attractions with new eyes.

"What a pretty foot you have, Clover," she said, looking at her sister's slippered feet.

"Not a bit better shaped than yours, my dear. Let us have a select little mutual admiration society."

"But mine are large," returned Mildred, sitting down and thrusting forth her slippers for inspection.

"So are you," suggested Clover.

"But isn't it strange that people never consider that, in speaking of a woman's foot? She must have small feet irrespective of her size, or else they had better never be seen or mentioned. In old novels a man sometimes keeps his beloved's slipper under a glass case. What a formidable piece of furniture my lover will have when he gets a glass case for mine."

"Foolish child! You are proportioned just right."

"Perhaps; but what I say is that the consensus of opinion decides that I ought not to be. Shoe men fall in with that idea. Dainty shoes are small shoes. I tell you fame and wealth awaits the shoe-dealer who becomes inspired with the idea that large women want pretty shoes too."

"You seem to have made Mr. Page have a delightful evening," remarked Clover.

"Yes; he didn't ask for one of my slippers, though. Fancy sterling cousin Page ordering a glass case!"

Clover smiled in answer to Mildred's laugh.

"What did you talk about?"

"Oh, weights and measures, as usual. I wasn't in the mood to be good, and I tried conscientiously to make a fool of our friend."

"Mildred!"

"No harm done; I didn't succeed. He made one of me instead. This has been what you might term an off day for your little sister."

"What do you mean? How did he make a fool of you?" Clover turned with so much curiosity in her gaze that Mildred rose quickly.

"I'll never tell you,—or hardly ever. Perhaps when we are both married."

Clover turned back to the glass, and Mildred was a little dismayed. The words had slipped out unthinkingly. Until this evening she had agreed in her sister's acceptance of the fact that her life could not be like that of other girls.

"Good-night," she said, standing back of Clover and meeting her eyes in the mirror.

"Good-night," returned the other.

Mildred kissed her cheek. "Do you like me?" she asked softly.

"Pretty well," Mrs. Van Tassel smiled. "Lots better than you deserve."

The younger sister went to her room satisfied. Arrogant and autocratic she might be to her slaves, but Clover's approval was the necessary sunshine in which her life blossomed.

Van Tassel had to put a guard upon his lips in the next days. He was trying to follow Clover's advice not to ask Mildred again to go to the Fair with him. It made the case harder, inasmuch as he could not help feeling that now she expected it. He noticed that she did not make outside engagements as much as before; but was oftener at home, either sitting about the piazzas in gowns which Jack thought the most becoming that ever a girl wore, or else romping with Blitzen and paying exasperating attention to Electra, who was fast developing into the most self-assured and exacting chicken of the Columbian year.

The following sort of scene was sometimes endured in anguish by the lover who was disciplining his lady to order.

Jack was one morning reading the newspaper on the piazza, Mildred sitting in the hammock, and Clover and Hilda training the morning-glories.

"Why don't I go to the Fair?" Mildred said, addressing the lake, resplendent with miles of diamonds.

Jack's hand closed on his paper in his longing to accept the challenge; not being at all certain that he would not receive a negative if he did, but still yearning to try his luck.

"Is it a conundrum?" asked Clover. "I can give a guess, if you like."

"Thank you; you're always so kind, dear. Come and go up in the Ferris Wheel with me, Clover. If you will, that will decide me."

"I couldn't, really. I'm glad I have been. One must go, of course; but twice, no, I couldn't." Clover passed near Jack, who threw an imploring glance at her behind his paper. "I can feel my hair whitening!" he murmured; but Mrs. Van Tassel frowned warningly upon him.

"What a pity you didn't say something about it before Robert went," said Hilda. "I think he means to go in the wheel today, as that is one of the things I can't bring my mind to do."

"But you will have a hundred chances, Milly dear.

Some of our friends are always going," added Clover comfortingly.

"Oh, don't trouble yourself," remarked Mildred with nonchalance. "I assure you I can go when I like," and she rose and sauntered into the house, followed by Hilda.

Clover laughed softly into the pink lips of a morning glory which she held in her hand.

"This may be very good fun for you," said Van Tassel, his unread paper dropped, "but let me tell you it is making an old man of me."

"Do your own way then, Jack, and live to repent of it."

"But I don't want to have to repent."

"Then behave as though you had some backbone. Remember Petruchio."

"Oh, that will do to say! Petruchio was married."

"All right. I wash my hands of you."

"No, no, don't, Clover."

Clover took pity on the clouded face.

"I'll give you a little bit of comfort, Jack," she said, gazing down at him knowingly.

"Angel!"

"Oh, it is only a wee, wee bit; but Mildred is uncomfortable."

"I should think that was wee," returned Van Tassel, his face falling.

"I don't know. It is the first time any man ever affected her that much."

"A very poor recommendation, I should think," remarked Van Tassel.

"Oh, Jack," Clover laughed, "I can see you would have had an awful time without me."

"I am having an awful time with you, Clover."

"Then gang your ain gait any time"—

"And may God have mercy on my soul, I suppose you mean," added Jack ruefully.

It was his habit to have flowers sent to the house almost daily, and Clover often wore his roses; Mildred never. Van Tassel asked her once if she never wore flowers, and she answered indifferently that she often did.

"I have never happened to see you with any on," he said.

"Indeed?" she returned with one of her characteristic smiles. "Then that must be because you never sent me any. Now don't look like that, Jack. If you should send me flowers, now, do you know what I should do with them?"

"Pitch them out the window, probably."

"No; for that would disfigure the lawn, and Clover is very particular about the lawn. I should present them to Aunt Love."

So Jack only gave one impotent look into her starry eyes, and continued to send his lavish floral gifts impersonally to the house.

But one morning Mildred came down with some sprays of heliotrope fastened in her dress. Van Tassel was delighted; but acting with blind faith in Clover, he did not appear to notice the concession. He had won several words of commendation from his mentor for the manner in which of late he had been playing his role. He had even called upon Mildred's friend, Miss Eames, in response to the latter's invitation, and had gone with her one day to the Art Gallery, and after coming home praised her discriminating and intelligent taste. It seemed to him an eternity since he had asked Mildred to go anywhere with him.

On this morning she waited for some remark upon her

decoration, but none came. Matters had become serious if such condescension was not going to be gratefully received. The family usually sauntered out upon the piazza after breakfast, and Van Tassel took his paper with him today as usual. He was alive in every nerve to the fact that Mildred had on a street dress, which meant the Fair. He wondered profoundly, as he always did, what her plans were and whom she was going with, but he gazed unseeingly into his paper, and was dumb.

All of a sudden, a sort of electric shock seemed to pervade the air about him. Mildred was standing at his side.

"Did you notice how perfect this heliotrope is?" she asked, looking down, not at him, but at the blossoms on the lapel of her jacket.

"It is pretty," he answered, wondering how soon his evil star would lure him on to say the wrong thing.

His apparently indifferent manner piqued her still further. "If you feel very good, and are sure you are going to be good all day, I will give you a piece," she said, separating one spray from its fellows.

Van Tassel sprang to his feet, and in a second Mildred's fingers were upon his coat.

The round world is just a rattle to her, and you are one of the bells on it that jingle when she moves you.

Clover's words were sounding warningly in his ears. He could not help it. He only prayed to jingle in tune, for moved he was to the depths of his being.

"You like heliotrope very much?" he asked, not daring to look below her cool, fair forehead.

"Yes. Sometimes, I think, best of all; but," with a sigh, "it goes quickly." And she dropped her hands and moved back.

"Like all the happiest moments of life," said Jack, and something leaped from his brown eyes that actually surprised Mildred, coming out of the long train of indifferent days.

Oh, if Jack is like that, she thought, and a new respect grew in her for the man who ruled himself, and refused to submit to her caprice.

"It is a clear day, Mildred. Let us go up in the Wheel," he said. "Have you made the trip yet?"

"No, but I have a new idea about it. I'm sure it will make me dizzy. It did Clover; and I think I shall be afraid, too."

"Don't give up going. I'm sure you will not be afraid. It is an absolutely steady, safe motion, and the changing view is unique."

"No, indeed; I wouldn't give up going, only I think I would rather go alone. I don't want any one to behold my weakness."

"Oh, very well." Van Tassel made a gesture of indifferent assent, sat down, and returned to his paper. The little incident of the heliotrope had done more to convince him of Clover's wisdom than all her sage words. Its perfume stole up to him as he sat reading the same line over twelve times.

Mildred moved away, outwardly calm, inwardly vexed with Jack for his ready acquiescence.

She went into the house and met Clover. "Going to the Fair?" asked the latter.

"Yes, I think so."

"Wait half an hour or so, and go with us."

"I don't believe you will take my way, for I am going in

the Wheel."

"With Jack?"

"No, alone."

"Mr. Page wants to go again. Let me ask him. He is upstairs writing a letter."

"Don't speak to him for anything."

"But I don't want you to go to the Midway alone, Milly. Hilda and both Mr. Pages and I are going to the Anthropological Building together. Do put off the Wheel, and come with us."

"No, I thank you. Our friend Gorham will be in his element, getting your mental and physical strength tested up there in the gallery. I wouldn't be in that revel for anything," and Mildred ran upstairs.

Clover entered the piazza.

"Is Mildred going to the Fair?" asked Van Tassel, looking up quickly.

"Yes. I do wish for once, Jack you had asked to go with her, for she is bound for the Ferris Wheel."

"I did."

"And she refused?" exclaimed Clover in surprise and exasperation. "Was there ever such an incomprehensible"—

"But she gave me this." Van Tassel exhibited his flower.

Clover looked interested. "Well, then, we are getting on," she said, much pleased. "Go on being an icicle, Jack. It is the only way. Don't for the world urge her to let you accompany her, even though I don't like her to go alone. In the first place she would only retreat as you advanced, and in the second it would probably be salutary for her to stick among the clouds of heaven for a few hours, so I won't worry about the Wheel."

Jack took his hat, lying on the chair beside him. "I think I will go on down," he said. "There is a bare possibility, you know, that I may meet Mildred. If she should be later than you expect in coming home, you would better think of me as being the trap than of the Wheel."

"You won't meet," sighed Clover. "What a foolish girl she is!"

To tell the truth, Mildred could not resist a certain suspicion of her own foolishness, as she emerged upon the piazza a few seconds later, ready to start. She was conscious of disappointment that Jack was not in sight. It was a warm day, and starting off alone was not inspiriting. It required all her pride to pursue her intention.

"You won't have a good time," prophesied Clover, and that strengthened her waning determination; so with a light response she set forth.

The Midway was a seething mass of humanity when she reached it, and she had hardly entered the street when she met her friend, Helen Eames. The latter greeted her eagerly, and began to talk about an entertainment Mildred had attended recently with Jack at her house.

Helen was voluble, and Mildred resented the tone in which she spoke of Jack, so she parted with her friend as soon as civility permitted, and passed on.

She began to feel that she was doing an absurd thing, to be forlornly and doggedly pursuing her way among the motley crowd, to the monotonous, rhythmic beat of drum, and the sing-song of strange voices.

Above their village the South Sea Islanders were pounding out their measures from a hollow log, and across the road the daintier Javanese rang muffled music from gongs and tinkling bells. Scenes and sounds had grown familiar to Mildred, but today she found neither truth nor poetry in them. Indian, Turk, and Bedouin passed her by, but she kept eyes ahead on the mammoth wheel, circling with ponderous deliberation. All she wished was to keep her word, take the skyward trip, and return home.

"All the girls are delighted with Mr. Van Tassel," Helen Eames had said.

Silly thing! Does she suppose I will tell him? thought Mildred, too absorbed in her own cogitations to note the "vera gooda, vera nice, vera sheep," of the jewelry venders, the stentorian exhortations to enter the dance houses and theatres, or the incessant "hot! hot! hot!" of those that offered the thin waffle-like Zelabiah.

Mildred did not like to find in her own heart the wish that Van Tassel had been with her, that Helen Eames might see him in his proper place this morning. She must indeed have fallen from her high estate if she could wish to display an admirer to another girl. All men were her admirers. It had been a foregone conclusion so long that she had never been obliged to harbor a thought of jealousy or rivalry, and she instantly challenged and condemned this novel weakness.

The Midway Plaisance was a strange place for introspection, yet Mildred's thoughts were sufficiently absorbing. People were always apt to turn and look a second time at her exceptionally vigorous young beauty, but she passed on today, totally unconscious of the glances bent upon her.

Might it be true that she had finally alienated Jack by her persistently capricious treatment? *All the girls admired him!* He did not fancy any of them, she was sure. If he cared for any woman, it was Clover; and then the girl coolly and impartially compared her gentle, sympathetic, tender sister with herself. Mildred possessed a clear head, and as she dwelt upon her own and Clover's characteristics, a sermon seemed preached to her amid that crowded babel, in a small voice which the noisy tongues could not drown.

How would it be possible for a man in his senses to prefer me? she thought, raising her eyes to a delicate, bell-hung minaret that pierced the cloudless sky. This novel humility impressed her with gravity.

But she had reached her destination. She moved up with the line to the ticket office that lay directly in her path, and bought her bit of paste-board mechanically. In a moment more the movement of her fellow-passengers had brought her to the base of the wheel. Those who have stood in that position know the effect of looking straight up. Mildred, already feeling small, experienced a painful physical sense of being overwhelmed. The monster had paused for its cars to be filled, and she shrank from the prospect before her with unprecedented sensations. If she allowed herself to be shut up in that glass cab, it meant that two flights of two hundred and fifty feet skyward must be taken ere she could regain her liberty.

"I believe I am trying to be nervous," she said to herself coldly. "I did not know I was speaking truth to Jack this morning."

Oh, if only she were not the vainest and most obstinate of girls, this trip would be a pleasure instead of a pain!

The faint, steady color in her cheeks faded, but she walked into the car determinedly, and taking one of its swinging chairs looked steadily through the glass front. The seats filled, the door was closed, and the scarcely perceptible motion began.

The roof of the next car began to swing into view. The inexorableness of the journey began to impress itself upon Mildred's mind. She was trying to turn away from the thought, when a well-known voice set her beating heart to throbbing faster.

"Why, this is fortunate," it said, with studied carelessness.

She started, and lifted her eager eyes. There was Jack Van Tassel looking down upon her, triumphant, but as usual uncertain of his reception.

It has been said before that Mr. Van Tassel was a good-looking young man; but the radiance which seemed to Mildred now to invest every feature of his face, and each dark hair of his head, was certainly the figment of an excited imagination.

"Why, Jack," she gasped, and clasped her hands tightly in her lap for fear they might tell too much.

"You are pale," he said, and stooped with tender concern.

"Why—the sun was pretty warm, didn't you think?" she returned.

Jack did think so. He had had considerable time in which to test it, dodging from one side of the Plaisance to the other in that crowd, where every one knows that his best friend had a faculty of dissolving from view even when he was supposed to be safely at one's side.

"Our poor heliotrope!" he said, glancing down at their decorations.

Mildred followed his gaze. The sprays on her jacket looked, she thought, much as she felt five minutes ago. "Let us throw them away," she answered, starting to withdraw the pin.

"Never," said Jack promptly, and the girl hesitated, then dropped her hand.

"Turn this way," he added. "See the University buildings,—a fine massive gray city that is going to be! Doesn't it seem strange to think that college will ever be venerable and have traditions?"

From this time their attention was fully occupied with the panoramic view. The crowd of sightseers in the Plaisance became a congregation of umbrellas and parasols, ever lessening in size, and whitened in patches where a number of faces were upturned at once to behold the gyration of the wheel. The strange colors and shapes in architecture brought from many lands stood in startling conjunction on either hand. Beyond stretched the Fair city with its winding waterways, held safe in the great azure crescent of Lake Michigan's embrace.

Mildred's eyes sparkled with interest and pleasure. The color had returned to her face, and her spirits to their natural level. When their car again neared earth she was glad, not sorry, that another circuit was in prospect to help her to a more satisfactory view of what had seemed but a tantalizing glimpse.

"The deed is done," said Jack, as at last the exit door of the car was opened, and the passengers passed from under the gigantic steel web and set foot on solid earth once more. "What is next on your programme?"

"I was going home," answered Mildred, rather hesitatingly.

"World's Fair finished?" asked Jack with a smile.

"I have seen almost everything in the Plaisance that I care for."

"But I haven't."

"What do you mean? Are you hinting?"

The girl smiled too, and somehow her expression was not so exasperating as at other times.

"Yes, I am hinting."

"Out with it, then. Speak up like a little man."

"Sometimes when I have spoken up like a little man you have made me feel like a little donkey."

"I don't see how you can like me at all, Jack," returned Mildred naïvely. "I made up my mind this morning that I was going to try to be more like Clover."

"Capital scheme!" exclaimed Van Tassel, with so much enthusiasm that Mildred felt disconcerted.

"I don't suppose the leopard can change his spots, though," she returned, rather stiffly.

"Let us go to Hagenbeck's and see," suggested Jack.

"It is rather far from here if we are going to do the shows with any system."

"Do you wish to, Mildred? Don't let me bore you."

"It only bores me to have you want me to be like somebody else."

Jack's lips drew together in an inaudible whistle, and it needed all Clover's warnings to aid him in holding the rein over himself. They were aimlessly walking east.

"But I honestly don't blame you," she added. "I have done nothing to make it pleasant for you here. In your own home it didn't seem necessary to treat you like a guest."

"You are right. There was no necessity in the matter; there isn't now. Perhaps you really wish to go home."

"Clover wouldn't go if she did wish it," Mildred smiled at him with a sidelong glance, "and so I will stay."

"Not with me," said Jack, lifting his hat and looking very firm as he paused in the road.

"Then you take it back that you wish me to be like my sister?" Mildred also paused, still smiling at him with her chin lifted.

"I want you to be honest."

"I am honest. I want to stay, you uncivil man."

CHAPTER 10

THE MIDWAY PLAISANCE

The magic carpet in the Arabian Nights which transported its owner from one country to another, remote, in the space of a few seconds, was the property of all visitors to the Midway Plaisance. Mildred and Jack spent a little time amid the Swiss Alps, the former amusing herself by picking out for Jack's benefit localities where she and Clover had traveled. Then they looked in at the Bedouin Encampment and saw an old woman making bread. She whirled the dough on one hand until it spread into a very thin sheet. This she flapped over a cushion and from thence transferred it to the top of an inverted iron basin, where it baked above burning sticks. It looked when cooked like a delicate cracker, as it was broken up and passed around to the spectators.

A gigantic black, clothed entirely in red from his high leather boots to the rope-like twists of cloth about his head, lay stretched on a divan beside another fire smoking a narghileh.

"The bread is coming this way," remarked Mildred apprehensively. "Let us go into that door and see what is there."

Jack followed her. "This room, Miss Bryant, is taken from a Damascus palace," he said. "I am surprised that you didn't recognize it at once. Observe these pieces of silver set into the walls, and the lavish number of mirrors. I believe a periodical lecturer appears in here."

"How much nicer to have it to ourselves, and guess about it. I have been standing so long, I can guess very closely what these gold-embroidered velvet divans are for," and Mildred stepped up on the dais at the end of the room and seated herself. The ceiling was lofty, and in the centre of the room a fountain played. Beyond it was another dais surrounded by divans. The floors were covered with rugs. Outside, two Bedouins fenced with curious swords, the handles wrapped with twine, waving their small brass shields meanwhile with ostentatious gestures as they deliberately stepped about. Increasing in concentration and swift fury to the climax of the play, they paused unexpectedly, and seating themselves on the ground, fell to rolling cigarettes and making coffee over the small fire beside which lay the immobile black.

Shrill and dull arose the rhythm of the flageolets and the tambours. The click of castanets told that the dark-eyed women were dancing.

While Mildred and Jack still rested, an Arab in loose robes came in, and going to the fountain bathed his face and hands and dried them on a purple silk towel striped with yellow.

"How nice of him," said Mildred, acknowledging this touch added to the picture.

As they were leaving, one of the Bedouins, the cloth from his twisted turban hanging about his shoulders, paused near them with a baby in his arms, a curly-headed tot of a year old, around whose big brown eyes were drawn lines of artificial black. Mildred looked gently upon the child, and the father, smiling with pride and pleasure, glanced from one to the other; so she patted the baby.

"She is very pretty," Mildred said, and he understood. His large gaze grew soft, and he nodded. Mildred looked at the dancing women with more interest. One of them, her chin tattooed with blue, was pointed out to her as the baby's mother.

A realization of the probable hardships and homesickness endured by these people in all the changes of scene and weather they had undergone assailed her; but it did not do to dwell too long on that side of life in the Plaisance. She only turned her sweetest smile once more on father and child, patted the baby's cheek, and followed Jack out.

To him it mattered little where they went. Each scene gained a glamour which, could the managers of the various enterprises have purchased it as a permanent adjunct to their attractions, would have ensured their fortunes. Passing from Arabia to the electric-lighted palms of the Moorish Palace, Van Tassel was prepared to admire everything. The labyrinth of mirrors which might in some moods have impressed him as a tiresome device, now triumphantly vindicated their right to be, by presenting him a hundred Mildreds so like the original as to be an embarrassment of riches. Even the wax figures above stairs were interesting. The rise and fall of the Sleeping Beauty's gentle breast was a marvel.

From the various tricks and optical illusions of the Moorish Palace they betook themselves to Hawaii, and stood together in darkness on the borders of a lava lake from whose centre shot living flames from the volcano's heart toward the lurid sky.

A priest, a shadowy figure, came forth among the gray rocks, and chanted a prayer to the dreadful goddess of fire. In the remote distance gleamed the peaceful blue waters of the Pacific. Jack would have been willing to stand for hours here by Mildred, in the weird dusky silence broken only by the monotonous chant, for the longer one lingered the more perfect grew the illusion; but she took him away presently, and in a trice the island of Hawaii had vanished and Egypt was gained via the western entrance to Cairo Street.

They passed in before the Temple of Luxor, in front of which a brazen-lunged American showman was reeling off a highly-colored description of the attractions within.

"Mummy of Rameses about the fifth on your right!" repeated Jack, laughing. "Let us postpone Rameses until he can be located a little more definitely."

"Yes, I want you to see an adorable Soudanese child," said Mildred, and they went over to the tent where the jolly little black baby hopped about among her elders, shaking the girdle of feathers and shells about her hips and dimpling with delight in the applause and laughter she called forth. More interesting than the Soudanese were the Nubians, who came in from the dark huts adjoining, and danced in the same tent. One of these in particular attracted Jack's eye.

"What a splendid woman, Mildred!" he exclaimed. "What an artist's model she would make."

The object of his admiration was tall, straight as an arrow, dressed in a long robe of white, and wore large hoop earrings. She had symmetrical features of haughty mould, and was very dark, with thick crinkled black locks free from the feathers, shells and twine, braided among the Soudanese tresses. She was an impressive figure standing immovable upon the stage among the dancers.

"Like a splendid bronze!" said Jack, gazing at the delicate proud face. The Nubian smiled, disclosing the most perfect teeth imaginable, and Van Tassel regarded her with growing admiration.

"I tell you, Mildred," he said enthusiastically, "if that woman could have been brought up in a different environment she would have been superb."

Mildred laughed. "What a pity that I am not a reporter," she said as they left the tent. "You could be worked into a sensational newspaper article, Jack. A young scion of one of Chicago's well-known families is maturing a plan to abduct the chief of the tribe of Nubians in Cairo Street. It is feared there will be an uprising, and so forth, and so forth."

"A feminine chief? I don't blame them."

"No, sir. Your superb bronze woman, your artist's model, is Mohammed Ali, the chief of the Nubians."

Jack looked incredulous. "You expect me to believe that?"

"Not if you wish to go back and inquire. It is true, though. Mohammed is a friend of mine. He was good enough, when Clover and I looked into his hut, to show us how he polishes those perfect teeth of his with a little stick. Did you ever see anything so shining? You can buy his photograph, if you like, at one of these booths, and keep it as a memento of Mr. Van Tassel's"—

"Look ou-at. Look ou-at for Mary Anderson," called a donkey boy in a blue gown.

"You wouldn't run over me, would you, Toby?" asked Mildred.

The boy trudging by through the crowd, showed his ivories in a smile of recognition, and urged his little white donkey onward in the narrow, crooked, brick-paved street.

Such a throng, such a noise, only the memories of the experienced can witness to. Camels swung along between the irregular houses, the warning cries of their drivers mingling with the monotonous sing-song of the venders in the closely packed booths.

Egyptian flower girls, veiled to the eyes, plied their trade. A conjurer pushed his way amid the gazers, a hen's egg sticking in his eye and another clinging behind his jaw. The rhythm of the Midway sounded from two drums slung at either side of a gaudily caparisoned camel, and was sung monotonously from the booth of the much-vaunted Oriental sweetmeat:—

"Alla gooda bum-bum,
Vera nice candy,
Beautifula bum-bum,
Vera good candy,"

repeated *ad libitum* by the swarthy Arab presiding.

Mildred and Jack glanced into the showcases as they passed onward, the former restraining her companion from purchasing specimens of brass work, filigree silver, ornaments, and embroidery. But once Mildred exclaimed with pleasure over a small hanging-lamp of dull silver.

"I will take it," said Jack to the instantly voluble salesman.

"Not for me; no don't," protested his companion.

"You must have a souvenir," returned Van Tassel, smiling over the word which had grown hateful by iteration to all Fair-goers.

"Please don't get it," said the girl; but the very tassel on their Oriental's fez was active in his zeal to wrap up the parcel for this gentleman who did not bargain.

The foreign fashion of changing a price by the beating-down process was one with which many Americans amused themselves when they found it was expected; but Jack was in that state of mind when an article which had the rare fortune to please Mildred was above rubies.

She dissembled her satisfaction, however. "If I had let you buy everything you have started to since we came into the street, we should have had to charter a donkey," she began.

"Look ou-at—look ou-at for Yanka Doodoo," bawled Achmet, the donkey boy, directly upon them.

"I don't like to feel that I mustn't admire anything," finished the girl as Jack stepped between her and the little quadruped who carried a much-excited and curled maiden of five.

"I like this lamp so much, I don't know that I shall let you have it," responded Van Tassel serenely, as he took the package. "Look up, Mildred. What a deep blue the sky gets between those irregular roofs."

"Only one of us can look up at a time, while the other keeps watch of the menagerie."

"There appears to be an extra crowd yonder," remarked Jack.

"Oh, that is the camel-stand. Hear the people laughing. How can anybody be willing to furnish so much amusement to the public as to mount one of those beasts? There is always just such a crowd there."

"Well, are we through here?" asked Van Tassel.

"What? Are you weary of Cairo Street?"

"Not if you are not; but it is rather warm, and there is a good deal of a mob, and I have inhaled enough attar of roses to last until my next incarnation. I thought perhaps you might be tired, standing."

"I am."

"There isn't a place to sit down, either," said Jack, looking around.

"That is just what almost every one thinks. I don't know how soon people will find out my enchanted palace, but they hadn't done so last week."

"Well, now, an enchanted palace is exactly what I am looking for," returned Van Tassel hopefully. "How did you learn the open sesame?"

"The open sesame is"—Mildred paused apologetically. "I am sorry to have to say it, but it is the only prosaic feature,—the open sesame is fifteen cents."

They moved along toward the crowd by the camel stand, and here in the noisiest, busiest portion of the winding street, Mildred led her companion into an open door which revealed a long, blank corridor. The dragon guarding it was a most commonplace American. Most people whose curiosity led them to look into the uninviting hallway were quickly frightened off by the placard stating the fifteen-cent admission fee. There was so much to see, and time and money were so limited, little wonder that the obvious attractions of the street decided them not to explore this side-show.

Mildred and Jack, leaving the din and bustle behind, passed the easily placated dragon, and at the end of the low, empty corridor found themselves in an open, floored court, out of which led a flight of stairs. A large earthen jar filled with water stood at one side over a smaller vessel into which the water filtered in crystal drops through the porous clay. Palms and lilies stood about, and edged the entire length of the staircase. It was very quiet here, and Van Tassel looked about him curiously.

Mildred gave him a smiling glance of mystery. "Let us go up and see Sayed Ibrahim," she said.

"Look here," returned Jack, frowning and smiling, "you are altogether too sophisticated."

"Sayed doesn't think so," answered the girl, and they proceeded upstairs. Entering a hallway where was a heavy bronze door of fabulous age and richness of design, they were met by a tall handsome Oriental in robes and fez, whose melting eyes lighted as they recognized Mildred. He bowed low.

"How do you do, Sayed Ibrahim; I have brought another friend to see the beautiful house."

He bowed again and held aside a portière of cloth-of-gold. The visitors passed within and found themselves in a spacious shadowy room with lofty arched ceiling. The windows were unglazed and shielded by curious hand-carved lattice work. Thick rugs were upon the floor, and small tables inlaid with pearl and ivory stood about. On a larger one were a number of tiny and precious coffee cups, held in little brass stands. Long-stemmed pipes hung upon the walls, and divans or cushions upon the floor invited one to repose. Rich portières divided the suite of rooms one from another.

The light was dim, coming out of the glaring street, and the colors in rugs and hangings were tempered in the wonderful Oriental weaving. There were no other visitors. Jack looked at the swarthy cicerone who stood ready to answer their questions.

"I do not wonder," he said to Mildred, "that you call this mysterious spot enchanted. It is a chapter out of the Arabian Nights."

"Yes; are you ready to come back to the nineteenth century? The nineteenth century in Egypt, you know. I wouldn't make your fall too sudden and profound."

Mildred moved to the broad window-seat which was covered with a rug, and smiled at the Arab. It was a language he understood as clearly as the Harvard graduate, and he hastened forward and threw open the lattice.

Van Tassel seated himself opposite Mildred, and together they looked down upon the madding crowd.

Their position was just opposite the camel stand, and from their height they commanded a view of the kaleidoscopic life of the street. The bystanders pressed about the cushions upon which the camels knelt to take on or be relieved of their burdens, and seemed to find never-failing entertainment in the behavior of those intrepid passengers who embarked for the adventurous journey to the end of the street and back again.

Mildred and Jack in their romantic eyrie held their sides with laughter over the absurdities enacted before their eyes.

"If any trip ever deserved the name of pleasure exertion, that is the one," said Mildred, wiping her eyes, while she watched two girls who evidently took their lives in their hands as they seated themselves on the cushioned back of one of the patient beasts. The Arab driver cried out, and tapped the creature on the neck.

"Now, then," said Jack, "see the ship of the desert let

out the reefs in its legs!"

Shrieks arose from the maidens at the first ascent, wilder and wilder cries and clutchings at the second and third, and by the time the animals had reached the stature of a camel and swung away, the whole crowd was uproarious, only quieting to observe the next pair embark.

"Miss Amelia Edwards says the camel is a beast that hates its rider," said Jack. "I wonder what are the private prejudices of the Cairo Street variety."

"As if you couldn't see!" answered Mildred. "It wouldn't be half so funny if the camels didn't curl their lips and look so supercilious all the time those idiots are shrieking so. 'What fools these mortals be!' is the sentiment their faces express chronically. Poor things! Just think, that they are only intended to kneel once or twice a day, and here they have to go down every three minutes. How they would execrate Columbus if they only knew how! Oh, look at that old lady! It is a shame to let her go," added Mildred. "They will laugh at her, too."

"Never mind. She will be the heroine of Perkins Point, or wherever it is, all the rest of her life."

"She looks scared, Jack. Oh, dear! her bonnet is falling off. I wish she wouldn't. Why, there are Clover and Mr. Page! Do you see them? Let us go out on the balcony." Mildred left the window-seat, and Jack followed.

"Is there a balcony? Why didn't you say so?"

"Because I am economical of my pleasant surprises." The watchful Sayed threw open double doors of the lattice work, and revealed a small, square balcony upon which the visitors stepped into the sunlight. The fanciful minarets and spires of the street gleamed against an azure sky.

Clover and Gorham had paused just below, also interested in the venturesome old lady, who was followed by cheers as her scornful camel bore her up the street.

Jack took advantage of the temporary lull that followed, to whistle the bit from "Carmen."

Clover instantly looked up and called the attention of her companion.

Mildred beckoned.

"Clover knows the way," said Jack.

"Most certainly she does. We Chicagoans aren't Fair visitors. We are Fair livers."

"Don't be so toplofty, mademoiselle. What am I, if not a Chicagoan?"

"Oh, a sort of deserter."

"'I deny the allegation and despise the allegator.' I am going to marry a Chicago girl, and live here all my days."

"Have you asked her?"

Van Tassel, perhaps reminded by the neighborhood of his mentor, forbore from replying to the saucy smiling eyes, and here Clover and Gorham appeared at the door of the balcony.

"Come out," said Mildred, "it holds five. Is this the way you visit the Anthropological Building?"

"Why, this is all right," answered Page. "'Midway Plaisance, Department M. Ethnology.' Look on the catalogue, and you will see this is all a part of the Anthropological exhibit."

"And apart from it," suggested Mildred, "which certainly is in its favor. I thought you would see enough ghastly pictures and graveyards and mummies in a short time."

"The exhibits in the gallery are wonderful and beautiful," said Clover. "I don't believe you know what you are talking about."

"I do, my dear. I have oh'd and ah'd over them all, from the dainty infinitesimal sea creatures on pink cotton to the mammoth. I felt so much obliged to him. He really made me feel small. Then the realistic cliff, with the birds and beasts artistically disposed, and the waterfall and flowing brook. I've seen them. How long have you been here?"

"Not very long. We have been watching the antics of the women on the camels, and the long-legged men on those tiny donkeys."

"A great deal of human nature comes out in Cairo Street," said Page with interest. "One sees a great variety of motives, and many grades of self-control by that camel stand. See that little woman going now to take a trip. Is it amusement she's after? Not at all. Note the determination in her face. Duty calls and she obeys. Dollars to doughnuts she doesn't scream, Jack."

"I'm out of doughnuts; but I'll bet you the supper she does. I haven't seen a quiet one yet."

"Done! You will see one now."

"That girl is from the East," said Mildred.

"I am sure of it," returned Page, gazing with pleased curiosity at his protégée, who stood waiting her turn; "but what brings you to that conclusion?"

"The trimming of her hat looks as if it were nailed on. They say all Boston women's bonnet trimmings are nailed on."

"She is a character," said Page. "Now I would like to know what her motive is in riding that camel."

Jack guffawed. "I am sure you would. You will be asking her the next thing we know."

"Well, it is no idle one, I'm sure of that."

"Perhaps she is a school teacher," suggested Van Tassel, "and wants to go home and tell her scholars how pitch-and-toss in Cairo Street differs from the usual game."

"There she goes," said Clover, and they all watched the fair-faced girl approach and mount a camel whose expression for utter boredom rather outdid its neighbors. At the driver's cry it gathered itself convulsively. The rider lurched forward. Her back was to the watchers on the balcony, but they could not hear a sound from her. She lurched backward, still without a cry, and they were not surprised when the camel swung around to see her face still set in its determined and composed lines while the crowd looked on in silence.

"I shall enjoy that supper very much, Jack," said Gorham.

"You haven't won it yet. Wait till she comes back. When his Nibs kneels down is the time a girl's lungs really come into play. After she thinks every joint in his body has doubled up there comes one unexpected plunge that fetches the most dignified of them every time. They say a sailor came in here the other day and after riding one of our humped friends, he said that the camel played cup-and-ball with him the whole length of the street, and only missed him twice."

In a few minutes, back came Gorham's heroine, still composed as she rocked back and forth clinging to the rope which the driver had handed her for a support.

"Now that supper hangs in the balance," remarked Page.

"I'm safe enough," returned Jack nonchalantly, "and I assure you my appetite is in prime condition."

The camel, slowly winking and holding his nose aloft,

approached his cushion, and began the series of spasmodic collapses which made its rider look as though at the mercy of a rocking chair gone mad. She pitched wildly, but valiantly held her peace. Even Jack had to admit that she did not make a murmur, and all his protests against playing off a dumb girl on him were unheeded as Page gazed benignly down on the young woman, who smiled sweetly and triumphantly as she rejoined her friends.

"Five minutes of four," said Mildred. "The wedding procession will soon pass. Aren't we fortunate to have the balcony? Do you see, other people are daring to visit the house and taking our window-seat?"

"Your widow-seat. That is pretty good," said Clover, turning toward the speaker with an arch smile. "We thought that was our window-seat, didn't we, Jack?"

She saw the color flash over her sister's face in the instant before the girl controlled herself. She wondered if Jack had seen the novel evidence of feeling before Mildred turned to him coolly.

"So you have been here before," she remarked. "Why didn't you mention it?"

Clover turned away to conceal her amusement. Jack in his embarrassment had implied all she could have asked from the disciplinary standpoint.

But now the attention of the quartette was claimed by the wedding procession, which was seen coming down the street, the camels nearly hidden under their gaudy, bulking trappings, and the din of the tom-toms filling the air. When the music, dancing, and sword play were ended, Mildred spoke to her sister.

"What have you done with Mr. and Mrs. Page?"

"They went to the Chinese theatre, and we have promised to meet them in Old Vienna and take supper there."

"Our dear Jack will have to take supper with us now," declared Gorham cordially.

"I suppose," said Van Tassel, addressing Mildred, "that Old Vienna is an oft-repeated experience to you?"

"At least I shall not pretend that it is a novelty," she answered without looking at him, and Jack was silent. He even colored, but it was not with proper contrition. It was a flush of pleasure that overspread his countenance as his brown eyes sent a quick glance into Clover's.

CHAPTER 11

OLD VIENNA

"How remarkable that you met Mildred," said Clover to Jack, after the four had wended their way out of Cairo and turned west.

"It was a lucky chance," replied Van Tassel.

"Where did you meet?" The fun in his face gave Clover her first suspicion.

"In the Ferris Wheel. Wasn't it a coincidence that we should have chosen the same cab? And I'll tell you in confidence, Clover that I think Mildred was considerably impressed with his Wheelship."

"Why should you make a confidence of that?" asked Mildred nonchalantly. "We are all impressed, aren't we?"

"Not to the verge of pallor, Milly."

"Don't call me Milly. No one does that but Clover."

"Were you really frightened, Mildred?" asked her sister with much interest.

"Why do you ask me? Ask Jack. He evidently knows

all about it."

"No, I insist on referring you to Mildred herself. She scorns petty deceits of all kinds. I cannot be relied on to tell the absolute truth."

Mildred looked at the speaker with a dangerous sparkle in her eyes. "Why don't you give Clover her present?" she asked suddenly.

"A present for me? Why, hurry," exclaimed Clover. "What new extravagance have you been committing, Milly?"

"It isn't I this time, it is Jack. He has bought you the most adorable little silver hanging-lamp you ever saw. Open it, Jack; or shall we wait till we are seated in Old Vienna?"

"You told him I wanted it, you naughty girl."

"No, I didn't." Mildred was bubbling over with mischievous satisfaction in Van Tassel's struggles to look bland. "It was purely spontaneous on his part. I even went so far as to urge him not to get it. Didn't I, Jack?"

Van Tassel's reply was scarcely audible; but they had reached the guard, who with puffed sleeves and feathered hat stood motionless, spear in hand, before the entrance to the Vienna of two hundred years ago.

Inside they found the Pages, standing before one of the many open shops which formed the first floors of the weather-stained, peaked, and turreted houses.

"Hilda is buying a spoon," announced Mr. Page as his friends approached; "but that goes without saying. I have kept careful count, and this is the seventy-seventh she has purchased while with me. Of course there may be others. I can't tell what pleasant surprises may be awaiting me when we get home."

"How was the Chinese theatre?" asked Gorham, while Clover and Mildred gravitated naturally to Mrs. Page's side to lend her their aid in deciding between the merits of two spoons she was examining.

"Immense; you must go."

"You mustn't go unless you want to be driven crazy with noise," put in Hilda. "Robert says I am deficient in the sense of humor, but you positively can't think in that place. There was a Chinese-American in the audience acting as an interpreter, and I suppose he saw that Robert was interested; so he just stayed with us, and put the crowning touch to the confusion by explaining the play at a pitch to be heard above the squealing music and the shrieking actors."

"Women's parts all taken by men, of course," explained her husband, "and they jabber in a high monotonous falsetto without any change of countenance except an occasional attack of pathetic strabismus. Two lovers meet after a separation of ten years. They start, then with two simultaneous squeaks fall backward in a swoon, feet to feet, and lie there with their elaborately dressed heads sticking up in the air, while a supe runs in with wooden supports which he tucks under their necks. The interpreter explained: 'Of course they cannot spoil their hair!' Ha! ha! It was great; and as for the costumes and hangings, they would stand alone for the gold and silver embroidery in them. Confess, Hilda, they were consoling."

"Yes, they were; and so was the baby we saw upstairs in the Joss-house. He was ten months old, with a black tuft of hair on top of his head exactly like the Chinese dolls, and was dressed in green silk trousers and a red silk shirt."

"You must have wanted to steal him," said Mildred.

"That is what his mother thought, I am sure. He lay

asleep in a little wagon, and when she heard me exclaim, she flew out from behind a curtain with a very suspicious expression on her pretty face. Yes, she was really pretty, and dimpled, and young; and her hands were loaded with rings. Robert, just look here one minute. Don't you think the filigree handle is the prettier?"

"My dear, I ate too many bananas once, and have never since been able to endure the sight of them. If you knew the sentiments of which a souvenir spoon inspires me, you would tremble."

"I will take the filigree one," said Mrs. Page, with a sigh of relief.

The six ate supper together at a table pleasantly distant from the fine German orchestra. Feathery bits of white cloud scudded over the blue above them. Picturesque gables and weatherbeaten façades illuminated with the decorations of a bygone time closed them in from the outside world with such an atmosphere of antiquity, that even the dignified beauty of Handel's Largo, as its stately measures pealed forth on the evening air, seemed an anachronism.

Mildred sat at Jack's right hand.

"What shall I put down for you?" he asked, looking up from the order he was writing. "I found nothing on the card injurious enough to be appropriate."

Mildred smiled slightly as she glanced over the menu.

"You deserved a worse punishment than that," she answered.

"It is true it was no great punishment. I should like to give Clover all Cairo Street if she wants it."

Clover was sitting opposite between the other men, and the music effectually concealed from her the above colloquy.

"Hurry up, Jack," she said, leaning forward; "They keep you waiting forever here. Give her bread and milk if she can't decide. It is good for the young."

While the party were waiting for their meal to be brought, Jack, now at ease in the situation, produced the silver lamp, which received much praise as it was passed about.

Gorham, Mildred's other neighbor, turned to her. "Your sister suggests that you must have practiced much self-control," he remarked. "She says this is just the sort of lamp you have been searching for."

"Do you hear that, Jack?" asked Mildred demurely. "I am afraid Jack does not appreciate me, Mr. Page."

Mildred, ever since the evening of her confidential talk with Gorham, had carried the half-nettled, wholly amused consciousness that he was regarding her with considerations of her search for that affinity she had described. She felt sure he would not repeat their talk to Jack; but if he should! The thought brought a stinging red to her cheeks.

Page was not thinking of her now, however. This little circumstance of the gift of the lamp impressed him. That Jack should, while with Mildred, buy this bauble which the latter coveted and give it to Clover, looked as though Hilda's convictions might be correct. As he caught a serene glance from Clover's violet eyes it suddenly seemed to him very improbable that an impressionable fellow like his cousin should not dream by day and night of that pure and beautiful face.

Jack was not worthy of her, he could not precisely state to himself why; and he ran over his acquaintances in his mind to see if he could find one the consideration of whom would rouse less antagonism. He had not succeeded when the waiter appeared with the supper.

"What are you indefatigable people going to do next?" asked Robert Page, lighting a cigar when their meal was finished. "I am extremely comfortable and good-natured now, but I warn you I shall turn dangerous if any one suggests the illumination. To be asked just to step over from Old Vienna to the Court of Honor sounds pleasant. It was played on me once when I was a tenderfoot; but I'm not to be roped into any such pilgrimage tonight. If I wasn't a married, man, I should sit right here and listen to the music, and see the Wheel go round, until it was time to go to my little bed."

"What nonsense!" remarked Hilda. "If you weren't married you would be urging me to go with you in a gondola."

"My dear, where would be the use? You know the gondolas are all bespoken by this time. What a sweet consciousness it is, by the way," Robert added, sighing restfully.

"We are going, though, some night," returned his wife. "Before we leave the White City, you must take me in a gondola and hold my hand."

"See the lengths to which this woman's frenzy for spoons carries her! Why, I'll hold your hand now, my dear. Any suggestion which presupposes so little exertion as that will find me in an affirmative state of mind every time."

Hilda glanced at his offered hand scornfully. "We haven't the stage-setting," she replied. "Be careful, Robert Page, or you will frighten Mildred out of getting married at all."

"Is that true, Miss Mildred? Oh, I don't believe it. You

are so level-headed you must see the situation in the right light. Did you ever hear the simile of the horse-car? When a man is trying to catch a horse-car and afraid it is going to escape him, he waves his arms, shouts, hurries, and disturbs himself generally. After he has caught the conveyance, if he continued to behave in the same perturbed fashion he would be set down as a lunatic. You see the point, of course?"

Mildred pursed her lips and shook her head. "You are a very audacious man," she answered.

"Now Jack isn't smoking," continued Page argumentatively. "That indicates the restlessness of the man who is afraid he will arrive too late at the street corner."

"It indicates that I am not going to stay here," returned Van Tassel.

"Whither away, restless one?"

"You will have to ask Miss Bryant. She is showing me the World's Fair today."

"Not after your perfidious behavior," said Mildred.

"Don't speak to me of perfidy!" said Jack with a grin.

"Well, shan't we all go somewhere together?" suggested Gorham.

"No, I think we shan't dear brother," replied Robert mildly.

"Do you want to stay, Hilda?" asked Gorham. "Aren't you growing tired of hearing Zwei Bier? Come with us."

"No, thanks. I will stay here until it bores me, and then I will give Robert his choice of selecting another souvenir spoon or taking me out."

So the other four left their seats and moved away to the martial strains of "Die Wacht am Rhein."

Clover found herself beside Jack a moment.

"It was a shame about the lamp," she murmured.

"What?" returned Van Tassel, looking uncomfortably into her roguish eyes.

"I saw how it was. Too bad; but that is another thing she will repent at leisure."

"How did you know?"

"By Mildred's impish dimple. She has one just above her lip that never shows except when she is in mischief. At first I was taken in; but after a moment I saw the imp, and then I knew."

"What a wonderful sight the Wheel is with its double row of electric lights," said Mildred to Gorham.

"What—yes; it has been rather warm," he replied; this irrelevance being due to the effect upon him of observing Clover's murmured colloquy with Jack.

Mildred stared. When she made a remark to a man, she was accustomed to find him attentive.

Page continued with another inexcusable speech.

"I wonder if perhaps Mrs. Van Tassel would like to go somewhere with Jack."

"I believe Jack considers himself otherwise engaged this evening," returned Miss Bryant with hauteur.

"Oh—oh yes." Gorham's eyes fell upon the speaker with an expression which suggested that he had just become aware of her, and until this moment had been talking to himself.

A light broke upon Mildred. There was but one possible explanation of such ignoring of her own preëminent right to homage.

They are both in love with her! she thought, and the slight pang that came with the idea surprised her.

Clover and Jack, with the laughter on their lips, stepped

forward and joined the others.

"Have you any wish, Mrs. Van Tassel?" asked Page.

"No, let us drift until something tempts us." They soon lost sight of Mildred and Jack in that stream of humanity which flowed in both directions along the Midway between the soft arc-moons. They left behind them the great Wheel, slowly revolving in sparkling light as though, sweeping through the heavens, myriad stars had caught thickly along its edges and were borne on to earth.

"Let me carry that precious lamp," said Page, taking Clover's parcel.

"I would not let Jack keep it, for fear he might give it to Mildred," she explained.

Her companion looked surprised.

"Jack is a little weak and indulgent where Mildred is concerned," said Clover.

Page did not know what to reply. Hilda had assured him in days past that no one could help seeing that Mrs. Van Tassel was unwilling Jack should ask Mildred to go to the Fair with him, and now this frank avowal of jealously perplexed him greatly.

"But what—what mystifies me, Mrs. Van Tassel," he said hesitatingly, "is that you should care for a gift—but there are limits to a man's right to express his thoughts."

Clover laughed out mirthfully. "Analyze me. I am perfectly willing, only it will necessitate exposing the fact that my sister is a very saucy girl."

Page regarded her so earnestly that he nearly stumbled over a wheeled chair that grazed him.

"I don't understand it at all," he said seriously.

"Of course not. Well, I will tell you. Jack bought this lamp for Mildred; and she, to punish him for some offense, forced him to give it to me in the way you heard. She doesn't know that I saw through it; but now I do not propose that she shall have the fun and the lamp, too."

Page found the Midway grow a trifle cheerier under this disclosure. "Of course not," he answered; then, after a moment's thoughtfulness: "That was a strange prank for your sister to play," he added. "I fear I shouldn't have known how to yield as easily to the joke as Jack did."

"Oh, he stuttered a good deal, poor fellow," laughed Clover. "Mildred is a spoiled child."

"Not so superficial, though, as one would at first believe," returned Gorham. "There is plenty of depth to her nature. Society educates a girl to seem shallow, that is all."

Clover looked surprised and pleased. She glanced at Page with quick, responsive feeling.

"It is very nice of you to see through Mildred," she said, and Page felt a strange glow under her approval.

The folly of Hilda, he thought, *in supposing this woman could be jealous of another!*

There was something too in the quiet joyousness of her sphere which assured him that whatever were her sentiments for Jack, she was not longing for his society now. She was content, he felt it, and the knowledge was bliss to him.

"I wonder how soon we are going to be attracted," remarked Clover, after they had walked a minute in silence.

Page turned to her suddenly. "What do you mean by that?" he asked so eagerly that the surprised color rushed to his companion's face.

"Why, we were waiting, weren't we, for one of these side shows to tempt us beyond the point of resistance," she answered, with the glibness with which a woman can skim over a moment which threatens too much.

"Well, to tell the truth I had forgotten what we were doing beyond sauntering together in this very interesting, motley crowd. Isn't it strange how completely alone we are in such a place?"

"Or might be, if it were not for the wheeled chairs," said Clover. "It isn't safe to become introspective here."

"Was I?" anxiously. "Have I been silent, Mrs. Van Tassel? My thought often play me tricks. Hilda is always saying that I am 'different.' I don't know just what she means, but if you would be kind enough to mention it if I do anything you don't like, I should be—it would be a great favor."

"You are very flattering," returned Clover, turning away to smile. "What a temptation you offer me!"

"Then I do offend you?" he exclaimed with frank consternation.

"No, no, I didn't mean that. I was only thinking what a temptation you hold out to a woman to mould a fellow-creature into the form she likes. But I know what an ignis fatuus that alluring idea is. Men do not alter themselves to please women."

"I should say," returned Page ruminatively, "that you are wrong. I know that Hilda has changed Robert in many ways, materially."

"By the force of years of influence, yes; but your brother did not know what was going on. I am certain of that."

"I should suppose," said Page earnestly, "that a man could not rest in the knowledge that he was doing something offensive to the woman he loves."

"Yes, you would suppose so," agreed Clover. "My knowledge of the truth is gathered from observation, not experience, as you know. I reverenced Mr. Van Tassel too completely to think of desiring to change him. In my married life it was myself I wished to alter; but I have seen a good deal of young married people, and—well, tell me, Mr. Page, did you ever hear Hilda say that she would be glad if her husband did not smoke?"

"Yes," replied Gorham, and said no more.

"Now I begin to feel a strong temptation, Mr. Page. How is it with you? Are you prepared to resist the Javanese village?"

"I have not been in there."

"Oh, you mustn't miss that. I wonder you have been able to pass that charming, fantastic, bamboo entrance. The lightness and simplicity of this life makes it to me the most charming in the Plaisance."

They entered the gateway and came suddenly upon the quiet attractions of the dainty straw village. Yes, it was still, here; still enough to hear the muffled music of the water-wheel. Clover and Page stood a moment in the hush, listening to its tinkle, and the plashing of the wavelets. A small, soft-footed Javanese occasionally passed them.

"I wish that I smoked," broke out Gorham suddenly.

"Here will be an opportunity," returned Clover. "You will be offered cigarettes at every turn in Java."

Page's seriousness was unmoved. "I want you to believe that I would give it up if you asked me."

Mrs. Van Tassel's serene heart quickened its pace, but she laughed. "Isn't it a pity that I shall have to remain incredulous?" then she hastened on, vaguely afraid of her companion. "Don't misunderstand me, please. I was not criticizing your brother a minute ago. Do you know you have formed a shocking habit of frankness in me? You have searched out my thoughts and opinions so many times that now you have only to suggest a subject and I pour out my ideas. I think I ought to have kept my observations to myself on this topic; but since I have said so much, I don't wish to leave you with the notion that I think your brother and men like him monsters of selfishness. A woman makes an absurd mistake to marry a smoking man, and then to be grieved because he refuses when she artlessly requests him to give up the habit; but a girl nearly always thinks that all she need do is to marry a man in order to make him over into anything she likes. I tell you, Mr. Page, it is the result of my observations that all the voluntary changes a man makes at the request of his beloved are made before—before he catches the horse-car."

Gorham smiled. "But I don't think Robert ought to smoke, since Hilda"—

"Pardon me. I am going to defend the absent. Did he smoke while they were engaged?"

"Yes."

"Very well. Now, do you wish to hear some words of wisdom?"

"Yes, indeed."

"Here they are. If Hilda disliked tobacco, she should have said so, then; and she probably did. When she found Mr. Page would not give up the habit, she should have weighed the question in her mind as to whether the matter of smoking were going to affect her happiness seriously. If she thought it would, she should have broken her engagement. The great point is, that if she decided to marry him she should have realized that she took him as he was, tobacco and all, and would be likely to have rather more than less of it for the rest of her life."

"A man is a selfish brute," remarked Gorham.

"Sometimes; but he has the same right a woman has to choose between his habit and his love; that is, if the woman speaks in time."

"Hilda does not particularly dislike cigar smoke," said Page, "but she thinks smoking is bad for Robert. I wonder if all men are as thick-skinned as you say. Now, there is Jack. Do you believe he would not fling all his cigars into the lake for—for you?"

"Yes, indeed; so long as there were plenty more to be had."

"No, Mrs. Van Tassel, be serious; and for the moment pardon personalities. If Jack were engaged to you"—

He waited, gazing at Clover. She smiled at him and said, "Well, if Jack were engaged to me?"

Page swallowed some impediment to speech.

"And you should earnestly ask him not to smoke, can you doubt the result?"

Clover shrugged her shoulders. "No, I am afraid I can't. Jack is a gentleman, and such an impulsive, affectionate fellow, I know pretty well what he would do, supposing of course that he were very earnestly and deeply in love with me."

"Which he is, of course." The dismal exclamation broke from Page unawares.

Clover stared at him. "Oh no, he isn't," she said gently, after a minute.

"What!"

"No, indeed. Jack and I always were good comrades, and always will be, I hope."

Page suddenly took both her hands excitedly, and laughed aloud.

"Pardon me," he said, sobering suddenly. "I was forgetting where we were." He drew her hand within his arm and they started to walk. "Pretty little light things these bamboo houses are," he continued. "What a gentle life they suggest. I don't know exactly why I am so glad to hear what you tell me, Mrs. Van Tassel. I was under a mistaken idea that you and Jack were—and it is no reflection upon Jack that I am relieved. He is a fine fellow. There is no man I like better; so it is—it is really difficult for me to explain why—why"—

"Never mind trying, Mr. Page," returned Clover, smiling softly at a cage of doves outside a cottage door. "It isn't necessary," she added demurely, "to label every feeling one has."

"It is a sort of habit of mine," he returned apologetically. "What is this long straw building?"

"The theatre."

"Yes; I have not visited it, but I hear it is interesting."

So they entered the well-filled hall just as the performance was beginning, and were fortunate enough to find seats near the stage. At both sides of the latter were placed rows of puppets with grotesque faces, featured like the masks worn by most of the actors. At the back of the stage were ranged the musicians, sitting cross-legged in rows before their highly ornamented instruments. These were soft-toned gongs, bells, and strings of strange fashion, and instead of being solely noticeable for rhythm, like most of the music of the Midway, one heard from this orchestra plaintive harmonies, and cadences which seemed but an amplification of the minor pleading in the water-wheel's play.

The curtained entrances at the side and back of the

stage looked too small and low to admit the actors, but there was room and to spare even for the men, and still more for the dainty brown dancing-girls who soon glided forth. They were exceedingly pretty and graceful, dressed in gold-embroidered velvet trousers to the knee, and short skirts. Their dimpled shoulders and arms were bare, and their fringed sashes were used to fling over their wrists in the fascinating monotonous gestures with which they pointed their little hands as they stepped about in their white-stockinged feet.

The performance was all in pantomime, the lines being read by some one hidden behind a screen in the centre of the stage. The orchestra men in their calico gowns and turbans often smiled at some sally of the clown; but Clover and Page did not need to comprehend in order to be amused. There was something tenderly comical in the pompous movements of the little people gesturing in stiff, studied fashion. From time to time the dancing-girls would appear, gliding hither and yon, and posing to the tinkling music.

"This is surprisingly pretty," said Page.

"I want one of those pretty girls to take home with me," returned Clover. "Aren't they the roundest, prettiest little creatures! Really, the whole thing seems strange enough to be a sight in fairy-land; and do you hear that enchanting rustle of trees above our heads?"

The light summer breeze was stirring the dried straw and grass that thatched the roof, with the lulling effect of wind in a forest.

"I am enchanted, I admit," answered Gorham.

After the play they walked about the village, among the houses where the little inhabitants sat upon their piazzas and sang, or talked or rested silently.

"I shall never see such a reposeful place again," said Gorham, when at last they passed out beneath the bamboo arch into the turbulent street. "I should like to prolong that experience indefinitely."

"You can repeat it," suggested Clover.

"I should like to believe that; but one seldom has so much enjoyment in the same space of time as I have had this evening. I feel grateful to you for showing me all that."

They passed down the remainder of the Midway and under the last viaduct. Walking north around the end of the Woman's Building, they stood a moment arm-in-arm by the lagoon, and watched the quiet boats glide by, then slowly began the homeward walk.

"You did not tell me," said Page, "what you knew Jack would do in our supposed case."

"Haven't we finished yet with the sins of smokers?"

"I don't know. Perhaps we have. Were you going to say that you believed Jack would give up the habit at the request of the woman he loved?"

"I was going to say that he would promise to. Yes, I am quite sure what Jack would do, for I have known men of his kind to do the same thing. His fiancée—I, for example"—

"No, say your sister; although he is not at all her kind."

"Why, what is the matter with poor Jack, Mr. Page?" asked Clover rather resentfully. "In what category do you place him, pray?"

"I place him high enough," returned Gorham hastily. "I only refer to a woman's fancy, and I have an idea that Miss Bryant would prefer a more sober, studious man."

"Why, I can't imagine what makes you think that!"

"It doesn't matter," said Page. "It can't hurt her at all

for us to engage her to him for a few minutes. You are not going to say that Jack would make a promise and break it? If you think that, you rate him lower than I do."

"He wouldn't mean to. This is about the way it goes, or the way I have known it to go. Supposing Mildred to be engaged to Jack, she might tell him she wished he did not smoke; that she disapproved it for many reasons. He would probably reply that he hoped she would not ask him to give it up, for if she insisted of course he should comply with her wishes. This would make such an appeal to her tenderness that she would forbear objecting awhile, feeling sure, poor thing, that her lover was completely in her power; but after a time, inclination and conviction both urging her, she would return to the subject. She might say, for instance, that she could not help wishing strongly that he would give up this habit, and that Clover had said no man would do it for any woman. At this Jack would flare up. How could Clover be guilty of such a speech! She had evidently never known any man who loved a woman as he, Jack, adored her, Mildred. He would die for her. It would be a pleasure to him to give up this comparatively slight gratification for the sake of proving his affection for his beloved. Great elation on the part of Mildred. Lying low on the part of Clover. Jack stops smoking, and is ostentatiously careless and cheerful. Mildred flatters him gratefully. He assures her that he does not care if he never sees a cigar again, and is glad if such a trifling sacrifice pleases her.

"Some day, perhaps before their marriage, perhaps after, it depends upon the length of the engagement, Jack, after dinner, lights a cigar with a friend. Mildred protests gently. He answers reproachfully. Of course she knows the habit is entirely broken up, she surely is not going to be puritanical and unreasonable because once in a while he lights a cigar as she would eat confectionery? She still feels uneasy, but is rather ashamed to show it. He puts his arm around her, tells her she is a nice little girl, and came just in time to save him from smoking to excess, and he thanks her for it."

"Well?" said Gorham, as she paused.

"Well, that occasional cigar soon becomes a daily one, or one of a daily half-dozen."

"Mrs. Van Tassel! How cynical you are!"

Clover laughed. "Oh no, not cynical. Jack was honest in his expectation to give up his pet indulgence. He reasoned himself into thinking his course was right."

"I can't believe it is always so."

"Always, Mr. Page," returned Clover, nodding wisely. "Men have died and worms have eaten them, but not for love. Men have given up tobacco and endured the torment it entails, but *not—for—love!"*

"I never wished before that I was a smoker," said Page musingly, "but I suppose it would be rather foolish to cultivate the appetite merely to deny it."

"A piece of braggadocio which would be sure to reap the reward of failure," replied Clover.

"Don't say that, or you will tempt me to experiment. My first cigar made me dreadfully ill when I was twelve years old, and my father counter-irritated my internal misery with an outward application; so I didn't try it again for some time. In the past year I have occasionally yielded to Jack's urgency and smoked a cigar, but it doesn't interest me. I forget about it, and it goes out."

"By all means let well enough alone," laughed Clover.

"Do you object to the use of tobacco?" asked Page

earnestly.

"In you I should," answered the other, her eyes shining in the darkness.

"I wish I could give it up," he replied simply.

CHAPTER 12

ON THE LAGOON

Mildred and Jack, when they discovered they had lost their companions, made no effort to find them.

"It is a great bore for more than two to try to keep together in this place. Don't you think so?" asked Van Tassel.

"It is very difficult, certainly," agreed the girl. "Isn't it strange to look about this wonder-world of a street and realize that it is just the Midway Plaisance? Recall the old driveway at this hour."

"Yes; early evening was its most populous time too; but even then, how quiet it was. What a wild idea it would have been to expect to see Turkish dancing-girls, half-naked Dahomeyans, and all the rest, living in those still, green fields. Have you been in to Hagenbeck's and seen the marvelous trained animals?"

"Yes; but it is a rather creepy pleasure to watch lions, tigers, bears, and leopards walking around that one solitary man and hissing threateningly at him even while they obey."

"The one moment when I found my breath short was

when the trainer made five lions lie down on the ground, and threw himself on his back upon them as though on a rug. He flung his arms out and caressed their great noses. I tell you, I didn't like him to let those beasts out from under his eyes."

"That was thrilling, I remember; but I felt for the lions sometimes, too. I didn't like to see them demean themselves. When one had to hold the end of a rope in his teeth and swing it to let a hound jump, it seemed rather small business to demand of the king of the forest."

When the two friends, stopping often by the way to watch some curious object of interest, reached the Japanese bazaar, they went in for a few minutes. By the time they emerged, the twilight had wholly faded.

"See your kings of the forest!" exclaimed Jack.

Mildred looked across the street. There in mid-air, apparently suspended like Mahomet's coffin, the iron cage above the entrance to the Hagenbeck arena was brilliant with electric light. Five great lions were within, and the strange effect, in the surrounding darkness, was heightened when the trainer, whip in hand, entered and closed the door behind him. In a shorter time than it takes to tell it, Jack and Mildred found themselves in the centre of an ever-growing crowd, all with upturned faces watching the wondrous apparition. The magnificent beasts glided lithely back and forth, watching the trainer, who, exciting them more and more by the whip which he cracked in the air, adroitly avoided being knocked down as they bounded about him, passing and repassing one another with increasing swiftness.

"A great advertisement," remarked Jack; then, as Mildred moved and turned her head, "Are you being uncomfortably crowded?" he asked.

"Never mind, it is worth it!" she said, rather breathlessly, as a big fellow, uncouth in his open-mouthed wonder, unconsciously shoved her against her companion.

Van Tassel drew her in front of him and placed his arm between her and the countryman. The latter still pressed, but feeling an obstruction firm as a bar of iron, turned his admiring countenance vaguely around toward Van Tassel.

"Well, I vum," he exclaimed. "Ever seen anything like that before? Wife and I never did. Them lions hangin' betwixt earth and heaven shakin' their manes at that feller, and he dodgin' around out o' their way as cool as a cucumber! It's wife's aim to tell the truth when we get home, and it's mine, too. It's both our aims; but we might's well lie. There won't anybody believe this."

"It is amazing," said Jack; "but you can see as well in one place as another. Would you kindly push the other way?"

"They're a-hunchin' us on this side too," explained the man; then continued to gape, oblivious of his surroundings.

The trainer placed a white and gold chair in the centre of the cage, and made one of the lions spring into it. The creature placed its powerful forepaws on the chair-back, and waved its graceful tail from side to side. Another of the beasts reared on its hind legs high above the trainer's head, resting its paws against the iron bars; and its roar resounded through the crowded street.

The trainer motioned the sitting lion from the chair, shot a revolver twice into the air, left the cage, and lo! The wondering spectators were gazing into blank darkness.

"Another dream over," said Jack into the ear so close to him.

The tightly hemmed-in mass of humanity slowly dissolved into its integral parts.

"They ought to have a packed house after that," remarked Mildred.

"Shall we swell the number?"

"Not unless you wish it," replied Mildred.

"I don't. I wish something else very much. Will you answer as meekly and civilly when I ask it?"

They had begun again their walk eastward.

"I don't know," came Mildred's honest reply.

"Oh, that is not encouraging."

"It is wise, though. I was brought up never to be afraid to confess that I didn't know a thing," explained Mildred.

"I want you to go with me in a gondola," said Jack. "Compare my humility with Robert Page's *sang-froid.*"

"A gondola will be even more difficult to catch by this time than a horse-car," suggested the girl.

Jack looked at her, but her piquant smiling face taught him renewed patience.

"Then you will not run much risk in promising," he answered. "Shall we leave it to Fate to decide? If we find a gondola easily, will you go?"

"Yes, indeed."

As they left the Plaisance and came around the Woman's Building, a sun-burst of fire in the east illuminated the sky.

"A salute to royalty," said Jack. "Queen Mildred has arrived."

The white light faded, to be followed by dazzling green, ruby, and gold, as one bomb followed another, to burst above the lake and cast abroad in the heavens fountains of jewels that rained down in glittering showers.

"Now, let us see if Fate is good-natured," said Van Tassel, leading his companion toward the nearest gondola-landing. A graceful willow hung above and obscured it.

"I must laugh at you, Jack," said the girl, suiting the action to the word. "The idea of expecting to find a gondola now, way over here."

"Stranger things have happened. Suppose," suddenly standing still and looking down into her eyes,—"suppose you should say that you wish it. Just for luck, you know."

"I never wish for impossibilities."

"Do you expect me to believe that?"

"Well, I try not to."

"But wish for this. You know it is possible to have strawberries in January."

"What a great boy you are still, Jack. Very well, I wish that two gondoliers may have been attacked by an unusual access of laziness this evening, have denied their craft to all applicants, and skulked over here away from the crowd, and that they may be waiting for us now in the shadow of the willow. Any more midsummer madness you would like me to indulge in?"

Van tassel led her down the bank. "Behold!" he said. "Mildred, what a witch you are! This is necromancy."

The girl stood with lips parted, for the waiting gondoliers sent their graceful craft to her feet. She put her hand in Jack's and stepped within. In a moment Van Tassel was beside her, and they had glided away.

The lagoon rippled in a light breeze. Along the edge of Wooded Island the sedges dipped in the waves. Here and there on the bank a group of water-birds showed white, as a neighboring electric light touched the soft plumage beneath which their heads nestled.

Jack wanted his companion to speak first, but she kept silence long.

"Is the sorceress enjoying herself?" he asked gently, at last.

Mildred returned his gaze as she leaned back in her cushioned corner.

"I am a philosopher," she answered. "I am being kidnapped, but I might as well enjoy it."

"Well, that is pretty good. I should say"—

"I don't want to hear anything you have to say. I am convinced that you are the most designing creature alive. Ask your minions to sing, please."

Jack longed that he might know the thoughts that flitted white-winged through his companion's mind as their boat glided on, to the gondoliers' song.

This ceased as they entered the Court of Honor, grown dusk now in preparation for the second playing of the electric fountains. Half the weary sightseers had gone home; no crowd lined the railings around the Grand Basin.

The rainbow jets sprang triumphant skyward. An invisible orchestra lent their colors richer meaning and beauty.

"Do you remember the song that Clover sang last night?" asked Jack, leaning a little toward his companion. "It suddenly came to my mind then as the water shot up. Those lines,—

> I share the skylark's transport fine,
> I know the fountain's wayward yearning,
> I love—and the world is mine!

Clover says that is a man's song. I don't agree with her. A woman may be angel enough to feel divine fullness of content simply in loving; but a man who loves must be loved again, or else feel that nothing is his,—nothing; there is no beggar so poor as he. Isn't it so?"

The earnest tone thrilled close to Mildred's cheek. She caught her breath quickly. "I—I don't know," she said, nervously surprised.

"Still true to your bringing up," remarked her companion, controlling himself with a strong will as he felt her shrink, and leaning back with a short laugh. "Not afraid to say you don't know, when such is the case. Well, I can only speak for myself. When I love and am loved I will agree with the poet,—I would even sing with her if I could:

> For soft the hours repeat one story,
> Sings the sea one strain divine,
> My clouds arise, all flushed with glory,
> I love—and the world is mine!"

Mildred was startled. What a lover Jack would make! He was not Clover's. She was sure of it now, but the thought brought no elation, rather a new, timid humility, which made her seem strange to herself.

She felt her companion's dark eyes upon her, and her usually ready tongue was mute.

Van Tassel did not know whether to gather courage or alarm from her silence as they sat there side by side. The gondoliers slowly propelled the boat, keeping in view of the fountains' tossing banners of liquid light.

"Tell me what you are thinking, Mildred," he urged, at last.

"I am not thinking. Do you ever come to such times? I do always in this spot. Perhaps it is because I have no thoughts to match such unearthly beauty. At all events I never think, here. I feel. I absorb."

"Yes, that is it," answered Jack simply.

"Give me the Peristyle," said Mildred, "and what I can see from it, and sweep all the rest of the Fair away if you like. I don't love many things in this world beside Mildred Bryant, but the Peristyle is one of them."

It was a novel speech from her, and in a novel tone. The low cadence of her voice had lost the laughter or imperiousness which usually characterized it.

Jack was silent for a time. "Are you warm enough?" he asked at last.

"Yes; but I think we had better go home."

"Aren't you comfortable?"

"Oh, certainly, and it was very kind of you, Jack to take so much trouble."

This gentleness alarmed Van Tassel more than any amount of coldness or impertinence would have done; but he fought off dejection.

"I have given you one thing, then, that you can't hand on to Clover," he said lightly.

The fountains leaped a last time and fell, dropping lower and lower, till only the white sea foaming about Columbia's barge was left. Soft radiance again lit up water and sculpture.

Mildred longed to be at home; and soon she and Jack entered a wagonette at the park gate and were driven to the house. When they arrived, the orchestra at the hotel was playing the music of Carmen.

"There is a delicate compliment to you, Jack," she suggested, as they ascended the steps.

"Yes; but must you go right in?" for she showed symptoms of leaving him.

"It has been a long day," she answered, lingering with an unusual gentle compliance from which he gathered no hope.

"You are tired," he said, with tender contrition. "I have had you so long, and yet—when should I be ready to let you go! Oh, Mildred,—is it any use?" he burst forth suddenly, in a low tone, seizing both her hands and holding them with painful tightness.

A fluttering and wild, loud peeping came from the tangle of vines near which they stood, and a small dark object half fell, half flew down past their heads to the grass below.

Mildred started. "It is Electra,—a falling star." She laughed nervously. "I am glad she fell, else I might be crying now instead of laughing. It would be such a serious unhappiness to me if I should cause you pain, Jack," she added brokenly. "You are so different from anybody else."

"I am answered," he said briefly and steadily; but he did not loosen her hands. "I am going to ask a great deal of you now, Mildred. Can you forget what I have said?"

"I—I am afraid not."

"Please try to; I will help you."

"Help me?" repeated the girl, bewildered.

"Yes, for everything between us shall be the same as before. Tomorrow morning you will say to yourself that you had a dream. That is all."

"Very well." The girl regarded him questioningly. "I hope you are not—are not thinking that I might—might speak of it?"

Jack threw his head back and gave an excited laugh before suddenly growing grave and gazing ardently into her eyes.

"Speak of it? What would it be to me, my darling, if everyone knew," he said with swift ardor. "I love—but the world is not mine. That is the whole story, and the only peace for you is to forget it."

Her head drooped under his look.

"I am dreadfully tired, Jack," she said faintly.

"Yes, dear, go, and forgive me." He kissed her hands passionately and released them. She passed into the house, her head and heart pulsing. Bewilderment was her chief sensation. The finality with which Jack seemed to accept defeat was so at variance with his manner.

She stole upstairs silently to her room, closed the door, and turned up the light. Then she went to her mirror and questioned her wan pale face with wistful eyes.

"I haven't expected it. I didn't know it was coming this time," she said, answering some thought. "Is Jack really so unselfish as that? Can he care for me enough to—and then cover his disappointment with gayety to save me pain?"

His loving words rang in her ears, her hands still felt the wild pressure of his, and the warmth of his kisses. No one had ever received failure so before. No man had ever dared to call her "darling." A look that was almost fear came into the eyes that gazed back from the mirror. How had Jack contrived to make himself seem victor instead of vanquished?

He had not even pressed his suit; he had not begged her to try to love him. How nobly he had spared her,—but how audaciously he had treated her!

The color was flowing back to her cheeks. Mildred could no longer study that face in the glass. She turned away, weary, perplexed, troubled by the restless beating of her heart.

"I will get to sleep as quickly as possible. He told me to believe it a dream. I must try to take it all as Clover would."

The thought of her sister was like calling up the image of a saint. She had not been the object of Jack's adoration, after all. How strange, strange! How much better it would have been for him. Not that Clover would have married him, but it would have been good for him merely to love her. Fevers, perplexities, could not come where Clover was; and with this thought came a great longing to breathe Clover's cool, wholesome atmosphere. Mildred slipped into a wrapper, and without pausing to think further, crossed to her sister's door. There was but a dim light within.

She spoke her sister's name very softly, not to wake her if possibly she might be asleep; but Clover herself in an instant opened the door.

"I thought I heard you come in, Milly."

"Why, what are you doing here, all dressed, in the dark?" asked the younger, entering.

"Thinking." Clover laughed. "It sounds amusing, doesn't it; but the music was pleasant and my window especially enticing. I felt rather tired when I reached home a little while before you, and meant to be asleep by this time, but here I am, you see."

"Let me come and think too," said Mildred; "Or rather, let me come where I can't think."

The two sisters sat down in the large bay window overlooking the lake.

"Haven't you had a pleasant day?" asked Clover.

"I've had all sorts of a day. How has yours been?"

"Delightful."

"You are my despair, Clover. Things are always delightful to you."

Clover heard the depression in her sister's voice, and wondered; her thoughts flew to Jack too, and she questioned what mood the day might have left him in. "Oh no," she answered, "but those nut-brown maids in the Javanese theatre would put any one into good humor. When they dance, you can no more help laughing than if you were being tickled with a feather. Such dear, cunning, absurd motions as they make, their little bits of mouths looking so serious all the time."

"You take such an interest in everything," said Mildred wistfully. "It is because you have 'a heart at leisure from itself.' I have never longed for that sort of a heart as I have today. For quite a while it has been slowly dawning upon me that I am more self-centered than most people; but today Gorham Page gave me the final blow."

"Mr. Page? Why, you astonish me. He has a high opinion of you. He was saying today how much deeper and more earnest you were"—

"For mercy's sake," exclaimed Mildred, flushing to her ears, "don't tell me what he said!"

"Why? Are you too conscientious to accept a compliment when you haven't a 'trade'?"

"I have plenty of 'trades.' Jack never talks about you without using superlatives."

"Dear Jack. He is far too appreciative," returned Clover, wishing it were light enough to see how her sister accepted this; "but you haven't told me how Mr. Page hurt you."

"No, it was the truth that hurt me."

"Mr. Page is a very good representative of that," smiled Clover.

"We were coming out of Old Vienna, and you and Jack fell behind to speak to one another, and I addressed Mr. Page. He looked at me vaguely, and answered at random. Well, it was the way that trifle affected me that made me see Mildred Bryant as I had never seen her before. I was deeply offended, yes, angry, that the important favor of a remark from my lips should be disregarded. Oh, Clover, the disgrace of it!"

The speaker's voice was unsteady, and she suddenly covered her face with her hands.

Clover leaned forward and put a hand on her knee.

"Isn't it beautiful," she said earnestly, "to find yourself shrinking from sin? It is so safe to condemn it in ourselves. Hatred of evil is only treacherous when we feel it for the mistakes of others."

"The worst of it was that I knew I should have felt less injured had it not been that another woman was what was preoccupying his attention. He was thinking of you, and I resented it. I couldn't live if I didn't tell you. It proved to me that I was growing into a regular—oh, a regular octopus. Everything must be absorbed to feed my vanity, and especially every man."

"Why, Mildred, I am so glad for you," said Clover simply, her cool tones falling on the other's scornful heat and extinguishing its fire. "We have to come to these places, you know, for we mustn't be left in our badness, and a little light is let in at a time as we can bear it."

"But I can't bear it," exclaimed Mildred wildly, "for it is second nature to me to be vain and exacting."

"You won't indulge it now."

"Yes, I shall."

"Not so carelessly as before. All this is what comes into the battle of life. One part of our dual nature loves our evils and the other hates them. You can have God's help if you ask it, you know, and you will find how little and how deceptive the progress will be that you make without Him."

"Your battle seems won, Clover."

"I am in one of the peaceful places now, and I am very happy and grateful. I wasn't given your tempestuous nature, dear, so our experiences always are and will be different. The Father in mercy let us develop as irresponsibly as the plants until we get such a glimpse into our souls as you had today; but then responsibility begins. It is sinning against light that warps and distorts us."

"I wonder if it would be good for me to be married," said Mildred musingly. "When girls are married, they haven't much time to think about themselves."

"It is good for every girl to marry when she truly loves a man who is unexceptionable," returned Clover, smiling at her own triteness. "But you remember the girl must ask herself, not Can I live with this man? but Can I live without him?"

"Then I should certainly never marry. You didn't do that, Clover."

Clover looked musingly out the window. "No; I didn't do that. I often think of that little ignorant girl who married dear Mr. Van Tassel. I don't know whether I did right or not; but at the time I thought I did, and that is all I have any concern with; but I was not in freedom. You are in freedom. The Can I live without him? ought to mean Can we be more useful together than we could apart?"

"Why, you don't leave a girl any comfort in thinking

about herself at all," complained Mildred, half in tears.

"There isn't much comfort in it, that is a fact," returned Clover, smiling. "You are tired, dear; go to bed now."

They rose, and Mildred took the smaller woman in her arms and their cheeks clung together. "I am unhappy, Clover," she said, with plaintive surprise at the fact.

"It is so restful," replied the other, "to think you have all eternity before you. Even if we only make a beginning here, it will be all right."

"Your words bring me comfort," said Mildred.

CHAPTER 13

THE HOTEL DANCE

It was Gorham Page's habit to drop in at the Van Tassel house before making his nearly daily visit to the Fair.

One morning, as he ascended the steps, his sister met him. "I hoped you would come," she said. "I want to be consoled with. Robert's foot has descended. We are going home."

"Oh, I am sorry," replied Gorham, taking the chair she offered him; "but can't some arrangement be made?"

"No. Robert has said 'positively;' and when he says 'positively,' I never waste any more nervous force. Poor, dear boy, he wants to stay as badly as I do, but we have been here longer than we expected already, and after all, I would rather go back than to give up the apartment and go to the poorhouse, which he says is the alternative."

"I must go to Boston before long," said Page. "Wouldn't you like to stay and go back with me?"

"Let Robert go home alone?"

"Yes."

"No, I thank you," with a firm shake of the head. "I shouldn't care for the Fair without Robert."

"That is nice," remarked Gorham, regarding her attentively. "I think I should like my wife to feel like that."

Hilda laughed. "Oh, that vague and shadowy wife of yours! Once I believed in her. Too bad that such a good-natured match-maker as I would have been, should be burdened with such an impossible brother as you. I have lost all my interest in you, and have transferred it to Jack."

Gorham smiled pensively, and struck the palm of one of his hands with the knuckles of the other. "You think yourself very clever about Jack, don't you?"

"It goes without saying that I am clever, of course, but this occasion does not demand much insight. If they were a trifle more secret in their chats in corners and their exchange of Masonic signals, I should think, perhaps, I was a treacherous guest to mention them; but they enjoy their little comedy, and are perfectly willing others should. I think it is unkind in them not to come out openly and allow me to give them my blessing before I go."

"I must say, Hilda, I don't enjoy hearing you use that tone about Mrs. Van Tassel."

"What is the matter with my tone?" asked Hilda.

"It is light," answered Page, with grave simplicity.

His sister stared a moment, then burst into laughter. "What crotchet have you taken now?" she asked. "Doesn't the match please you?"

"It is not a match. You are laboring under a false idea. If Mrs. Van Tassel should ever distinguish a man in the way you are speaking of, it will come to our knowledge in a different manner from the one you describe. We are talking in low tones in a corner now; but we are not sentimentally interested in one another."

"An unanswerable argument," said Hilda good-naturedly. "You needn't take the matter *au grand sérieux.* I am profoundly grateful to Mrs. Van Tassel, and think her one of the most charming women I ever knew."

Page's countenance, which had been grave to sternness, relaxed until slowly smiling, he looked into his companion's eyes and beamed mutely upon her.

Hilda noted the change with private astonishment, and determined to experiment.

"She is so refined," she added after a pause.

"The perfection of refinement," said Page.

"And very graceful."

Gorham nodded. "It is a pleasure to see her move, is it not?"

"She has plenty of spirit too, and wit."

"Yes, indeed. In whatever company she is, she makes her mark."

"And it is never a black and blue one either," responded Hilda, passing her handkerchief over her lips as she returned the rapt gaze of the earnest face drinking in her words. "There is so much in that. Her wit could never hurt. Her uniform, considerate kindness is her most prominent trait."

"Yes," responded Page, faithfully antiphonal. "Only a pure, true heart like hers could prompt such behavior."

"There is a subtle charm and stimulus in her society."

"And a restfulness, a satisfaction. It is hard to word it, but you have felt it; you recognize it. One can only say, it is good to be in her presence."

Hilda pushed back her chair so suddenly that her companion started. "Gorham Page," she said, gazing at him with sparkling eyes, and rising, "don't you see what has happened?"

"No," he answered, removing his fixed gaze and pushing aside the vines, the better to peer about.

"Not out there!" exclaimed his sister.

"Oh," he answered mildly. "I thought perhaps Blitzen had killed Electra."

Mrs. Page burst into laughter. Peal after peal broke from her, and she clasped her hand to her side.

Robert appeared on the scene.

"It is time you arrived," said Gorham, vaguely smiling. "I haven't the least idea what ails Hilda."

Mrs. Page dropped her head on her husband's shoulder.

"Gorham thought—thought—that perhaps Blitzen—had killed Electra," she gasped.

"How intensely amusing," remarked Robert. "This girl is tired to death, Gorham," he went on, patting his wife's convulsed shoulder. "She thinks she doesn't want to go home, but I know it is time. Mrs. Van Tassel urges our remaining. What a spirit of sunshine she is! If ever there was an angel in a house, she is one."

Hilda lifted her head, to look at Gorham's face. She found it beaming upon his brother with tender delight, and falling back she relapsed into another spasm of laughter.

"Stop this, stop this," said her husband, giving her a little shake.

"I am really afraid Hilda isn't well," said Gorham with concern. "I am sorry if she is too tired, for I wanted to see if you all wouldn't like to come over to the dance at the hotel tonight."

"That is sensible, profoundly sensible," remarked his brother. "What could finish off a day at the Fair more appropriately than a dancing party!"

"You've got to go, Robert," said Hilda, wiping her eyes.

"It will be lovely. We will smoke on the piazza, and watch the others through the windows."

"Yes, I know how you enjoy looking on at a dancing party."

"Yes, thank you, Gorham, we will come," continued Mrs. Page relentlessly. "I shall just go down to the Court of Honor for one last look," she added sighing. "I will go up in that little balcony at the corner of the Electrical Building, and gaze once more down the stately, spacious square. I shall see the peacock-blue lake through the columns of the Peristyle, look up into the Italian sky roofing all, and say my prayers or sing the doxology; then I shall come home and pack. Oh, Robert, how can we leave it all!"

That evening Jack entered the parlor and found Clover leaning back in an armchair. He dropped into a seat beside her.

"You look fitter to adorn some marble shrine in the White City than to decorate a humdrum, mortal home," he remarked, regarding her thin gown approvingly.

"I believe I never saw you before in a dress-suit," she answered lazily. "You look very neat, my dear. That is what mother used to say to us to suppress our vanity, when we were in festive array. It is rather amusing to see Fair pilgrims in evening dress, isn't it?"

"Where is Mildred?" asked Van Tassel, looking about.

"She will be here directly. If my sister were entirely costumed at any appointed time, I should be anxious about her."

"I haven't had a chance to confess before," went on Jack, low and hastily. "I spoke to her too soon, after all. I need a keeper."

"Oh, Jack! I'm sorry."

Clover looked dismayed, and her tone was heart-felt.

"The milk is spilled, though; there is no going back. Didn't she tell you?"

"No, indeed. When did it happen?"

"The night we took the gondola ride."

"Days since, then. You are a wonder, Jack. Are you going to stay here and live it down?"

"I am going to stay here if you will let me."

"Let you? It is your home. Oh Jack, I am afraid of your tone. You haven't given up. I must tell you, though, that Mildred would be honest, uncompromisingly honest, in a serious matter like that. She is not a coquette."

"I know it."

"If she doesn't love you, you do not want her."

"I don't know whether she loves me or not, and I don't believe she knows any better."

As his handsome, frank eyes looked up at her, Clover's heart swelled with the approval and admiration she felt.

"We must relax to it," she said involuntarily.

"Or brace up to it," he replied, with his brilliant smile; "but it is too late now for the Petruchio act, Clover. I have literally and figuratively given myself away."

"Yes," said the other simply; "what you have to do now is to leave her in freedom. The Lord loves you both alike. If he does not give you Mildred, it will be because that marriage would stand in the way of your real advancement."

"Do you really believe that?" Van Tassel regarded her in curiosity and surprise.

"Why, Jack, think it out some time. How can it be any other way?" she answered, speaking hastily, for she heard a rustle on the stairs; and a moment after her voice ceased,

Mildred came into the room.

She was dressed in a pale violet gown, which revealed her superb neck, and she pulled long gloves up over her bare arms as she came.

Jack sprang to his feet. How could she help liking the homage in his eyes?

"I know I haven't kept you waiting," she said brightly, "for Mrs. Page's light is till burning, and of course it will take her some little time to wake up Mr. Page."

Hilda's feet, in their little black satin slippers, came flying down the stairs as she spoke.

"Is Robert in a hammock?" she exclaimed apprehensively. "I meant to stick them both full of pins, but I haven't had time. That poor dear man has done a lot today, in spite of all my warnings. I expect he will sleep from here to Boston when we get started. You two girls look perfectly lovely. I shall wake him up with that information."

As they were all finally setting out, Gorham Page came up the walk.

"I thought I would wander down and make sure of you," he said to Clover, as he turned back beside her.

"You were sure of us," she returned. "I have not danced for five years. It seems to me I should never have thought of it again but for your invitation."

"You do not care for the amusement, then?"

"Clover Bryant used to care greatly," she said, smiling; "but perhaps Mrs. Van Tassel has forgotten how to dance."

They found the long, spacious piazza of the hotel gay with promenaders.

Robert Page groaned. "How marvelous is the endurance of man and woman kind," he remarked. "How many of these people do you suppose have been doing the Fair today?"

"You mustn't talk about the Fair," returned his wife. "It is fortunate for you that the diversion came up, else I should have spent this evening weeping because I have said good-by."

"Have you come over here with the notion that I am going to dance?" asked Robert mildly.

"No, I haven't the least idea you will. I wouldn't ask it, since you were foolish enough to tramp miles today."

"How could I help that, my dear, with the awful 'last chance' sensation hanging over me?"

The orchestra in the hotel parlor began to play. Jack Van Tassel came up to where the husband and wife were sitting.

"Are you going to dance, Hilda?"

"Apparently not," she answered gayly.

"Give me this, won't you?"

"Oh, you don't need to. Why, where are Mildred and Clover?"

"They are sitting over yonder. They have many friends here. It seems to me this is rather a peculiar way for you to treat my invitation."

"No, Jack," said Robert, with a heart-rending sigh. "The old man will have to dance once. 'Let it be soon,' as the song says. Come, my love, weary and footsore, let us tread the dreamy maze together."

"Robert really wants to dance," said Hilda to Van Tassel confidentially. "The music inspires him. I haven't the heart to refuse. Thank you. Perhaps later we can have a turn."

"Now, wasn't that sweet of Jack and exactly like him?" asked Hilda, when they had drifted in among the floating couples. "He was afraid you were going to be immovable; and the very first dance, when of course you would suppose he would ask Mildred"—

"Or Mrs. Van Tassel, according to your theories."

"My dear, I am shaken on my theories. I may have been wrong. I hope I have been. What do *you* think, Robert?"

"I can't tell any of my thoughts while I am dancing, Hilda. Don't ask it. If you do, I shall probably step on your foot. I have the greatest sympathy with the man who, when his partner insisted on talking to him in a round dance, replied as follow: Yes, two, three; one, no, three; one, two yes; and so forth."

"What a goose you are, dear; but you dance as well as you ever did, if you have forgotten how to say sweet nothings during a waltz."

"Pray remember how much more breath I used to have. The spirit is willing still, but the flesh is too many for me."

"There go Gorham and Clover," said Mrs. Page with some excitement, pausing in the dance, and taking her husband's willing arm. "Robert, I want you to watch Gorham tonight," she added impressively.

"More mysteries?" returned Page plaintively. "I don't see anything out of the way about him. He is rather stunning in a dress-suit."

"I wonder if Clover thinks so," responded Hilda significantly.

"Oh, you are only marrying him again," remarked her husband, with an air of enlightenment. "If all your plans succeeded, I don't know what would become of Gorham. He couldn't even take refuge in Utah, for I understand the Mormons are discouraging plural marriages."

"You can chaff, Robert; but mark my words, some day you will look back to this evening and exclaim over my cleverness. I haven't told you all I know. I have proofs, if I chose to"—

"Yes, my dear, your fate is the common one of those who cry 'Wolf' too often. I've heard your proofs before." Then squeezing his wife's hand against his side, he added, "There isn't another Hilda for poor Gorham, so how can I take a breathless interest in his prospects?"

Mrs. Page was mollified, of course; but she shrugged her shoulder. "I don't understand how you can see those four people together and not weave romances. Now, for instance, I am burning to know why Mildred and Jack are not dancing this first dance together, instead of with Lieutenant Eames and his cousin. I dare say poor Jack lost his chance by coming to take care of me."

But Hilda was wrong. A little circle of friends had gathered about Clover and Mildred as soon as they appeared on the hotel piazza, and Mildred saw at once in Jack's quiet withdrawal that he did not intend to ask any favor for himself. She liked this in theory, but it half-vexed her to find herself alertly cognizant of his every movement even while she chatted and laughed with her other friends. She saw him approach Hilda, and wondered if he were asking her to dance; then, when the latter moved away into the hotel with her husband, Mildred talked volubly to Eames in order to prevent his having an opportunity to offer himself for her partner. These dances were informal. There were no printed programmes. She wished to give Jack time to return to their group and claim her before the lieutenant should.

How exasperatingly deliberate his motions seemed to

her, as he sauntered along!

"I can easily believe what you say, Mr. Eames," she said glibly. "The papers print a great many of the amusing blunders that are made, and I am sure they are not exaggerated, by my own experience. There were two women standing near me in front of the Manufactures Building the other day, and one said to the other: 'Oh, look at that big statue of Liberty; do you suppose it's solid gold?' 'No!' replied the other scornfully, 'it's holler. If that was solid gold it would be worth ten thousand dollars.' Then this sophisticated one turned to me. 'Can you tell me where the Court of Honor is? Is it in the Administration Building?' I answered that this was the Court of Honor, and I suppose I gestured generally, for she looked down at the Basin and then at me with a pitying smile. 'Oh no,' she said, 'that is the lagoon.'"

Why *would* Jack stop to look in at the window? How slow he was! "Oh yes, and, Mr. Eames, was there any truth in that story I read about the battleship? Somebody says, you know, that although it looks so solid and impressive, an angry man could do it considerable damage with a crowbar, and I read lately about some country people who were visiting it. While they were exploring, the ship's bells rang, and coincidentally the whistle of a neighboring tug began to blow. The story said those poor people thought the boat was going to start and they rushed for the gangplank, panic-stricken. One man fell into the water, and a woman broke her ankle. It ought not to be amusing, but it is."

"Ha, ha," responded Eames, "there is a grain of truth in it." Jack was drawing near. "The rest is the reporter's imagination. I can tell you what was the foundation of that yarn." Jack approached and stood near the speaker. "Won't you dance this with me, Miss Bryant, and I will initiate you into some of the methods of newspaper men as discovered by the officer-of-the-day at Jackson Park."

They moved away, and Helen Eames, who had audaciously escaped a would-be partner in the hope of this very event, fell to Jack's lot.

She was a vivacious, jolly girl, and a man was not obliged to talk much while with her, so Van Tassel yielded to her determination to detain him at her side as long as was feasible.

Mildred, promenading with her partner on the piazza after the dance, passed them sitting near the water where one could see, down the curve of the lake, the fireworks of the White City bursting in starry brilliance. Far out upon Michigan's breast shone a row of steady lights, beside which, as on a liquid boulevard, the illuminated passenger-boats plied up and down.

Van Tassel was playing with his companion's fan, and laughing as though he were well entertained, at the moment Mildred passed by.

The sight did not please her.

It is all my vanity, she thought. *I am glad Jack isn't one of the sort of men who stand around in corners and watch one tragically.*

She had danced several times when Clover, left near her by Gorham Page while he went to bring her a glass of water, addressed her.

"Milly, you haven't danced with Jack once," she said, with hasty reproach.

"Haven't I?" Mildred raised her eyebrows.

"But aren't you going to, dear?"

"Not unless he asks me, darling."

Clover stared, then turned away to smile. She had not often seen Mildred in such an ill-humor.

"Poor, dear, unconscious Petruchio," she reflected. "I wonder if he is building better than he knows."

Here Page returned with the water, and she could say no more, even if she wished. Moreover, Gorham now addressed Mildred, to claim the dance for which the strains of the Washington Post March were already sounding assertively.

Jack had this two-step with Hilda, and when it was over he brought her to a seat near those which Mildred and Gorham had taken on the piazza.

"Mildred," remarked Hilda, "this young man does know how to dance."

Van Tassel bowed until the parting in his hair was visible.

"That is nice," returned Miss Bryant languidly.

"The fireworks are over," continued Hilda. "That awful word 'nevermore' is hanging over everything for me to-night. I meant to be out here to see the last piece, but I wasn't,—that superb volcano, or whatever name they try to describe it by. I want you all to think of me with compassion every time you see it hereafter. Where do you suppose Robert is?"

"Perhaps I ought to know," suggested Gorham. "I will hunt him up if you will allow me, Miss Mildred."

"I'll go with you," said Mrs. Page. "It is rather cool here to sit still after dancing. You will excuse me, Jack? I think I ought to let poor Robert off now, and take him home."

It was the first time Mildred and Jack had been alone

together since the memorable evening.

"May I have the next dance?" asked Van Tassel abruptly.

"If you like," answered the girl carelessly. "Haven't you had enough dancing?"

"I haven't had any," he answered briefly; and Mildred told herself that the demon of her vanity had received what it craved, so warm a sensation of satisfaction stole around her heart.

"I thought I would make myself safe before one of your other friends espied you here; but if you are tired"—

"I am never tired—physically," said the girl, with a slow smile.

"I was only going to say that I would be content to sit out the next with you; although we have not danced together since that night in the boathouse." Jack smiled. "Do you remember what you told me?"

"Oh yes. You made that child very happy. She owes you a dance."

"These surroundings are strange. Have you been thinking of it?"

"Yes. Only last year this ground was a tangle of goldenrod and willow-trees. How many times we have gone bathing on that beach! It was as good a playground for jolly youngsters as could be imagined; and now"—

She paused.

"Now, the music has commenced," suggested Jack, rising. "In consideration of the manner in which I have effaced myself so far, you should allow our dance to begin promptly."

They entered the parlor by the door which leads from the east piazza. She put her hand in his, and they glided away over the polished floor among the pillars with their vine-like wreaths of electric lights.

Amid the scattering groups which, outside, watched the dancers through the windows, was one spectator who was seeing a conventional dancing party for the first time in her life. It had suddenly occurred to Robert Page that it would be worth the exertion of going after Aunt Love to see her view this pretty scene; and when Hilda and Gorham reached the front entrance of the hotel in their search for Robert, they found him ascending the steps with Miss Berry.

"The young ladies did ask me if I didn't want to come over, and I thought I should feel out o' place," she said; "but Mr. Page, he just made me, so here I am."

"Now, come to this window," said Robert, "and tell me what you think of that."

The others clustered around Miss Lovina, as she murmured and exclaimed in her surprise. "I never approved o' dancin'," she said. "I never saw any before. Mr. Gorham, do you remember that hall in the New York Buildin'? That must be temptin' to young critters when it's lighted up, and the music's a-playin'. Why," eagerly, "see Miss Mildred and Mr. Jack. My, don't they go pretty! And there's Mrs. Van Tassel herself and some feller. Why," turning suddenly upon Gorham, "why ain't you in there dancin' with her?"

"I have danced with her twice," he answered. "I mustn't be a monopolist, although it is a temptation. She is by far the best dancer here."

Upon this Hilda pressed her small satin shoe against her husband's foot, and he obtusely moved it out of her way.

"Well, I declare," exclaimed Miss Berry, gazing in ever-warming admiration, "if it ain't enough to make a body want to be young and pretty. To think this is the real, wicked thing itself, and I ain't shocked. What's the matter with me, Mr. Gorham?"

"Considering you prejudices and traditions, it is a little odd. Perhaps it is because you cannot associate an idea of evil with anything you see Mrs. Van Tassel engaging in."

Here Mrs. Page again endeavored to gain her husband's sympathy, with the result that he exclaimed, "Where *would* you like to have me put my feet, Hilda?"

"Why don't you go in there and dance, Mr. Gorham?" pursued Miss Berry.

"Am I so young and pretty that you want to see me? Well, if Hilda is willing to favor me."

"Oh certainly, so long as Robert doesn't care to go home. *Au revoir*, dears."

"Now, then," Aunt Love turned upon her companion argumentatively, "are you perfectly willin' a man should put his arm around your wife's waist?"

"On the contrary, I should object seriously."

"How about that, then?" Miss Berry gestured toward the hall.

"For a man to place his hand on a woman's waist to steady and support her is not to put his arm around her. There are too many other things for a couple to think of in guiding themselves successfully through a crowd of dancers to allow of their usually being conscious of the intimacy of their position. Don't be afraid to admire the dancing, Aunt Love. It can be abused, like everything else; but it is an excellent exercise, inculcating grace, strength, and good manners."

"Well, now, I'm goin' to tell some folks I know what you say. Ain't your wife just as light as a fairy, and don't your brother look handsome tonight? No, sir, there ain't any folks here as good-lookin' as ours."

When the waltz was finished, Gorham Page and Hilda approached Clover and told her that Aunt Love had arrived. She excused herself from her partner to go with them, and soon afterward Gorham walked home with her.

"Thank you so much for coming," he said, when he was bidding her good-night.

"I am sure we have all to thank you," she answered. "Isn't it hard to be reconciled to letting your brother and Hilda go? We have been such a pleasant party."

"Yes," returned Page, looking down at her as she stood in her white wrap, an unconsciously adoring expression in his eyes; "this summer is an experience that one could wish would never end. Going away," he smiled vaguely, "leaving you, having these weeks come to an end, is almost as difficult to grasp in prospect as the thought of death."

Clover laughed softly. "We won't borrow trouble," she said. "Good-night."

CHAPTER 14

DRESS PARADE

"Do you think Jack enjoyed himself?" asked Clover, when her sister crossed the hall to her room that night for the usual last word before retiring.

"I suppose he did. How anxious you are about Jack all the time! You make an absolute fetish of him. It used to mislead me."

"Did it?" Clover smiled, and turned back to her dressing table.

"Yes, indeed, and no wonder. It is a good thing, however, that I was mistaken, else I'm sure there would have been coffee and pistols ordered for two. I want your opinion, Clover, on a delicate question. Supposing a man of some strength of character spends a whole evening at a dance following about after a woman, smiling pensively at her face, or the back of her head, or her shoulder, or whatever of her he can get to smile at, and finding spots of vantage from which he can behold her dance when he is not dancing with her himself. Supposing he flies about to bring her glasses of water, and wraps, and fans, and performs all the other offices which are usually the privilege of her partners, driving said partners to the last pitch of exasperation. What, I ask you, is the matter with that man?"

Clover turned her tender glance upon her sister, marveling that the spirit of mischief could be so rampant in her eyes.

"Dear," she said reproachfully, "that man is very deeply in love."

"That is what I supposed myself," replied Mildred demurely; "but I wanted to be sure I didn't exaggerate."

"Too seriously so for you to make merry over it," continued Clover, shaking her head.

"Well, if you aren't a pair of you!" exclaimed Mildred, bursting into laughter, which she endeavored to repress out of consideration of the lateness of the hour. Then she seized her sister's astonished face between her hands and kissed her on the forehead. "I suppose there isn't another man in the world beside Jack Van Tassel, is there?" she asked facetiously. "How glad I am, I am not setting my cap for Gorham; I should be wildly jealous."

"Oh—Mildred. I didn't know that any one noticed"—Clover was as red as her namesake, and looking everywhere except at her sister.

"Noticed! Why, my dear, Gorham was a perfect spectacle. I fancy everybody in the room noticed except himself. He doesn't know what is the matter with him, either. He asked me once, when we were out on the piazza, if there wasn't some malaria here. He isn't able to sleep of late, and his appetite isn't right." Mildred went off into a peal of laughter.

"Hush. Do please hush, Milly," implored Clover, crimson in her agony. "Supposing Hilda should hear you and come in. She will. Oh, *please*."

"He said he thought he should take—oh dear, I'm hurting myself—he thought he should take quinine!" Mildred wiped her eyes; "and I said—I was of the opinion—oh my! that something sweet would help him more; extract of Clover, perhaps."

"Mildred, tell me instantly you didn't say that!"

"Well, not quite so much as that; but he tempted me dreadfully."

"Go to bed, Milly. Go to bed straight off. It is late."

"All right; but isn't it funny?" pleadingly.

"No. I do not think it funny at all."

"Oh, you must; that big, absent man, vainly mooning round among his data"—

"Well, if you will only go away; perhaps—it's a little— There, I have turned the gas out. You will have to go."

"I am about to set up a Gorham to match your Jack," said Mildred irrepressibly. "I am going to see that you treat the poor man right, and help him diagnose his symptoms. I am going to give you reproachful glances and him tender ones. I shall have to tell him they're tender, though"—But here Clover succeeded in pushing her over the threshold and closing the door upon her.

The following day Mr. and Mrs. Page took their departure, the latter more reluctant than ever to leave so many objects of interest.

"Ain't it lonely without 'em?" said Aunt Love that night to Clover, after dinner. "I don't know but you'll want to ask Mr. Gorham over here to help fill up the gap," she suggested rather timidly.

"No, I think we won't disturb his arrangements," replied Clover quietly. "I suppose he can't stay here very much longer any way."

Miss Berry went to the back door to give Blitzen and Electra their supper, and arbitrate between them while they ate it.

"She won't ask him over. H'm!" she soliloquized, arranging two dishes of scraps, while the two pets barked and chirped expectantly. Then she seated herself on a step to watch their proceedings.

"That looks like it," she continued in her own thoughts. "Well, if this is what he's been waitin' for, thirty odd years, I don't feel to blame him. Now you get back, Electry. Blitzen ain't a-goin' to stand everything. Sometimes it does seem's if you had the most cheek of any critter in feathers. Well, look at that now!" for Blitzen, exasperated at a raid upon his plate, jumped at the chicken, who quick as thought hopped on his back, and clung to her perch by means of claw and wing while the terrier raced in a mad circle.

Aunt Love's hearty laugh rang out as she watched Blitzen's fruitless efforts to disembarrass himself. At last he lay down and rolled over, and Electra, squawking excitedly, ran back to her plate.

She was not pursued. The terrier ever afterward regarded her as something uncanny, and so far as possible refrained from acknowledging her existence.

An event of general interest during the Fair summer was the visit to the Exposition of the West Point cadets. Cro' Nest itself is scarcely more immovable from its position among the Highland of the Hudson than these pets of Uncle Sam; but it is a matter of history that they and their paraphernalia were transferred to the Philadelphia Centennial, and now again with much form and ceremony their camp was set up in the green plain adjoining the Government Building on the shore of Lake Michigan. They arrived one dazzling afternoon, which began serenely calm, but toward evening gave the guests a northeast wind which sent white-capped waves rushing landward, and shook the tents in the new company-streets.

Starting from the Terminal Station, the young soldiers marched through the streets of the White City, preceded by their famous band, and as they proceeded looked neither to the right nor the left at the widely noised marvels surrounding them, but kept eyes front as though still treading their own quiet, elm-lined avenues, while the waiting crowds cheered and cheered again the elegant precision of their movements.

In an hour, gray-coated sentinels were again walking post in this new Camp Sheridan, alertly conscious of their routine business and apparently without a thought of the surroundings beyond the camp.

Mildred Bryant felt considerable interest in the cadets, and assumed much more. "Helen Eames says that no matter how good a time a girl may have, she can never have as good a one as if she had spent a summer at West Point," she announced to Van Tassel one day, on the occasion of their being together. She felt that he made these occasions rare, and at times the fact touched her. At others she said to herself, "He is getting over it."

"Then why don't you go there?" asked Jack. "I don't know who has a better right to the flowers of life."

"I did think of getting Clover to take me next summer, but now, wonder of wonders, the mountain has come to Mahomet. Don't you want to go down to parade tonight?"

"Yes; I don't know just how to make you comfortable, though. The mob is something marvelous. I looked over their heads a minute last night, but being in the sixth or seventh row, concluded the game wasn't worth the candle."

"Ah, that is where the convenience comes in of having a military friend," returned Mildred gayly. "We shall not need to mingle with the *hoi polloi*. Won't you come too, Clover?" as her sister entered the room.

"Where?"

"To see dress parade this evening."

"Yes, I am going. Mr. Page has already asked me."

"I don't believe you had better try to get along without me. Jack and I are going to meet Mr. Eames on the steps of the Army Hospital at a quarter before six. There is a great crowd."

"Thank you. Perhaps we will be there. Did you hear Aunt Love's comment last night? She said that in the afternoon she ran into an impassable throng near the Administration Plaza, and after vainly trying a long time to get through, she finally found the attraction was only a lot of school-boys drilling. If those important young heroes could have heard her scornful tone!"

When Clover had left the room, Jack spoke again. "Since you have an appointment with Eames, I withdraw, Mildred. I don't see why you asked me."

"He said I might bring my friends," she replied. "Do come, Jack."

Van Tassel looked straight into her eyes, and smiled with an expression which seemed to the girl both brave and hopeless.

"Won't you?" she persisted.

"Of course," he answered.

In the afternoon, Clover walked to the Park, and entering back of the Texas Building, walked down the northern avenue of State buildings. The usual crowd was flocking in and out of Mount Vernon, but she crossed the street to New Jersey's charming home, and entered. It was entertaining a large number of sightseers, note-book in hand, who jotted down their inventories. Clover wished she might look over the shoulder of one woman, with a harassed but determined countenance, whom she met in the cozy east room downstairs. She wondered how this anxious one would be able to transfer to paper the charm of its quiet comfort, with the breezy foliage waving near its half-closed green blinds and casting shadows on the dainty white curtains.

It was all familiar ground to Clover, so she went upstairs and seated herself in a corner of the deep, luxurious sofa which commanded a view, down through the open gallery, of the front door.

People came, looked, commented, passed into the dainty blue chintz bedroom, emerged smiling, and went away.

Many had appeared, climbing the stairway with various degrees of toil, before the figure she awaited came into view. This one sprang up the steps alertly, with a serious expression, which brightened to pleasure at sight of her.

"Have I kept you waiting?' he asked eagerly. "I came around from the Cliff Dwellers by the Intramural road, and we had a stoppage of several minutes. I have been very anxious."

"I am sorry for that," answered Clover, as Page seated himself beside her. "I thought you knew that I am always content in this house. I should move down here and live, if they would let me. I have been fancying that I was holding a reception as the visitors came and went. I wonder if any pilgrim to the Fair has a soul so dead as not to covet this house."

"I didn't know you liked it so much," said Gorham, as though the fact were of serious importance. "Perhaps you would enjoy having tea here."

"Tea in the New Jersey Building? What a pleasure! But why do you tantalize me?"

"I think we can. The lady manager from New Jersey is a near relative of mine. Excuse me a minute and I will try the magic of her name."

Page went downstairs, and in five minutes returned.

"The house is mine, practically," he declared, smiling. "I herewith present it to you."

"How delightful! And the tea?"

"Is near by." Gorham went to one of the locked doors on the east side of the hall and knocked. Presently he ushered Clover into this exclusive nook, and the door closed behind them.

It was an appetizing little supper that was shortly set before them on the daintily clothed round table.

"You have gratified one of my pet ambitions," said Clover. "Now I shall always feel a small proprietorship as well as a great affection for this house. I am really breaking bread at its board."

"You spoil your friends by the pleasure you make it to contribute a little to your happiness," returned Gorham, his eyes resting upon her with the utmost satisfaction.

"This room is as charming as the rest," remarked Clover, looking about at its ruddy decorations; "and the remoteness one feels from everything confusing, or noisy, or soiling, can only be appreciated by those who do not live in the midst of a large well-kept park. I amused myself while waiting for you by searching for the fewest words that will describe the faces of Fair visitors. I decided upon 'tired' and 'pleased.' Not 'delighted;' they are too weary for that,—but just 'pleased.'"

Page looked away and considered the idea, as Clover had intended he should.

"Do you know Mildred gives us the opportunity to find good places at parade under Mr. Eames' wing?" she suggested after a minute.

"Oh, I am glad to hear that. I don't quite understand what makes the cadets such a fad. No; one can't call it a fad either, for there is no sudden interest in them, they are always lionized. Since they have been here, I notice that people go hours before the time for parade for the sake of securing good places, and then wait patiently; so I have been wondering this afternoon how I could fix it for you to get a view of the ceremonies. It will be very pleasant to have Mr. Eames' assistance."

"Then comes in that awful word again," laughed Clover. "We shall have to hurry a little."

Page sighed unconsciously. "Is this very good tea?" he asked, as they finally rose from the table. "I am not a connoisseur."

"Very nice indeed."

"I thought it must be. I never enjoyed any tea so much in my life."

"Then we are very much obliged to each other, aren't we?" said Clover gayly, and consulting her watch, she reminded her companion again of the hour of the appointment, and they hastened away.

They arrived at the hospital steps just as the others were leaving.

"Oh, you loiterers," was Mildred's greeting.

"Don't you see our breathless condition?" returned Clover. "How can you have the heart to reproach us? How do you do, Mr. Eames? We are very grateful to you. What a hopeless throng that looks like!"

"Let me take some of those camp chairs," said Gorham, suiting the action to the word.

Mr. Eames led his party towards the officers' tents. They had to force their way through serried ranks of gazers, who were held back with difficulty by the blue-coated sentinels from the camp of "regulars" near by. The sentinel saluted Eames as he passed, and the lieutenant stood still and allowed his friends to file before him to the reserved places before the officers; tents. There they found Helen Eames, who welcomed them radiantly, fixing cordial eyes on Jack in a manner not lost upon Mildred. The latter did not enjoy this effusiveness. She did not wish to marry anybody, but at the same time she did not like to have any other girl try to appropriate her especial friends.

However, her attention was soon momentarily distracted by the novel sights before her, and the usual questions began to flow.

Eames was most willing to answer them. Before long the band marched out upon the plain, and the evening's ceremonies had begun. The cadets, a shining assembly, marched forth from the company-streets and fell into line.

The band, playing The Thunderer, marched up and down the plain before the motionless ranks, and one to whom the West Point forms were familiar asked himself if it must not all be a dream. Here were the same camp, the same cadets, the same band; but where were the mountains, the huge old elms, the river?—instead, the Government Building, the Fisheries, the Battleship, and Lake Michigan.

To Mildred the very sight of the band was not thrilling from all it implied, but she soon found herself absorbed in interest and admiration.

Once she turned around to Jack, who stood behind her.

"I think I must go to West Point, after all."

"Indeed, you must. It is perfectly lovely," exclaimed Miss Eames. "There, you see, that is the adjutant now, advancing to the officer-in-charge;" and she proceeded volubly to explain the tactics which followed.

"I think I shall have to know some cadets," remarked Mildred, turning to Eames.

"That will be very easy; and when you know one, you will know all. They can talk only on one subject," was the rather stiff reply.

Mildred was perfectly aware that the young lieutenant admired her. She saw that her proposition was displeasing to him; but what she did not know was that he had not yet recovered from that profound fall which results from exchanging the chevrons of a first-class man for the shoulder-straps of a second lieutenant. That young officer must indeed have a seared conscience who can lay his hand on his heart and declare that he entertains only cordial sentiments for a cadet of the first class when their ways chance to cross.

"You refused to attend the cadet ball with me at the New York Building tonight," added Eames reproachfully.

"Why, of course; in my ignorance. Wasn't it stupid of me? Oh, what are they running for? Isn't that pretty? Wouldn't you like to be a cadet again, Mr. Eames?"

"Heaven forbid!" exclaimed that officer devoutly. "I am waked up by reveille yet. Hope I shall get over it some time."

"Mildred is contracting cadet fever, Mr. Van Tassel," declared Helen, looking up at Jack in a way which Miss Bryant noted resentfully, in spite of her preoccupation.

I never before noticed how objectionable Helen's ways with men are, she thought. *I know Jack wishes she wouldn't look at him like that.*

"I suppose so, Miss Eames," replied Van Tassel. "I am trying to find out what it is that is so fetching about those all-conquering youngsters."

But Jack need not have tried. No male civilian under forty was ever known to discover it.

"What is cadet fever?" asked Mildred, "and what is the microbe; a bell-button? I haven't one yet."

The "double-timing" companies had retreated down the streets of camp, and the cheering crowds of spectators quieted. Many of them moved toward the lake shore; for in a short time it had been learned that the cadets would next march to supper preceded by the drum corps; and any ceremony which they performed, no matter how simple, drew a curious throng.

"What is the matter? What are they going to do now?" asked Mildred.

"Going to the Clambake to supper," replied Eames.

"Then I am going to the Clambake to supper," announced Miss Bryant.

"I think you would not enjoy it," said Eames shortly.

"I know I shall," responded Mildred, with her glorious smile.

"I am sorry I shall have to leave you," remarked Helen. "I have a number of friends among the first class. They were yearlings when I was at the post. I have promised to attend the festivities with one of them tonight. Do come and see me, Mr. Van Tassel," holding out her hand. "Remember you owe me a game of tennis. I assure you, you would not beat all the time. Are you coming with me, Fred?"

"I believe not, unless you want me. If these people are determined to go to the Clambake, I think I shall have to go too; but remember, you are to save a two-step for me to-night."

"*Au revoir*, then;" and Miss Eames, her last glance for Jack, moved away.

"We won't go with Mildred," said Clover, "for we have had tea recently, and aren't hungry yet. You would never guess where, either. Good-by, Mr. Eames. We are all greatly indebted to you."

"Indeed we are," said Gorham, shaking hands cordially with the lieutenant. "That was a most interesting sight. I congratulate you on being one fit to survive that tremendous training. This is the show side, but I know something of the other."

"Where did you have tea; where?" demanded Mildred, smiling into Gorham's serious face. He instantly smiled back. Those cold, abstracted eyes of Page's had learned a new look recently, as though so much sunshine had warmed his heart that there was an overflow.

"It would make you so discontented with the Clambake, dear," suggested Clover with mischievous deprecation.

"Why, I *will* know."

"The New Jersey house."

"You selfish creatures! Aren't they?" exclaimed Mildred, calling upon Eames and Van Tassel to witness.

"Yes, we are," laughed Gorham, as he and Clover turned away. "We know it."

Mildred, her companions on either side of her, began her walk northward. Eames wished cordially that Jack would remember an engagement. Jack wished sincerely that he knew what Mildred wanted him to do. Unconsciously fulfilling the lieutenant's desire, he spoke:—

"I suppose I really ought to be at home attending to some correspondence I have been putting off, instead of loitering at the Clambake."

Eames answered without giving Mildred time to speak. "I shall be most happy to take Miss Bryant home after her curiosity is satisfied." Van Tassel's jealous ears detected the eagerness in his polite tone.

"But supposing my curiosity is not gratified by the time you are obliged to go and array yourself gorgeously for the evening? No, Jack, I am sorry for you, but Mr. Eames is engaged elsewhere."

"It need not be for some hours yet," protested the lieutenant.

Mildred shook her head firmly. "I couldn't think of allowing you to assume the care of me in addition to all your other responsibilities this evening."

"Very well," said Jack. "When it comes to a matter of letter-writing, my conscience never requires very much soothing."

When they reached the Clambake, two cadets were just issuing therefrom. Their hands went up in an instant salute to Eames, who had for the moment preceded his friends.

"I suppose there is a great deal of eating and running being done tonight," remarked Jack.

"But where are they?" asked Mildred aggrievedly, as they entered the busy, noisy eating-room.

"The cadets mess upstairs," returned Eames, with latent

satisfaction. "Did you suppose they fell in here with the general company? You don't know much of military discipline, Miss Bryant."

"Never mind; if they are going to run up and down that staircase all the time, as they are doing now, I shall see a great deal of them."

"There isn't much order tonight," remarked the lieutenant. "The cadets own the Fair for the moment, and permits have been issued *ad libitum.*"

But supper had scarcely been brought to the three friends when, with a grand clatter on the bare staircase, the remainder of the corps came hurrying down, walked out the door, and quickly forming in ranks, marched back to camp.

"Now, does that pay for mingling in this drove of people and getting half-served?" asked Jack, with disdain.

"Fully," exclaimed Miss Bryant, with enthusiasm. "Without those absurd straps around their faces, one can see what beautiful creatures they are."

"Well, I'm glad," returned Van Tassel shortly.

"I am resigned to your interest in the cadets," said Eames, "if it brings you to West Point, for I am likely to get a detail there next year."

Jack took no part in the animated discussion that followed.

"Don't look bored, Jack," said Mildred at last. "Ask Mr. Eames questions, as I do."

"There isn't any need. You have covered the ground. You are mistaken about my being bored. This is my expression when I am absorbing stimulating information."

"Then he should abstain from stimulants. Don't you think so, Mr. Eames?"

They arose from the table, and going out into the arc-lighted street, walked slowly west.

When they reached Brazil, Mildred declared her desire to go into the building.

"I suppose I ought to leave you," said Eames reluctantly, "but perhaps if you remain in the grounds I may meet you again."

"What is going on?" asked Van Tassel.

"Several things. A procession of illuminated boats in honor of the cadets, a concert by the West Point band outside the Michigan house, illumination of all the State buildings and dancing in many of them, but notably New York, all for the cadets. You will be likely to hear enough of those young men and see enough of them if you remain, Van Tassel."

"Oh, we can't," smiled Mildred demurely, as she gave her hand to the lieutenant. "We have important letters to write."

The "we," even in jest, was music to Jack. He turned to her as they ascended Brazil's steps. "Well, are you ready to come back to civil life?"

"Haven't I been civil all the time? And you," reproachfully, "were going to leave me."

"Only out of regard to Eamse."

"I think you might have more regard for me than for him."

"I have. I thought you knew it."

Mildred did not answer. They had reached the large salon which was the second floor of Brazil's home, and from thence ascended the spiral iron staircase leading to the roof. Mounting another short flight of steps, they entered one of the four towers, and standing between its white pillars looked down on the enchanting vision of early evening in the White City,—the sum of imaginable loveliness.

The imposing façades of its palaces were now pure but not dazzling; the green trees and flowering shrubs of Wooded Island were hung with thousands of fairy lights; the long, bridge-spanned canals wound away into distant mysterious vistas, where tower on tower still rose far as the eye could discern; and, queen above all, stood the flamy curves of the coronet of Administration.

The columns of the Art Palace were mirrored in the lagoon, and near and far upon the water's breast lay little boats, gay with lights, in readiness for the procession soon to take place; their chains of colored globes faithfully reflected in the depths below.

Distant bells were chiming; from one of the boats the tinkling melody of a mandolin floated up to the watchers in the lofty tower; all else was still, as though the peerless scene were indeed something supernatural, evoked for a moment's breathless rapture, and fated to disappear forever.

Neither Mildred nor her companion spoke for a time.

"Once you gave me your hand when we lived such an experience as this together," said Jack at last, withdrawing his gaze and looking at Mildred in the twilight.

She hesitated, then extended her hand frankly. "So I will again," she answered, with an effort at her old air of good-comradeship. "I am a great believer in handshaking."

Van Tassel only looked at her without accepting the favor, and shook his head slowly. "No," he said, as though to himself, "I cannot be satisfied with it."

Mildred blushed as her hand dropped. "You said," she returned low and swiftly, "that everything should be as it was before."

"Yes, I did, because I was inexperienced. I have never been in love with any one else, and I didn't know how it was going to be. I have become better acquainted with myself since that night and can speak with more intelligence. I find myself hoping, even though I say over every day that there cannot be the slightest hope for me, because you know me well, and by this time the truth would be evident to you. If it were in my favor you would tell me, wouldn't you?"

The girl gave him one fearful glance, and looked away.

"You would, of course?" he said, with sudden excitement, seizing the hand he had refused. "Mildred, I love you! I love you! I do not say it to you every hour, but I think it with every breath. You would not make me wait one moment if"—

"Oh, how can you, Jack? Why must you love a girl so unworthy?" She shrank closer to the railing. "I told you,—I tried to warn you,—I told you that I do not love anybody but Mildred Bryant."

Before she ceased speaking, Van Tassel had released her and recovered himself.

"And the Peristyle," he added steadily, "you are forgetting that."

She did not smile, and her lips quivered.

"So long as my only rivals are your sweet self and the Indians, Helmsmen, *et. al.*, who view the country from the top of the Peristyle, I cannot despair. Perhaps I ought to, dear, but I can't."

Mildred wondered if her companion were really so pale as the shadows made him appear.

"Hope springs eternal in the human breast, and I am

going to hope until you announce your engagement to me. Then, until I receive your wedding cards, I shall look to see you find that engagement a mistake. And if you are married," Jack paused; "I don't know. My mind turns blank when it occurs to me that you might marry another man."

"I am not worth it. I am not worth it," repeated the girl.

"Have I made you unhappy? Shall I go away? Will my presence be a burden to you now?"

"No." Mildred looked at him piteously. "I think I have a stone in here instead of a heart," she said, pressing her side, "but stay with me and—and keep the others away. I don't need to tell you how much I like you, Jack. If only it were safe to say what you want me to when I only like you, and value you, and respect you more than any other man"—She paused, unable to proceed.

He turned to her, tender consideration in his tone.

"That is a great deal, Mildred. I must try not to forfeit it."

CHAPTER 15

IN THE PERISTYLE

The next morning, before seven o'clock, Miss Berry, while busy arranging matters in the dining-room preparatory to breakfast, was summoned by a maid to the back door with the word that a gentleman wished to see her.

To her great surprise, it was Gorham Page who stood waiting on the path.

"Well, well, Mr. Gorham, ain't the days long enough for you?" she asked, smiling, as she came out of the door. "This is new manners for you. Go 'way, Blitzen. Look out, Mr. Gorham, his paws must be wet."

"I didn't want to disturb the house by ringing the bell," explained Page, "and I knew you would be likely to be about by this time. A very unfortunate thing has occurred;" he looked annoyed as he spoke. "I have received a sudden call to St. Louis by a client I cannot neglect, and the business requires that I should spend the whole day in town before I go. Mrs. Van Tassel has promised to go down to the Fair with me this morning on the Whaleback. I want you to explain to her how seriously I regret breaking the engagement. I am really very much put out by the necessity."

Miss Lovina smiled as she broke a twig from the maple under which they were standing. "Ain't you comin' back at all?" she asked.

"Why certainly I am coming back," replied the other severely.

"Oh," remarked Miss Berry innocently. "I thought perhaps you wanted me to say good-by to 'em for you."

"No, indeed; nothing of that kind. I may be detained a week or ten days, but I wanted Mrs. Van Tassel to understand that no trivial circumstance would deter me from taking the boat trip with her and Miss Bryant as we planned. I would—I would give a great deal not to be obliged to leave."

"Mrs. Van Tassel won't lay it up against you," remarked Miss Berry.

"No, I dare say not," said Page abstractedly. "I mustn't wait," he exclaimed, after a moment's reverie. "Tell her, Aunt Love, how sorry I am; put it strong. I thought I would see you instead of leaving a note, for writing is so formal; and oh, by the way, tell her if she forgives me and understands the situation, how glad it would make me to receive a word from her to that effect. This is my address," thrusting a card into Miss Berry's hand.

"What's the use?" asked Miss Lovina, her shoulders shaking in a laugh. "You know you're always forgettin' girls. If you should get a letter signed Mrs. Van Tassel, you'd scratch your head and say 'Van Tassel? Van Tassel? Where have I heard that name before?'"

"This is no time to joke," he returned hurriedly. "I trust you to deliver my messages faithfully. Don't make light of the matter. Good-by;" and with a hasty bow Page moved briskly away.

Miss Berry looked after his departing figure with some exasperation.

"I hope I do him an injustice," she murmured, "but it's my opinion he hasn't found out yet that he's lovin' a woman instead o' worshipin' a saint. I don't want to be profane, but I must say I'm reminded of Ann Getchell's brother. He used to say that he liked a fool, but a darned fool he never could stand."

Clover and Miss Berry sometimes began breakfast before the other and sleepier members of the family appeared on the scene. This was one of those mornings; and while Clover poured the coffee, Aunt Love embraced her opportunity.

"You can't guess who's been here already," she began.

"No; tell me. Don't make me guess. The day is too new."

"Now you look just fresh and bright enough to guess anything." Miss Berry gazed affectionately at her as she spoke.

"I saw Mr. Page going down the street," said Clover, as she set a steaming cup on the waitress' tray. "Could it have been he?"

"Yes; but you'd never 'a' guessed him, would you? He come over to get me to tell you that he's called away on important business, and regrets very much breakin' his engagement with you this mornin' about goin' on the *Christopher Columbus*."

Clover's transparent skin flushed, but she looked coolly into her informant's eyes. "He does not see us again, then?"

"Mercy, yes, in a few days he does"—

"Lena," said Clover to the maid, "please tell Katie to keep the other things hot for a while. Miss Bryant and Mr. Van Tassel are both a little late. I will ring when I want you."

The moment the door had closed behind the girl, Clover's face changed. "Tell me all about it," she said.

Ain't it a pity that gump can't see her this minute? thought Aunt Love. *Even he's a darned one, I guess he'd get a glimmer o' sense.*

"Why, he was the most distressed bein' you'd want to look at," she returned, "just 'cause he couldn't stay and go with you on that boat. You'd think he'd never seen a sign o' the Fair,—not that he said a word about that, he was all taken up with the disappointment o' not goin' with you." Aunt Love was determined to make the most of Gorham's behest to "put it strong."

Clover's face had quieted, and she was occupied in stirring her coffee.

"I told him I guessed you wouldn't be overly hard on him, and he told me to ask you, pervided you did forgive him, to write and tell him so to this address."

Clover looked up quickly as she accepted the card.

"How long will he be gone?"

"A week or ten days, I think he said. Mercy, if I've forgotten anything he told me, I shall need the prayers o' the con'regation. Strange," continued Miss Berry slyly, "that I haven't ever seen anything so severe about you that Mr. Gorham should look all beside himself at breakin' a light, triflin' promise to you through no fault o' his."

"I will write in three or four days," said Clover musingly. "That will divide the time." Then she looked up, and met Aunt Love's eyes fixed on her with an expression that made her glance away. "He's a none-such," said Miss Berry. "I guess you better let him off easy, Mrs. Van Tassel."

"Oh, yes," returned Clover with some confusion. "I will ring for the breakfast now, Aunt Love. We will not wait any longer."

Gorham Page came home to his hotel in St. Louis a few days afterward, tired and enervated by the excessive heat, and requiring to remember all his philosophy not to anathematize the fate which had snatched him from the feast spread upon the shores of Lake Michigan. A little later in the season, during the Congress of Religions, the gentle Dharmapala was riding upon the lagoon one evening, where his snowy silken robes seemed more in place than the close-fitting black of his companions. Looking about him in the waning light where all was melody, harmony, and beauty, he said:—

"All the joys of heaven are in Chicago."

This sentiment of the lovable Singahalese, Page would have echoed, had the anachronism been possible. A sort of chronic yearning and dissatisfaction possessed him, and the heat in St. Louis being a tangible discomfort, he dwelt to himself upon the superior vitality in the air of the lake region, and laid his discomfort at the door of the weather. It was his custom, as soon as he entered the hotel, to inquire for letters; and today he received one in a feminine handwriting.

The clerk noticed the expression of his face as the missive was handed him.

"That fellow can't sing 'The letter I looked for never came,'" was his comment.

Gorham's sensations, as in his room he opened the

square envelope with religious care, were of a chaotic nature, which required analysis. He even went so far as to hold the folded sheet a moment and look at the opposite wall with an effort at introspection; but the insistent desire to possess himself of those written words engulfed all other considerations.

The letter was gentle and friendly like the writer herself. It compassionated him on the fact which Chicago papers reported, of a hot wave in St. Louis; and described her sight of a great Maharajah, the nabob then visiting the Fair, who, resplendent in cloth-of-gold robes and pale green turban, passed in state with his suite about the grounds. Jack had surveyed him, and with democratic audacity dubbed His Highness, "that chocolate duffer."

The little letter closed with these words:—

"I am alone in the house; even the servants are away. It is rather a desolate sensation; and yet some people profess to feel more keenly the loneliness of being in a crowd of strangers, than that of being entirely by themselves. The former is your sort of loneliness at present. I wonder if you dislike it? I wonder—you always seem so sufficient unto yourself, so much more a man of intellect than of heart—I wonder if you ever feel, as I do more and more strongly every day, our dependence on each other?"

There was nothing more save the conventional ending. Page scarcely glanced at the signature. Something seemed to mount to his head, as his eyes dwelt fascinated upon the last sentence recorded. The sweetness of his instant interpretation of it so possessed and intoxicated him that no other thought could obtain entrance. All the processes of his system seemed arrested for one overwhelming moment, then the pulses, reacting, sent the blood boiling through his veins.

Mechanically he rose, and going to the bureau began throwing articles of clothing into an open valise near by.

Recollecting himself, and duties still undone, he stopped these premature preparations and, the valise happening to be the object under his vision, he gave it the most prolonged amorous gaze that ever fell to the lot of insensate leather. Then catching up the letter again, he read it over and over.

That evening a messenger boy ran up the Van Tassel steps, and five minutes afterward Clover was smiling and frowning in perplexity over a telegram addressed to her.

I shall come back at the first possible moment.

Gorham Page.

Aunt Love had brought her the message, and she in her mystification read it aloud. Something in Miss Berry's glance, as she met the young woman's eyes, made Clover's color rise finely.

"You need not speak of this to Mildred," she said after a pause, with dignity. "I—I do not quite understand it."

I don't either, thought Miss Berry, discreetly moving away. *Either he's even more kinds of a gump than I thought, or else he's come to his senses with a crash. I always knew when Gorham Page did start out to love a woman somethin' had got to break; and it ain't goin' to be his heart now, thank the Lord. What a pair they will make! My, My!"*

Page returned on the second day toward evening. He hoped fate would favor him by sending Mildred and Jack to the illumination that night. It did not occur to him that

Clover might have gone too until he neared the house. Then the thought brought dismay. He had schooled himself for days to work and conquer among dry-as-dust details of his profession. Now, it seemed impossible to wait a matter of hours.

There was no one on the piazza when he ascended the steps, and the evening being fine, the fact appeared sinister. Miss Berry answered his ring at the bell.

"Oh, it's you, is it?" was her greeting. "Glad to see you back, Mr. Gorham. It hasn't seemed right not to have you runnin' in every day."

"It is good to be here again; but I am afraid you are alone tonight."

"Yes, the young folks are down to the Fair, as usual." Miss Berry's keen eyes saw the disappointment in the earnest face. "I s'pose like as not you wouldn't feel like goin' down any way, wore out as you must be with all that heat."

"I would go gladly, if there were any chance of meeting them; but the people you want to meet are the ones you do not happen upon at the Fair."

Miss Lovina looked at him with a shrewd smile. "Then I guess you'll give me a good mark for once; for it happened to come over me that you might get home tonight, and I said as much to Miss Mildred. I asked her where they'd be, and she agreed to stay by one o' the big horses till the illumination was over."

"What time is it?" asked Page with sudden haste, wringing Miss Lovina's hand cordially.

"Oh, you've got time, I guess," observed Aunt Love, with a comfortable chuckle. "Now haven't I got a head for somethin' more 'n cookies, Mr. Gorham?"

"If I should stop to compliment you as you deserve, I should miss the appointment," was the hearty response, as the young man lifted his hat and hurried down the steps.

The boy in the driver's seat of the Beach wagon just passing did not bear even a faint resemblance to any conventional idea of Cupid; yet surely no power less than that of the pudgy winged creature could have sent that conveyance exactly at the moment it was needed. Page felicitated himself on the occurrence; and in the whole history of the Fair it is doubtful whether better time was made by a pedestrian than his record tonight between the Sixtieth Street entrance and the Court of Honor.

But for all his haste, when he reached the giant horses his friends were not there. He rushed from one to the other with frantic energy, but in vain. No familiar face and form rewarded his search.

The Grand Court was lighted. The first playing of the electric fountains was over—perhaps for some time. Page was too dispirited to look at his watch. For him the surroundings were stale, flat, and unprofitable. He was just about moving away with a sense of disappointment which he condemned as unreasonably keen, when there loomed up before him a vision more beautiful to his eyes than the most lovely sculptured angel in the neighborhood.

"Well, Jack," he exclaimed, taking his cousin's hand, "here you are! I was just looking for you."

Van Tassel smiled at the eager reception.

"Thought we had flown, did you? So we have, a little way. The girls are sitting over yonder. Mildred has been sending me on periodical scouting expeditions, lest you might come down. Glad to see you back. Business go all right?"

"Yes, I'm all right, thanks. Didn't quite get a sunstroke."

Van Tassel was striding along to keep pace with Gorham, who had instantly started in the direction Jack indicated. The latter smiled, and did not make a further attempt at conversation until the settee was reached where Clover and Mildred were waiting.

"You did come," said the latter, pleasantly. "We thought you might hunt for us."

"It was so kind of you," exclaimed Page gratefully, as he greeted them both. "Now I can draw a long breath."

The four exchanged a few commonplaces concerning his trip, and then Mildred changed the subject.

"We have cards for a reception at the Woman's Building tonight, and we have been in a dozen minds about going: but I think it would be pleasant to look in."

Gorham glanced tentatively at Clover. He had not been gazing at her this evening as was his wont, and Mildred observed the change. "It would be pleasant," he said, without enthusiasm. "Don't let me detain you, of course. I haven't been here for what seems to me a very long time, and I don't feel inclined to go indoors. Do you especially wish to attend the reception, Mrs. Van Tassel?"

"No—in fact"—

Mildred spoke quickly, for she felt her quiet sister's embarrassment. "The truth may as well be told, Mr. Page. Just previous to your appearance she had flatly refused even to approach the Woman's Building; so she cannot put on airs about relinquishing a pleasure."

"Then we might divide," suggested Page, with so much alacrity that Mildred smiled; but the smile was fleeting. She had risen, and was standing behind her sister. Now she placed a hand on her shoulder.

"Oh, my friends, look!" she cried suddenly, lifting her hand toward the east. The moon was rising behind the Peristyle. Deep in the soft sky it shone between the lofty white columns and cast a silver sheen across the summer lake.

"This is Greece, and that is the Mediterranean!" exclaimed Jack.

Mildred after a moment of gazing, stooped and dropped a light kiss on her sister's cheek. "Good-by, Clover."

As the other two moved away, Clover and Gorham rose simultaneously. "I believe we had the same thought," he said, looking at her with happy eyes.

"Mine was to go to the Peristyle," she answered.

"And mine."

She took his offered arm; they started down the half-deserted walk, and quickly came one of the magic changes of the place. The lights vanished, and the colossal moonlit gateway of the Peristyle gained new majesty.

"At last I can thank you for your letter," said Page.

"Were you glad to get it? I am afraid it was not much of an epistle."

"As if any word you would write could be anything but precious! It breathed of you in every line. All things are made new since I read it. My whole life, all my powers, every worthy thing I may ever attain, are yours. Is it possible that you are really going to accept them, that you can care for *me*, Clover?"

She felt his strong arm tremble under her hand, and it thrilled her; but she was silent, and his impetuous speech rushed on.

"I have had to hold under with an iron will all my

thoughts, the contradictions, the hopes and fears, of the last few days. Last night I dreamed of this. We were walking together somewhere, and the moon shone on the water. I asked you to marry me, and you looked at me pityingly and said—No. I reminded you of your letter, but still you shook your head. Clover!"

He spoke her name with tender appeal. They drew near the Peristyle and, stopping within, walked slowly down the wondrous vista of fluted columns beneath the clusters of flower-like lights.

"My letter?" she repeated softly. "How could you value that trivial little letter so much? What was there in it? I do not even remember."

Page stood still, to look in amazement into her face; but even in his surprise it did not occur to him that she might be resorting to subterfuge.

"I have the letter here," he said simply, thrusting his hand into an inside pocket. "We will see."

Clover crimsoned to her throat. She did not wish to see the letter. She suddenly feared it. What trick had been played upon her? Could Mildred— Oh, impossible!

Gorham unfolded the sheet before her reluctant gaze. Then with sudden haste she took it from him, opened it, and read the closing lines. Her breath came freer.

"Oh, yes," she said, smiling in her relief. "I wrote that."

Gorham unconsciously received the paper into his hand. He was scrutinizing her face. "What did you mean by those words?" he asked.

"Why, nothing," she answered, surprised and affected by his agitation,—"nothing except what I said. Let me read it."

"Those last words," said Page briefly, indicating them.

Clover read obediently aloud.

"I wonder—you always seem so sufficient unto yourself, so much more a man of intellect than of heart—I wonder if you ever feel, as I do more and more strongly every day, our—dependence." The voice gradually lowered, then paused; Clover cast one beseeching, troubled glance up into her companion's face. It was as pale as hers was glowing.

"We always have been so impersonal. Of course I meant people in general," she finished, low and quickly.

Page gave her a sad smile. "We have theorized and speculated together a great deal, I know. So this was only one more speculation, was it?"

"Why, Mr. Page!" said Clover, scarcely above the breath that was failing her. "How could you think"—

"I don't know now, myself," he answered with simplicity. "I suppose I was so suffused with love of you that this one hint at reciprocation set my head aflame, and brought on an attack of emotional insanity. I ask your pardon; but all the same, Clover, I am not ashamed, and I cannot regret it. It was my good angel who held your little hand while you wrote that, for it gave me moments of such happiness as I never knew before, and perhaps never shall again."

Clover wanted to speak and could not. She thought if he would move, or take his gaze from her face, her courage might rise. She lifted her eyes, but only far enough to note that the electric fountains were flinging their jets of color aloft; the water taking new shapes each moment with bewildering grace and rapidity.

"I never thought of you before as a woman whom it would be right for a man to ask to come down beside him; I did not know that my heart was reaching out toward yours until that day of the letter. Would you mind telling me, Clover, how long you have known that I love you?"

Clover drew a long, involuntary breath. "I did not know it," she said at last, looking up at him bravely; and when once her eyes were held in that compelling gaze, she did not wish to escape. "I only—hoped it," she finished.

The fountains fell and vanished. The dainty flame-blossoms in the remote sculptured nooks overhead still added their soft radiance to that of the moon. The lovers were alone in that colossal aisle, that pillared temple, where for one transcendent moment they stood heart to heart. It was the period of shadow in the Court. At the other end of the lagoon, far away through spaces of darkness, the gemmed dome of Administration lifted its cameos and starry crown against the heavens. From the distance of the lighted Peristyle the deep surrounding shadows gave a supernatural effect to this single lighted edifice, whose triumphant angels seemed to move in the waving illumination thrown over them from flaming torches. It was an aerial castle, with no affinity for earth; and exalting vision such as visited the prophets of old.

"Earlier in the evening," said Page, almost too deeply moved to speak, "I would willingly have turned from the Court of Honor. I could not find you, and its company of angels was incomplete. Now, heaven itself lies here. I ought to be a good man, my darling. You will help me. It is a debt I shall owe forevermore."

CHAPTER 16

THE NEW YEAR

The reception at the Woman's Building proved attractive. It was late when Mildred and Jack returned home that night. All was still about the house. They parted in the usual friendly fashion, which both sought to make easy, and each felt to be constrained.

Mildred went quietly to her sister's door and listened. All was still. *Then she has been at home some time,* thought the girl. *Good! That speaks volumes. Poor fellow, I'm sorry for him.* The *frou-frou* of her dress as she turned away almost drowned the voice that spoke her name. Not quite, however. She turned the handle of the door.

"Did you call me, Clover?"

"Yes; come in."

"Oh, I can't go to sleep. I don't want to."

The speaker put out her hand, and drew Mildred down on the side of the bed. The latter's eyes widened in their effort to penetrate the darkness.

"Something did happen, then?"

"Yes, it is all right," answered Clover, and her soft, glad tone pierced to her sister's heart.

"What do you mean by that?"

"He does love me!" What a different voice was this from the one in which she had said the same words about Jack Van Tassel four years ago!

"Of course; but, Clover, surely you don't love him!" exclaimed the other, aghast.

For answer, Clover took the hand she held and pressed it firmly between her own. "With every beat of my heart," she said slowly.

Mildred stared, then abruptly pulled her hand free and threw herself face down upon the pillow, her muffled sobs causing Clover considerable distress.

"Dearest, you needn't be so troubled."

"I can't help myself! I hate to think of Gorham taking you away from me!"

Clover slipped her arm around the recumbent form. "Gorham can't take me away from you. You should know that."

For several moments, Mildred remained inconsolable.

"I am so disappointed, Milly." Clover interspersed her words with loving pats. "I thought you would be as happy as I am."

"I am never as happy as you are," answered the other. "I know this is abominable, but I've got to be selfish this once. I'm just envious and miserable, Clover. Why should you always be blessing people and I, never? Because of Jack, my heart is heavy and it hurts me all the time."

In an instant Clover sank her joy in loving compassion. It was the first admission concerning Jack that Mildred had ever made.

"My poor darling, I am so sorry," she said feelingly, "and I do not see that you have done any wrong. Instead, you have been true to yourself. Anything else would have been a dreadful mistake."

Mildred was so surprised that she stopped crying suddenly. "Then Jack has told you?" she said without lifting her face, a belated sob struggling in her throat. "Yes. Shouldn't you prefer to have him go away?"

"No, not unless he wishes it. I would rather he stayed."

"Things will come right for you, dearest. They always do when one is trying to live up to her standards, and to do the best she knows how. Perhaps I have made you feel that even I thought you ought to marry him. If I have, please forgive me for adding to the cruelty of your position. I ought to have known that you would be glad, too, if you believed you should accept Jack."

Mildred rose to a sitting position. "Let us forgive mutually," she said, wiping her eyes. "I am mortally ashamed of myself for bothering you at such a time. Wait till tomorrow morning and see me redeem my character by my treatment of Gorham." She stooped and kissed her sister. "Why should I blame him, when I know that I would not look at any woman but you if I were a man?"

Aunt Love was a happy woman next day. She was quite a heroine in the small family jubilation.

"All my life I shall owe you twelve added hours of happiness," Page said to her, when she gave him a kiss.

"Well, Mr. Gorham, you know I always was good to you," she responded radiantly, and contented herself all day by drawing Mildred off into corners to discuss this and that detail of "his" and "her" behavior during the past weeks; "trifles light as air," but "confirmation strong" to Aunt Love of a good time coming, and which she dwelt upon with such profound delight and secrecy that Mildred had not the heart to refuse her an audience for all the asides she chose to make.

Gorham Page allowed himself a brief period in which to realize his happiness before returning to Boston, but his energies now turned willingly toward his work as the means by which he could soonest carry Clover to his own home and hers; and before he left, it had been arranged that they should be married the following spring.

The day before the one set for his departure, Jack came out to Clover, who was sitting with some fancy work on the piazza. Page was at the hotel, writing business letters.

"Gorham says your cigars are too strong to be good for you," she said, looking up as he struck a match.

"Yes, he has let out from the shoulder lately," returned Jack, puffing his cigar alight.

"Do listen to him, Jack," said the other pleadingly. "Don't injure your health."

"What is my health good for?" asked the young fellow, dropping down on the edge of the piazza, upon which he extended one leg, while he embraced the other knee as he leaned against a pillar.

"Don't talk that way," said Clover. Van Tassel had never heard her use so acute a tone, and he was surprised on looking up to see her eyes swimming. "It is wicked when one has friends who love him as yours do you."

"All right, Clover. Thank you. I *am* listening to Gorham. This cigar that I have here"—he removed it from his lips, and regarded it through contracted lids—"might have become sauerkraut by a little different process of handling." He smoked a minute in silence, then said: "Mildred has gone away, hasn't she?"

"Yes; she has gone to spend a day or two with Helen Eames. Helen has been urging her all summer."

"I think I'll go back with Gorham tomorrow," added Van Tassel briefly.

"Why, Jack!" Clover dropped her work and gazed at him.

"Yes, I'll go back." The young man flipped the ash from his cigar off into the grass.

"Do you feel that you have seen the Fair?"

"Yes, too many Fairs." Jack smiled rather dolefully as he glanced up toward the blue eyes.

"I can't urge you to stay," said Clover sadly.

"Oh, perhaps I'll come back," remarked the other cheerfully, "when I get my second wind, as it were. The first supply has been about knocked out of me."

"You don't look well."

"Oh yes, I am well enough."

"You have behaved like an angel, Jack."

He laughed. "I feel a little like one of those angels on the side of the Transportation Building,—the sort you can pass under a door without touching their buttons, you know."

"Did you plan to go without saying good-by to Mildred?"

"Oh no."

"I'm glad of that. It would hurt her."

"No. I will run up to the Eameses this evening and kill two birds with one stone. I ought to say good-by to Miss Eames. She has been very kind to me. That is," looking up inquiringly, "if you and Gorham can spare me on your last evening. How is that?"

There was dew again in the violet eyes. "It does not

seem right for me to be happy when you are not, Jack," Clover said, unconsciously clasping her hands together. "If I could only say something that would stay with you as a comfort! I am afraid to seem to preach when my own lot is what it is. You are plucky and have plenty of self-control, but I hope you will not try to lean only on your own strength. We can all have faith that, so long as we do right, the outcome will be the best thing for us, whatever it is."

"I'm not kicking," said Jack quietly, "but I am going away because I believe it is the best thing both for Mildred and me."

"Does she know your intention?"

"No. It is rather sudden. I only took it today. I have stayed here long enough to bring things the way I want them if it were on the cards. Now, I will do the next best thing."

A couple of days afterward, Mildred returned from her visit. She came breezily into the room where her sister was sitting.

"Oh, I am so glad to see you!" exclaimed Clover, starting up and kissing her.

"Let us look at you," said Mildred, holding her off and scrutinizing her with bright, audacious eyes. "No, they are not red," she continued; "I thought I might be coming home to a Niobe."

"They are both gone," said Clover plaintively.

"Yes." Mildred turned away to a mirror, and began removing her hat-pins. "I have been kept so busy consoling Helen Eames that I couldn't come home any sooner to dry your tears."

Her sister looked at her inquiringly. Was there any bravado in this disappointing gayety? Apparently not.

Mankind loves a lover, and Clover, especially loving this lover, felt tempted to resentment; but might it not be that Mildred indeed felt more light-hearted than for months past? Why should she be blamed, if she found relief in the knowledge that her home was free from a presence which had been in a way a constant reproach?

"I wish Jack did care for Helen Eames," returned the elder, unconsciously sighing.

"Yes; wouldn't it be convenient?"

"I'm glad you've come home, Milly. The house has seemed so empty."

"Oh, but what lovely flowers!" exclaimed the latter, espying a great bowl of roses in a shaded corner. "Why didn't you tell me?"

"They are not yours, my dear." Clover smiled at her bouquet. "They came last night."

"They are beautiful. Did brother actually remember to have such a sweet substitute sent you on your first lonely evening? I am proud of him. What else interesting has happened?"

"Nothing, I think. Gorham received a characteristic letter from Robert just before he left. He gave it to me to keep, with one that came from Hilda. Perhaps you would like to see it?"

"Indeed, I would. Nice, jolly Mr. Page! I wish they lived next door."

Mildred took the letter Clover handed her. "I'm going to read it aloud. It probably says nice things about you.

"Dear Gorham,—So you have won that sweet woman! blessings on you, my boy! I may be partial, but I believe you are somewhere near good enough for her. Truth compels me to state, however, that your gain is my loss, owing to the overweening satisfaction it is to Hilda. In an evil moment, I underrated her prescience when she prophesied this happy event, and the consequence is that I am considering living at the club until the first blush of her triumph passes over. It flavors the matutinal oatmeal and the after-dinner coffee. I cannot indulge in a short nap without encountering a tall nightmare in which the wife of my bosom pops out from unexpected corners and exclaims 'I told you so!' She sits opposite me now, writing a letter to go with this. I know those are burning words that are growing with such swiftness. I can almost hear the paper hiss. However, I am just as pleased as she is. Please give Clover my love,—you see I am not slow to use my privilege in naming her,—and tell her I am sure the world will be a better place for such a home as you and she will make in it. Indeed, I feel more than I can say on the subject.

"With kind regards to all,

"Your brother,

"Robert."

With the early autumn came the Parliament of Religions,—the congress which, among the many that preceded and followed it, proved, to the general surprise, to be the one of greatest interest to the public. Miss Berry was indefatigable in her attendance; and her young ladies were often with her. The names of those Orientals, whose words she listened to as to music, were impracticable to her; but their dark faces and graceful gestures were fixed in her mind forever. Aunt Love was one of thousands whose complacent generalization of "the heathen" received a blow.

Clover did her share in the entertaining of some of these

scholarly delegates from the far East; and Mildred found a totally novel *sauce piquante* in the society of a handsome coffee-colored Indian, who wore a pink silk turban and mouse-colored robe, and talked transcendental philosophy in the purest English while gazing at her from long, beautiful eyes.

Lieutenant Eames had rejoined his regiment, whether or not hiding a heart-wound, Clover did not know. Mildred said nothing. October, the busiest, gayest month of the Fair, came on. Such of society as had hitherto been obdurate, now returning from seashore and mountains, made one united, belated rush for the widely extolled Exposition. The climax of attendance during one day came on October ninth, Chicago's own celebration, the anniversary of the great fire, when more than seven hundred and fifty thousand persons were in the grounds. The effect, when one could rise to a slight eminence and look down, was such as is observed in a trap so full of flies that there is only a general stir and movement among the mass; no form is visible.

The day was faultless. Not a cloud flecked the azure against which shone the groups of the Agricultural Building, that one edifice which interposed no roof between its superb statuesque decorations and the revealing blue of the firmament. The three mammoth fountains at the end of the Court of Honor played in dazzling sunshine, filling the air with crystals.

Clover and Mildred were present, attended by the Pink Turban, splendid in his unconsciousness of being regarded on all sides as a sort of embodied apotheosis of the Midway.

The ceremonies of the day began with what Clover's

chair-boy naïvely called a procession of "the hussies," although the Chicago Hussars might have taken exception to the term. From that moment until late evening, the interest was not permitted to flag. A tightrope-walker in cavalier costume ran and pirouetted high in the air before the Peristyle, the scarlet and gold of his costume showing jewel-like against the pure columns.

A large chorus sang national hymns. The young liberty-bell pealed. Hundreds of children in fancy costumes marched around the lagoons; but the magnitude of the crowd defeated its own entertainment by the fact that the procession of elaborately prepared floats could not force their way through the avenues.

It was all very wonderful, but greatest of all was the fabulous splendor of the night display. The Van Tassel party viewed it from the roof of the New York Building. Surely, Chicago had earned the right to celebrate herself by bombardments of colored fire, if so it pleased her, and she did so this evening on a scale which trebled previous efforts, and made the heavens as luminous as on that night, twenty-two years ago, when she was the victim instead of the instigator of her pyrotechnics.

Once more the city meant to distinguish the World's Fair by novel and striking accompaniments to its intrinsic grandeur. It was intended that its close should be attended with a metaphorical flourish of trumpets; but close upon this last day, shame and affliction visited Chicago in the murder of its mayor, and all festivities were renounced. The last hours of the existence of the Dream City were mournfully quiet.

"A bubble is always most beautiful just before it vanishes," Mildred said to Clover, as they stood together in the

Court of Honor on that afternoon, waiting for the fateful moment.

"It never looked more lovely," replied Clover.

They spoke softly, as in a holy place, and with one accord looked up at the infinite message in carven letters, the significant legacy of the summer's grand experience:—

"Ye shall know the truth, and the truth shall make you free."

A strain of solemn sweetness sounded through the harmonies that poured without ceasing from the orchestra in a neighboring pavilion, touching every heart in that waiting throng.

The rays of the low-hanging sun shot for one moment past the side of the Administration Building, gleamed through the waters of the fountain, and traveled a swift path across the lagoon to illume for an instant the golden Republic.

"It is the swan-song!" exclaimed Mildred.

A long, sullen roar sounded from the east. It was the first peal of the salute which bade the Dream City vanish. The sisters clasped hands, as they had once before in the selfsame spot. The eyes that had sought each other, dark with excitement and anticipation, that day, now saw through mists of tears. The myriad flags they had seen unfurled in gladness now with one accord slipped down from sight, and the music died as the message from the cannon's mouth told the country around that all was over.

Jack had been with them on the opening day. Mildred could recall how earnest and handsome he looked, standing with his hat off, carried away by the spirit of the occasion. A great wave of compassion swept over her heart, and mingled with the yearning and sense of loss in the air. The weather was chill now and cloudy. She was glad to slip her arm through Clover's and hurry home.

Soon after this, Aunt Love returned to Pearfield. There was some discussion as to whether she should take Blitzen; but that sagacious animal, as was usual when anything inimical to his interests was in the air, seemed fully aware of her doubts, lost his high spirits, haunted her like a silent ghost, walked when she walked, sat when she sat, and whined as he gazed at her, until the persecuted woman yielded to his mute entreaties. Electra stayed, and remained the heroine of her latticed enclosure,—an additional reason for Blitzen to prefer returning to his native heath.

Aunt Love's farewell was by no means a sad one. She was radiant as she remarked how soon Clover would be her neighbor.

"And in that way we'll get you, too," she said to Mildred; but that young woman demurred.

"Of course she will come," said Clover.

"I'm not sure," persisted the younger.

"Well now, my dear," said Miss Berry in parting advice, "don't you wander through the woods too long and take up with a crooked stick at last; but, whatever you do, marry a man o' your own color, who wears a hat and coat instead of a turban and a bath wrapper. Remember that."

"I don't know," responded Mildred, with a teasing smile. "The Pink Turban says he has a pair of very handsome diamond earrings. Perhaps, if I should have my ears pierced, he would let me wear them a part of the time."

"Go 'way!" exclaimed Miss Berry, with a repudiatory gesture.

The old Scotch housekeeper soon returned, joyful to be back again, and felicitating herself that the Fair was safely over; and life might have been supposed to move on as before, but it did not.

Clover had come into a new state of existence, the deep, constant joy of which she never expressed in words. Except for the framed photograph on her dressing-table, Mildred might have believed her equable sister to be unchanged in thought as well as habit; but Mildred's own mode of life was noticeably changed this season. The winter was a hard one. Cold weather set in during November, and the reaction from the great business activity of the year before caused a depression cruelly felt among the poor. Charitable work was the order of the day, and Mildred entered into it heart and soul.

"Slumming was never so fashionable," she said; and thus lightly accounting for the new direction of her energy, she learned novel views of life, which would modify her character in all time to come. Clover was her efficient aid, and her friend Helen Eames sometimes went on these expeditions too, under the shadow of her wing.

It was a grievance with Helen that Mildred never of her own accord referred to Jack, and if questioned, made brief replies. Mr. Van Tassel was a Chicago man and belonged here. He was, in Helen's own phraseology, "perfectly fascinating," and not to be lightly dropped. She intended to keep herself posted as to the probabilities of his return; but Mildred early nipped her plans in the bud.

"We can't reckon on Mr. Van Tassel as a Chicagoan any more," she said. "He is reading law very earnestly now in Boston, and he has lived there so many years, it is home to him. Besides that, he is devoted to Clover, and when she is married to his cousin, that will be another tie to keep him at the East."

Upon which Miss Eames grew thoughtful, and fortune shortly after throwing in her way an invitation to visit a friend in Boston, she incontinently dropped her pilgrimages amid Chicago's back streets, and departed on the most limited train available.

Soon afterward, Mildred received a gay letter from her. Mr. Van Tassel had called, and had been one of the theatre party her hostess had given the night before. She was having a charming time, and hoped dear Mildred would not take something in those dreadful basements before she could return to help her again.

"Wouldn't it be strange," Clover asked, when her sister showed her the letter, "If little Helen should catch Jack's heart on the rebound, after all?"

Mildred returned her look with unusual gravity. "Are men's hearts so unfaithful, do you think?" she asked seriously.

"Sometimes," answered Clover, "when they despair; and women's, too."

"Then they are unworthy," Mildred said quietly.

No winter ever suffered more than this by contrast with the summer. In public print and by private hearsay, the bitter needs of the poor surrounded one. The corpse of the White City lay wrapped in a winding-sheet of snow. The sisters never entered the grounds from the afternoon its spirit departed. They looked askance, in passing, at the buildings, with their cold, silent surroundings, where so recently all had been life and warmth. The same domes and façades unprepared under the cold sky. One could only say as he does in glancing tenderly and sadly at a dear, dead face: "How natural it looks!"

Little wonder that plans were innumerable for preserving a portion of that dream of beauty, to be resuscitated and to become the joy of one more summer; but the work of spoliation had begun, and would march on inexorably.

"Miss Mildred has grown awful quiet, Mrs. Van Tassel," said old Jeanie one day in confidence. "It's wrong you're doing her, I'm thinking, letting her quench all her bright spirits in those holes she visits."

"I think not, Jeanie," Clover replied. "Miss Mildred is having a deep experience; but we can't help the sorrow in the world except by coming close to it."

"I saw tears in her eyes the other night," whispered Jeanie profoundly, "and I asked the poor child why, and what do you suppose she answered?"

"I suppose she had the heartache over some of our new friends."

"Maybe; but if she did, she wouldn't acknowledge it. She said 't was because the Chicago Beach Hotel was closed for the season, and there couldn't be any dances there!"

But she had been quick to observe the alteration in Mildred. Sometimes she hoped that Jack's absence had wrought the fulfillment of his desire, but she did not seek to probe her sister's feeling. If unseen influences were expanding the entrance to the holy of holies in the young girl's heart, what right had she to interfere? Sometimes she feared Mildred was depressed by the prospect of a marriage which would break up this home. Whatever the cause, the fact remained that her sister's interest in society had waned, and the part she kept up in it was perfunctory, and did not extend beyond those efforts which courtesy demanded. She had never been more companionable with Clover, however, and the latter had never enjoyed her so much.

Thus matters stood when the New Year was ushered in. The day was clear and bright, and many thousands took advantage of the fact that Jackson Park passed back today into the public jurisdiction. Curiosity seekers and vandals poured down the strangely mute Midway Plaisance and through the avenues of the Park. Clover and Mildred did not swell the number who gayly parodied "After the Ball."

And now was to come the long pull and the strong pull of winter. Mildred wondered in her own mind why the prospect should look so very dreary. No other season had ever seemed like it. Doubtless it was her new and close acquaintance with the griefs of others that had changed the world, and made life a novel sort of struggle.

The new year was less than a week old when Clover received a letter from Jack, announcing his intention to make them a call.

"I won't give any excuses," he wrote; "I admit that I am coming simply because I want so much to see Mildred and you that I believe I shall do better work after indulging in that pleasure."

"Loyal as ever," said Clover, looking up, and Mildred did not raise her eyes from her work, but she was smiling.

Jack had said he could not set a precise time for his arrival, but that in a few days they might expect him to drop down.

When his determination had been taken, Van Tassel pushed forward his preparation with all haste, and his restlessness did not quiet until he found himself, in the early evening of the eighth of January, walking down the old familiar home street once more. As he reached the corner, he suddenly observed that clouds of smoke mingled with large red cinders were rolling up from the south.

Must be a fire in the Fair grounds, he thought. *I wonder if the girls know.*

They were coming out of their door, with their outside wraps on, when Van Tassel came up the steps, and they gave him a greeting in which excitement and cordiality mingled.

"There is a fire in the Fair," they all three said at once.

"You will take me down there, Jack," exclaimed Mildred. "Clover was going, but she hasn't been well and she ought not to."

Clover protested faintly, suggesting some of the rites of hospitality for Jack's benefit; but he would hear nothing save carrying out Mildred's wishes, and after taking a moment to deposit his bag in the hall, he set off beside her.

"How is Gorham, I wonder?" murmured Clover with a comical little smile and plaintive raised eyebrows, as she looked after the figures retreating into the dark. "I feel as if I had been in a whirlwind." She looked toward the once gay hotel; now, its many sightless eyes gazed blankly southward. "I will go there," she exclaimed with sudden determination; and reëntering the house, she called Jeanie, and made her hurry into her wraps. The housekeeper obeyed, with many a fussy groan over her mistress' caprice, and soon they were walking northward.

They ascended the dark stairway to the piazza of the hotel, and peered through the door at the office, where one dim light showed. Clover was a bit frightened, but she knocked on the glass. A man appeared behind the office desk, and, picking up the lantern which was the vast hotel's single attempt at illumination, advanced through dark spaces, casting strange shadows on the marble floor as he came.

"May we look at the fire from here?" asked Clover, wishing Gorham were with her rather than Jeanie.

"Yes; I see they've got a fire down there," the man remarked imperturbably, but he stood back for them to enter, and then clanged the heavy door behind them. It echoed in the big empty hall, and Jeanie looked so discomfited that Clover smiled, though she herself thought the situation rather eerie.

The last time she had stood here, the place had been ablaze with electric light, and gay with music and guests. She had ascended with her friends to a balcony to view the lighted White City in the zenith of its beauty, and to revel in the fiery marvels which mirrored themselves in the lake. It flashed into her memory how enthusiastic the crowds had been over the rising of a slender cylinder of light which poised itself aloft, then slowly unrolled until the stars and stripes appeared in the heavens. She could hear again the patriotic salutes from a congregation of boats as Old Glory sailed away across the lake.

Now, all was hushed and dark. A second man, who appeared in the office, struck a match and lit another lantern, by whose light he proceeded to pilot the two women upstairs.

Jeanie muttered and grunted to such an extent that Clover relented after the ascent of three flights, and the old man led her to the window of one of the white-sheeted bedrooms, from which she eagerly looked.

"Oh, Jeanie, I am sure it is the Peristyle!" she exclaimed, gazing horror-struck on the volume of fire and smoke visible through the bare ribs of the Spectatorium. "What will—what will Mr. Page say!" Involuntarily she pressed her hand on her beating heart, seeming to hear the roar of those cruel flames.

Meanwhile Mildred and Jack had caught a train, which they left at Sixtieth Street. The young man was glad that the tension of his anticipations had been relieved by the unconventional circumstances of his welcome. To be joined with Mildred in the present excitement was far preferable to the doubtful home evening he had looked forward to. Arm in arm they pressed forward against the cold lake wind toward the shore, and did not pause until they had neared the Music Hall.

Only once Mildred spoke as they hurried on. "I am afraid," she said breathlessly, "that it is the Peristyle."

"It looks like it," said Jack briefly. The hoofs of galloping horses smote the hard ground, and the puffing of fire-engines was borne to their ears before they reached the scene of confusion. There they stood still, Mildred clinging with both hands to Van Tassel's arm, her wide, horrified eyes fixed on the blazing Casino, the building into which the Peristyle merged at the southern end, as it did into Music Hall on the north.

The lagoon was coated with a thin sheet of ice, across which the sparks, after circling around the head of the golden goddess, whirled up the Court of Honor in lines of fire.

Above, the wind bore the glowing brands swirling over the great neighboring buildings. Streams of water fell with no quenching power into the flames.

"Why don't they bend all their energies to saving the Peristyle?" exclaimed Mildred.

"That is what they are doing now. See?"

The dauntless firemen were fighting the flames at close range. A dozen streams of water at once were directed upon the Peristyle; but in vain. The walls of the Casino crashed in; devouring tongues of fire fastened upon the first noble pillar and ate upward.

Van Tassel felt his companion shudder in her furs, and put his hand on hers. The crowd that had gathered in the very spot where they cheered the summer's pyrotechnic display were strangely motionless and silent, watching with fascinated eyes and saddened faces as the fire crept upward, leaping from pillar to pillar, ascending toward the statues which stood serene and fair above smoke and flame long after the watchers expected them to succumb. At last, each white figure in turn, seeming suddenly to become aware of its environment, wavered on its pedestal, hesitated, and with one shrinking look below, plunged downward into the fiery chasm.

"Jack!" gasped Mildred, shivering from head to foot, her dilated eyes never leaving the heart-rending sight.

For an instant, free of smoke and illumined gloriously, shone out for a last time the heavenly promise:—

"Ye shall know the truth, and the truth shall make you free."

"The Quadriga!" groaned Van Tassel, for the grand arch was seized upon, and swiftly melted away in the furnace. No search-light of the summer ever compared in grandeur with the effect that succeeded to the crumbling of the staff below the famous group, the pride of the noble Peristyle. The iron skeleton supports, laid bare, were invisible in the night. Columbus, his chariot, the outriders with their banners, and the spirited horses led by maidens, stood triumphant in the vivid light. It was a sight of supernatural beauty. In the glare of the leaping flames the snow-white horses seemed to stir restlessly and paw the air, as they arched their necks and gazed proudly down into the glowing chasm.

"Jump, oh, jump!" cried Mildred; then, unable to endure the impending catastrophe, her nerves strained to the utmost, she turned with a wild movement, and sobbing, hid her head on Jack's breast.

He put his arms around her.

"The—the Peristyle has gone!" she exclaimed chokingly,—"gone back—to heaven!"

"Yes, darling," he answered close to her ear. "My rival. forgive me, but you are making me so happy I can't realize anything except that I have you in my arms. What does it mean? Only that you are overwrought?"

Mildred lifted her face slightly, but away from the burning pyre.

"Your rivals are all gone, Jack," she said, as steadily as she could speak. "Even I do not count."

Half an hour afterward, Clover heard them enter the house, and hurried down to the parlor.

When she pushed aside the portière and entered, she paused in amazement and her heart leaped up, for Jack's arms were about Mildred and his lips were pressed to hers.

They saw her, and in another instant she was beside them, her hands clasped in theirs.

As she gazed at her sister, mute for joy, Mildred regarded her with a tender version of her beautiful smile.

"I believe," she said, "this lifts the last cloud from Clover's horizon."

"Yes," answered the latter rather unsteadily; "the world never looked so bright to me as now. I think heaven itself must have grown happier tonight," she concluded, her face aglow.

MORE GREAT LAKES ROMANCES

MACKINAC
by Donna Winters
First in the series of *Great Lakes Romances*
(Set on Mackinac Island, 1895.)

Her name bespoke the age in which she lived . . .

But **Victoria Whitmore** was no shy, retiring Victorian miss. Never a homebody, attending to the whims of her cabinetmaker Papa, she found herself aboard the *Algomah*, traveling from staid Grand Rapids to Michigan's fashionable Mackinac Island resort.

Her journey was not one of pleasure; a restful holiday did not await her. Mackinac's Grand Hotel owed the Whitmores money—enough to save the furniture manufactory from certain financial ruin. It became Victoria's mission to venture to the island to collect the payment. At Mackinac, however, her task was anything but easy, and she found more than she had bargained for.

Rand Bartlett, the hotel manager, was part of that bargain. Accustomed to challenges and bent on making the struggling Grand a success, he had not counted on the challenge of Victoria—and he certainly had not counted on losing his heart to her.

The Captain and the Widow
by Donna Winters
Second in the series of *Great Lakes Romances*
(Set in Chicago, South Haven, and Mackinac Island, 1897.)

Lily Atwood Haynes is beautiful, intelligent, and ahead of her time . . .

But even her grit and determination have not prepared her for the cruel event on Lake Michigan that leaves her widowed at age twenty. It is the lake—with its fathomless depths and unpredictable forces—that has provided her livelihood. Now it is the lake that challenges her newfound happiness.

When **Captain Hoyt Curtiss**, her husband's best friend, steps in to

offer assistance in navigating the choppy waters of Lily's widowhood, she can only guess at the dark secret that shrouds his past and chokes his speech. What kind of miracle will it take to forge a new beginning for *The Captain and the Widow?*
Note: The Captain and the Widow *is a spin-off from* Mackinac.

Sweethearts of Sleeping Bear Bay
by Donna Winters
Third in the series of *Great Lakes Romances*
(Set in the Sleeping Bear Dune region of
northern Michigan, 1898.)

Mary Ellen Jenkins is a woman of rare courage and experience . . .
One of only four females licensed as navigators and steamboat masters on the Western Rivers, she is accustomed to finding her way through dense fog on the Mississippi. But when she travels North for the first time in her twenty-nine years, she discovers herself unprepared for the havoc caused by a vaporous shroud off ***Sleeping Bear Point***. And navigating the misty shoals of her own uncertain future poses an even greater threat to her peace of mind.

Self-confident, skilled, and devoted to his duties as Second Mate aboard the Lake Michigan sidewheeler, *Lily Belle*, **Thad Grant** regrets his promise to play escort to the petticoat navigator the instant he lays eyes on her plain face. Then his career runs aground. Can he trust this woman to guide him to safe harbor, or will the Lady Reb ever be able to overcome the great gulf between them?
Note: Sweethearts of Sleeping Bear Bay *is a spin-off from* The Captain and the Widow.

Charlotte of South Manitou Island
by Donna Winters
Fourth in the series of *Great Lakes Romances*
(Set on South Manitou Island from 1891-1898.)

Charlotte Richards' carefree world turns upside down . . .
on her eleventh birthday, the day her beloved papa dies in a spring

storm on Lake Michigan. Without the persistence of fifteen-year-old Seth Trevelyn, son of the island's lightkeeper, she might never have smiled again. He shows her that life goes on, and so does true friendship.

When Charlotte's teacher invites her to the World's Columbian Exposition of 1893, Seth signs as crewman on the *Martha G.*, carrying them to Chicago. Together, Seth and Charlotte sail the waters of the Great Lake to the very portal of the Fair, and an adventure they will never forget. While there, Seth saves Charlotte from a near fatal accident. Now, seventeen and a man, he realizes his friendship has become something more. Will his feelings be returned when Charlotte grows to womanhood?

Jenny of L'Anse Bay

by Donna Winters

Special Edition in the series of *Great Lakes Romances*

(Set in the Keweenaw Peninsula in 1867.)

A raging fire destroys more than Jennifer Crawford's new home; it also burns a black hole into her future. To soothe Jennifer's resentful spirit, her parents send her on a trip with their pastor and his wife to the Indian mission at L'Anse Bay. In the wilderness of Michigan's Upper Peninsula, Jennifer soon moves from tourist to teacher, taking over the education of the Ojibway children. Without knowing their language, she must teach them English, learn their customs, and live in harmony with them.

Hawk, son of the Ojibway chief, teaches Jennifer the ways of his tribe. Often discouraged by seemingly insurmountable cultural barriers, Jennifer must also battle danger, death, and the fears that threaten to come between her and the man she loves.

ORDER FORM

Customer Name ____

Address ____

____

____

Available while supplies last.

Quantity		Total
	75-8. *Mackinac*, $6.95	
	76-6. *The Captain and the Widow*, $6.95	
	77-4. *Sweethearts of Sleeping Bear Bay*, $7.95	
	79-0. *Charlotte of South Manitou Island*, $8.95	
	78-2. *Jenny of L'Anse Bay*, $7.95	
	80-4. *Sweet Clover: A Romance of the White City*, $8.95	
	Subtotal:	
	Michigan residents include 4% tax:	
	Postage-add $1.05 for first item, 50¢ for each additional (maximum - $3):	
	Total:	

Send check or money order to:
Bigwater Publishing
P.O. Box 177
Caledonia, MI 49316

READER SURVEY—*Sweet Clover: A Romance of the White City*

Your opinion counts! Please fill out and mail this form to:

Reader Survey
Bigwater Publishing
P.O. Box 177
Caledonia, MI 49316

Your Name: ______________________________
Address: ______________________________
____
____

In return, we will send you a bookmark, the latest issue of our *Great Lakes Romances® Newsletter*, and while supplies last, samples of note cards and/or stationery depicting an historic Great Lakes scene.

1. Would you like to read more books by Clara Louise Burnham?

YES_____ NO_____

2. Do you know of other books published prior to 1906 which you would like to buy in reprinted editions?

Title Author

____

____

3. Where did you purchase this book?

____

4. What influenced your decision to purchase this book?

_______Front Cover _______First Page _______Back Cover Copy

_______Title _______Friends _______Publicity (please describe on next page)

____

_______Other (Please describe)___________________________________

____

5. Please indicate your age range:

_______Under 18	_______25-34	_______46-55
_______18-24	_______35-45	_______Over 55

If desired, include additional comments below.